AND THE TEMPLE OF TIKAL

ADAM GUILLAIN

ILLUSTRATIONS BY RACHEL GOSLIN

Milet

Milet Publishing Ltd
6 North End Parade
London W14 OSJ
www.milet.com

First published by Milet Publishing Ltd in 2004
Copyright © Adam Guillain, 2004

ISBN 1 84059 394 6

Adam Guillain has asserted his moral right to be identified as the author of this work, in accordance with the Copyright, Design and Patents Act 1988.

Cover and chapter illustrations by Rachel Goslin.

Milet's distributors are as follows:

UK & Ireland
Turnaround Publisher Services, Unit 3, Olympia Trading Estate, Coburg Road, London N22 6TZ

North America & Latin America
Tuttle Publishing, 364 Innovation Drive, North Clarendon, VT 05759-9436

Australia & New Zealand
Tower Books, Unit 2/17 Rodborough Road, Frenchs Forest NSW 2086

Global Language Books, PO Box 108, Toongabbie NSW 2146

South Africa
Quartet Sales & Marketing, 12 Carmel Avenue, Northcliff, Gauteng, Johannesburg 2195

Printed in Great Britain by Cox & Wyman

BELLA BALISTICA

AND THE TEMPLE OF TIKAL

Every child is born with a nahual. The nahual is our double, something very important to us. It's usually an animal. The nahual is the representative of the earth, the animal world, the sun and water, and in this way the child communicates with nature. We often come to love the animal which is our nahual even before we know what it is. There is not one world for humans and another one for animals, they are part of the same one and lead parallel lives.

Rigoberta Menchú
From *I, Rigoberta Menchú, An Indian Woman in Guatemala*
Rigoberta Menchú won the Nobel Peace Prize in 1992

"I wish I was a bird," Bella mumbled to herself as she carefully made her way down through the branches of the tree. She had always felt drawn to birds. Even before she learnt to talk, Bella would call out to them . . .

Bella Balistica and the Temple of Tikal

CHAPTER ONE

MYSTERY BIRD

"I can't run any faster," Bella panted, as she frantically dragged herself up Oxleas Mount. Her only hope was to get to the brow of the hill and find shelter at the café. She shot a terrified look over her shoulder. To her horror they were catching her up.

"Damn that Mrs. Sticklan!" she yelled, as yet again her shoes failed to grip on the tarmac when she tried to accelerate, causing her to stumble. Bella would have been able to run much faster in tracksuit bottoms and trainers but Mrs. Sticklan, the newly-appointed headteacher at Hawksmore Primary, had introduced very strict rules regarding school uniform. All the girls had to wear these hideous brown and orange A-line skirts and slippery leather shoes. These weren't the only rules that Bella found hard to swallow.

The thud of stone missiles all around her alerted Bella to a new danger. Eugene Briggs in particular was an excellent shot with a catapult; it wouldn't be long before one of his gang made a direct hit. She decided to get off the main path and wade her way through the dead leaves and winter-worn woodland towards the old watch tower.

Bella had tried to leave school at the end of the day without getting into another fight, but when Eugene started stuffing his grubby hands through Charlie's red hair and calling her a 'ginger nut', Bella had flown off the handle as usual.

"Leave her alone, you big fat oaf," she'd shouted, squirting apple juice into Eugene's face. A fight was inevitable. But Bella Balistica needed to work on her insults. Eugene was anything but fat. He was as lean as he was mean and he prided himself on finding the cruellest thing to say to anyone.

Initially, everything had been going according to Eugene's plan. Bella had taken the bait, then Connor Mitchell had snatched Charlie's school bag and started running off with it down Jackson Road. As expected, Charlie had chased after him while the rest of the gang closed in on Bella.

"Guess what *I* saw this morning?" Eugene mocked, taking a step closer to Bella.

"What's that then, Briggsy?" sneered Roland Richardson, as he swung his bulbous belly and wobbly thighs right up to Eugene's side. Roland knew perfectly well that Connor and Eugene had caught Bella singing to the birds in Oxleas Wood. It was time to hammer the embarrassment home. Eugene relished moments like this. He loved toying with his victim before he pounced. Bella Balistica was the bane of his life. No one came back for more in the way she did. It wouldn't have been so bad if she just stuck up for herself, but she had to stick her oar into everyone else's business too, including his dad's. It was getting boring. He grabbed her scruffy black hair.

"On your knees, pig-face," he snarled, pulling her down towards the kerb. Bella dropped her schoolbag.

Bella had once turned her nose up and flared her nostrils at

2

Eugene in a gesture of defiance. Since then, he'd teased her that she had a nose like a pig. "You have the nose of a princess," her mum would reassure her. But Bella wasn't so sure. Refusing to buckle, she tried to push Eugene away, but his arms were too long.

"No wonder your mother gave you away," Eugene hissed. "I'm surprised anyone adopted you."

Bella was furious. She threw a fist towards Eugene's face, but it was no use – his arms were simply too long. Then, in a moment's inspiration, she flung herself onto the ground, causing Eugene to lose his balance and stumble forwards.

"Stop her!" Eugene howled.

Bella rolled to the kerb and pulled herself up. Grabbing her school bag, she swivelled round to make her escape but ran straight into Prakash Malik. She was surrounded. Luckily for Bella, Prakash was so caught out by the ferocity of the collision, he toppled back just enough to let her slip through and sprint away.

"Prakash, you idiot!" Eugene shouted as he pulled himself up and glared at the stunned faces around him. Prakash went red and looked down to his boots.

"Sorry, Briggsy," he muttered, worried in case Eugene should decide to turn on him too.

Eugene quickly turned to Winston Geoffrey, the fastest runner in his five-boy gang. "What are you waiting for, lanky legs?" he snarled. "After her!"

And that's how Bella Balistica found herself running up Oxleas Mount at dusk pursued by a gang of the meanest boys at Hawksmore Primary.

"Ouch!" Bella yelped as the first stone stung the back of

her right leg. "I hate school uniform!"

If she'd been allowed to wear thick socks and trousers instead of this horrible skirt, the sharp stone wouldn't have cut her so badly. She wanted to stop and throw something back, but she was outnumbered. With the cold, easterly wind lashing against her face and causing her eyes to water, Bella gritted her teeth and picked up speed. If Winston Geoffrey caught her up and saw her watery eyes, he would be sure tell the gang. "Sissy," they would call her. "Cry baby."

But Bella never cried. Not in front of boys. For an eleven-year-old girl of average height, Bella Balistica was tough.

Very few people walked their dogs on this side of Oxleas Wood, partly because of the steep climb, but mostly because of the foreboding reputation of the old watchtower. Tucked away in a small clearing, the medieval ruins were a well-known sanctuary for wild birds and rodents as well as the odd local tramp. It was a creepy place at the best of times, but on a dark December afternoon with the bitter wind wailing through the trees and biting into your legs and ears, it was chilling. People said that the old oak tree by the tower had once been used for public executions. According to local legend, on certain days of the year, ghosts would return to re-enact these hideous events, haunting all those who set eyes on them. There was even supposed to be a mad phantom who appeared on the balcony every night at dawn. It was no wonder then that Bella's mum didn't allow her to walk to school this way. But Bella loved these stories. They were the very reason she played here.

The oncoming wind was getting too strong to fight. Bella

knew that she had to hide – and fast. With the strength of a gibbon, she yanked herself up into the old oak tree just in time to see Eugene and his gang dart into the clearing. Surely they would see her.

Bella was used to standing out. She was from Guatemala, a small country in Central America just south of Mexico. She wore colourful Guatemalan headbands, with which she irritably attempted to sweep away her unruly hair and then complained to high heaven when they got confiscated because she fiddled with them in class. The fiery passion evident in her dark, sparkling eyes during these outbursts alluded to a wildness of spirit that was even more striking than her Mayan features. Quite simply, Bella Balistica was unlike any child Hawksmore Primary School had ever seen before.

"Can you see her?" gasped Eugene Briggs, panting as he trailed Winston Geoffrey into the clearing. Bella was nowhere to be seen.

"We'll wait for the others to catch up," he told Winston. "Search the whole area. The little witch must be around here somewhere."

The bare branches of the old oak offered Bella little camouflage, and if it hadn't been for the autumnal colours of her uniform, she would have had little chance.

"She's too fast," moaned Prakash, stumbling onto the scene totally exhausted. He bent over and rested his hands on his thighs while he attempted to catch his breath.

"Prakash, you're pathetic," Eugene lamented. "And where's Ratty?" Eugene had nicknamed Roland "The Rat" because of his crabby moods and mean-spirited behaviour – attributes well suited to his role in the gang.

"Coming," Roland wheezed, finally making it into the clearing only to flop to the ground in a heap.

"Get your fat arse into gear and start looking!" Eugene ordered, picking up a stone and throwing it directly at him. Reluctantly, Roland and Prakash followed Winston's lead and started to explore the clearing. Through the windswept branches, Bella watched as Eugene picked up a fallen stick and began thrusting it into the undergrowth. Sometimes when Eugene furrowed his brow, his eyelids would narrow until they looked as slitty as a snake's. She shook with anger to think how he would make friends with new children just so he could torture and reject them later. He was like a boa constrictor who slowly coiled around his prey before he suffocated and devoured it.

Like his father, Ted Briggs, Eugene was skinny and pale-skinned with an unkempt mop of shaggy blond hair. He was easily the tallest Year 6 boy in the school, which meant he always made the football and basketball team and stuck out in class assemblies. He wore trainers most days, even though this wasn't allowed, and tied his school tie with a huge knot, which allowed him to defy the rule about top buttons being done up. Every day he wore the same brown crew-neck jumper, which he never seemed to take off, even for P.E. It drove Bella mad that while Mrs. Sticklan would make all the other boys wear V-necks in class and green short-sleeved T-shirts for PE, Eugene appeared to be exempt. In fact, as the son of Ted Briggs, the chair of the school of governors, Eugene got away with murder.

The Briggs family ran a pet shop at 48 Eltham Gardens, just off the Well Hall Road, where they sold exotic pets. At the back of the house there was a large private aviary which could only be viewed by making an appointment. There had been a school trip to visit it last term, but Bella had refused to go on principle. "I don't think it's right to lock up animals," she'd told her teacher, Mr. Alder. "Especially birds."

Unfortunately for Bella, she'd made her opinion known to Ted Briggs by standing up in the middle of one of his boring assemblies and shouting him down about his abuse of animal rights. "I want you to make her life hell!" Briggs had roared after the assembly, prowling around Mrs. Sticklan's office like a demented werewolf. "Then, when she's as miserable as she can be – I want her out!"

Bella's mum was so upset about the abusive phone call she'd received from Ted Briggs following the incident that she'd complained to the local education authority. To Briggs, this impertinence was a declaration of war.

Right now, Ted's son, Eugene, was pulling back bushes and probing them with the thorny stick in his hunt for Bella Balistica. "If she's made it through to the café, we won't be able to touch her," he snarled bitterly. "There'll be too many people around."

"But it's December, Briggsy," exclaimed Connor Mitchell, rejoining the group after burying Charlie's schoolbag in a tall wheelie-bin at the end of Jackson Road. "The café is closed and boarded up until March."

Eugene and the other gang members grinned with pleasure as all around them a clammy smog of condensing breath and sweaty jumpers polluted the freshness of the dusk. "Then she must be here," mused Eugene slyly, taking a packet of chewing gum from the inside pocket of his bomber jacket.

"We'll find her."

In the tree, Bella shivered as she watched Eugene thoughtfully draw himself a stick of gum before passing the packet on to Connor Mitchell. Seeing Connor was a double-edged sword for Bella. The good news was that Charlie had probably got away. The bad news was that Eugene and Connor had the tracking instincts of wild cats. "They catch rabbits and cut off their tails just for something to do," Charlie had told Bella only the other day.

"Hunting me down in the woods is going to be a positive pleasure to them," Bella trembled as she tried to manoeuvre herself higher into the tree without giving herself away. Bella knew that Connor Mitchell could be particularly brutal. Rumour had it that he once put a large rat into a box with his pet guinea pig. At school he was always in trouble, partly because his short spiky hair and bony features made him stick out like a porcupine on stilts, but mostly because he was so cruel. From the uncertainty of her hiding place, Bella felt scared.

It gets dark in the woods long before it does on the street. Bella could hear the flapping wings of the returning sparrows and starlings as they started to gather around their nests in the rafters of the watchtower. She looked up from her high position in the tree and saw a glorious red and green bird, rather like a parrot, disappearing through a small crack just below the gutter.

The dusky-red sunset was already fading when Eugene ordered his gang to spread out and encircle the tower. "She must be hiding inside," he announced, striding up to the wooden doors and rattling the handle as hard as he could. The doors and windows to the old watchtower were always locked and boarded up, but it never seemed to stop people getting in. Angrily spitting out his gum, Eugene started to kick violently at the door while Connor and Winston forced open the shutters of a downstairs window with a chunky branch and scrambled in. Seconds later there was a bone-chilling scream. Bella felt the hairs on the back of her neck stand up. Amidst a flurry of flapping wings and terrifying squawks, Connor and Winston jumped from the window and bolted like demented chickens.

"Run!" yelled Connor at a blood-curdling pitch.

There must have been a hundred pigeons in the first wave of the assault alone, followed by a flock of starlings and sparrows. And chasing them out with an ear-piercing shriek, Bella was amazed to see the strange, colourful bird she had just glimpsed slipping into the tower. Seeing the bird at close quarters allowed Bella to appreciate the iridescent blues and greens of its exceptionally long tail. It reminded her of a bird she had seen in a glossy holiday magazine about Guatemala. "No," she said to herself. "It can't be."

From her viewpoint in the tree, Bella watched as Eugene and the boys all turned and ran for it over the brow of the hill, past the café and down through the meadows, chased by the mysterious bird and the harassing flock. "I wish I was a bird," Bella mumbled to herself as she carefully made her way down through the branches of the tree.

She had always felt drawn to birds. Even before she learnt to talk, Bella would call out to them from her buggy. The fact that she'd been born with legs and arms and not claws and wings was often a source of disappointment to her as a young child. Even now, she loved to lie in the garden and gaze at the local bird life.

"You'll grow your own wings and fly away one day," her mum would say. "All children do."

"Don't talk rubbish," Bella would retort. "I'm not flying anywhere."

The idea was ridiculous.

Or so she thought.

CHAPTER TWO

THE PENDANT

"I'm home," Bella shouted grumpily, barging through the front door. Her crashing entrance set off the "Jingle Bells" music in the seasonal doormat. She hissed at the startled cat who'd been dozing at the foot of the stairs and sent it squealing up to the landing.

"You're not being mean to the cat again are you, Bella?" her mum shouted from the kitchen. "She's not killed anything for months now." Bella and her mum had hundreds of arguments over the murderous tabby. If her mum wanted another fight, Bella was raring to go.

"Are you ready for your tea, Bella?" her mum called. "I've made a lamb casserole."

Bella had been hoping for chicken nuggets and fries but, breathing in the delicious smell of coriander and rosemary, it was difficult to be cross. She threw her schoolbag down under the small Christmas tree in the hall and ran through to the kitchen to find her mum sitting at the table, peering through her metal-rimmed glasses into a well-worn recipe book. Bella guessed her mum must have been home for a while because she'd changed out of her midwife's uniform into a T-shirt and jeans and had her long black hair tied back with one of Bella's colourful Guatemalan scrunchies.

"Hi, darling," her mum greeted her, cheerily looking up. "Come and give me a kiss." Bella felt her anger subsiding. Whatever happened at school, it was always good to be home. She went up to her mum and gave her a kiss on the cheek.

"Charlie called,' said her mum. "She's bringing her homework over after tea." Bella felt relieved. She needed to be sure Charlie was alright after the incident with Connor Mitchell.

Bella's adoptive mum was known as Annie, although her real name was Anna Balistica. Annie's father was Spanish, which accounted for her beautiful olive skin and silky black hair. Charlie's mum had to stand on a chair to change a light bulb, but Annie was so strikingly tall, she could do it standing on the floor. Although they argued, Bella loved her adoptive mum. She was older than most of the other mums but was really cool about bedtimes and TV (unless they were eating). They always did nice things together at weekends, even if she couldn't always take her to watch Charlton Athletic play football when they had a home match. When she did have to work over the weekend, Bella would usually go to Charlie's house. It was great, not only because Bella and Charlie had a good time anyway, but her mum would miss her so much that she'd want to spoil her afterwards. Sometimes this would mean taking her to her favourite shop, The Quetzal, in Greenwich and buying her a present. The shop specialized in imported goods made in Guatemala, and Bella had a whole collection of toys made by orphans who lived on the streets there. Her favourite was a small orange bus carved out of wood. She kept it on her bedside table by her alarm clock where she could admire it and gaze at the figure of the happy, smiling driver, waving from the tiny cabin. She'd tried tipping him out of the bus, but the glue was too strong.

"How were the rehearsals for the Christmas concert?" asked her mum, getting up and going over to the fridge for some juice.

Bella answered by scrunching up her nose. It was the Monday of the penultimate week of term. The whole school was a mayhem of singing rehearsals and making things ready for the Christmas concert next week.

"Mr. Alder wants me to be the narrator," she replied. "But I told him to pick Rahina. She never gets a speaking part."

"You're very fair, Bella," her mum told her proudly as she poured them both a juice and sat back down. "I guess you get chosen all the time because you're so extrovert."

Bella knew that "extrovert" was parent code for "loud and noisy". She looked over her mum's shoulder at the recipe book as she sipped her drink.

"Would you like me to make you and Charlie some chocolate cake later?" her mum asked her, taking off her spectacles to reveal her emerald-green eyes.

Normally Bella would have been excited about the cake, but tonight she was too upset to talk about puddings. She simply shrugged her shoulders and made for the door.

"Oh, and that Guatemalan folktales book you found on Amazon arrived today," called her mum, lifting up the recipe book to reveal a brown package.

Bella was back like a shot. She ripped off the packaging,

tipped out the book and turned directly to the blurb on the back cover to check it was the right one.

"It's all about a three-headed jaguar who guards the great Temple of Tikal," her mum told her. "I know the story well, only this looks like a more modern version."

Secretly, Bella was excited. She loved gory adventures with fire-breathing monsters and treasure but loathed the fact her mum knew more about these stories than she did. "I hate stories about monsters and hidden treasure," she lied, "they're stupid." But she couldn't wait to read it.

Seeing the cut on the back of Bella's leg, Annie got some cotton wool from a drawer and went over to the sink to wet it under the warm tap. "Come here, darling, let me wipe that nasty little cut for you."

"No!" snapped Bella. "It's only a scratch. I'll do it myself."

Bella's mum looked thoughtful. She worried about Bella much more than she let on and was trying hard not to get cross with her just because she was tired from work. But it was difficult. Bella could be so stubborn and argumentative sometimes. She handed Bella the damp cotton wool.

"You look tired, Bella," she said kindly, as she watched Bella wipe away the dirt from her wound.

For a moment, Bella was subdued, as if she too had things on her mind. Her mum kissed the back of her head. What she didn't say was: "What *have* you been doing? You're late, your uniform looks filthy – and why are there bits of bark and moss in your hair?" That would have been a mistake.

"Better go upstairs and put your clothes in the wash," she suggested. "Dinner will be ready in half an hour."

Bella chucked the dirty cotton wool into the bin, grabbed

a chocolate biscuit from the tin in the cupboard and ran through the house clutching her new book. As a rule, this kind of snacking before dinner would spark a row, but tonight her mum let it go. She could see her daughter was in a bad mood.

"Mind the Christmas tree in the living room," she called after her through the thud of pounding feet and clinking baubles. "I love you. Come and talk to me about it when you're ready."

Annie knew that Bella kept her problems to herself. It was hard for her to accept sometimes, but the more she might ask Bella about the things that made her unhappy, the less Bella would say. Annie felt that as long as she sent out subtle, sympathetic signals that she was always available to talk to, Bella would open up when she was ready. Sometimes she did.

The mottled grey tabby dived into the dirty washing basket the second she felt the tremor of Bella's bounding footsteps on the stairs. Dropping her school clothes all over the landing, Bella went to her bedroom and changed into her Charlton Athletic football shirt and jeans. Eugene's dig about her real mum giving her away had hurt her feelings. She wanted to know more about her birth mother, but Guatemala was a long way away.

"All I know," Bella's mum had told her a thousand times, "is that your mother was an orphan. She was born in the Santa Maria orphanage in Quezaltenango just as you were."

This made Bella feel indescribably close to the mother she'd never known. Tragically, an infection picked up in childbirth had taken her mother's life only a few days after Bella was born. Although this made Bella feel sad, it also gave her something she could cling onto. But of her father, she had very little to go on.

"They say he was a great football player," Bella's mum had told her. "But one day there was an earthquake, and that was it. He was never seen again. Over a thousand people just disappeared. It was on the news, in the papers – everything." Bella's mum had kept a scrapbook with all the articles about the earthquake she could find. Bella looked at it sometimes when she wanted to think about her father.

It was a horrible feeling not knowing who her real parents were. Somewhere deep inside, Bella hung onto the distant hope that her father had somehow survived. She fantasized that he'd been separated from her mother by powerful natural forces and that he was, even now, trying to fight his way back to find her. She was determined that one day she would visit the orphanage in Quezaltenango where she was born and find out everything she could about them.

Bella and her adoptive mum lived at 14 Birdcage Crescent, a small semi-detached house near Shooters Hill in southeast London. The house didn't have much of a garden at the front, just a place for the bin and the battered old Mini, but at the back there was an apple tree and a small bird table. Inside the house, there was a big living room and kitchen downstairs, and two bedrooms, a bathroom and a small spare room upstairs. Her mum was a keen photographer and used the spare room as a darkroom. Bella had been on at her mum for months to get a digital camera to use with the computer and printer, but Annie was much happier with her own way. She had even bought Bella a camera last summer when they'd gone snorkelling in Tenerife. "It's waterproof," she had told Bella excitedly.

Bella had used it on the trip but soon lost interest. Secretly, it upset her mum that she just left it on the attic floor with an unused roll of film in it, but she didn't say anything.

Last year, a builder had put down wooden floorboards and fitted a skylight in the attic. Bella loved the woody aroma of newly-cut timbers and rafters – it was a smell that made her feel all warm and cosy inside. Her mum had recently had a pull-down ladder fitted, which meant it was easy for Bella to get up and down there whenever she wanted. Apart from a hammock, a mirror and an old wooden chest that her mum had shipped back from Guatemala, there was very little else in the way of furniture in the attic. The chest was covered with beautifully-carved pictures of jaguars and tropical birds and was full to the brim with clothes and artefacts from her mum's backpacking days. Bella often played in the attic for hours, rummaging through all the photographs and knick-knacks. "I hope you're not making a mess up there," her mum would shout.

But her mum never came up uninvited. The attic was Bella's space, and unless Bella called for her to catch some "hideous spider" and dispatch it to the bottom of the garden, she rarely ventured up the steps. Actually, these spider trips happened more often than Bella cared to admit. Bella loved animals but, brave and fearless as she otherwise was, she had an absolute phobia of eight-legged, web-weaving arthropods – especially hairy ones. Her worst scenario was a fast-moving hairy spider scuttling through her hair. Whenever Bella saw or sensed the presence of a spider, she would scream blue murder and her mum would have to rush up to the attic fearing some awful accident had occurred. Like her fear of the dark, Bella knew it was stupid, but she couldn't help it. Spiders aside, the attic was her favourite place in the whole house.

There was almost half an hour before teatime, so Bella took her book, pulled down the metal ladder and clambered up into the attic. Sometimes it could take a few moments for the lights to stop flickering and come on after she'd pulled the cord, but Bella never waited. She always knew exactly where to put her feet. She had to. Despite the new timber, there was still the odd creaky floorboard to avoid if she wanted to come up in the middle of the night without waking her mum. She pulled herself up into the hammock and avidly explored the illustration on the cover of her book. The fearsome three-headed jaguar shooting dragon-like flames across an ancient tomb at a petrified archaeologist certainly whetted her appetite. Bella guessed that the large sparkling emerald the archaeologist clutched in his arms would be his undoing.

"Fantastic!" she sighed with glee, turning immediately to the first chapter and eagerly starting to read about the empire of King Kabah.

When she wasn't reading, Bella would often lie in the hammock and stare at the portrait that hung from a rusty nail on the far wall. It was an old oil painting like the kind you might see in a church, only this one was of a beautiful Guatemalan woman in her traditional Mayan robes standing before a great pyramid. The colourful patterns woven into her long, wrap-around skirt and top were dazzling and made her clearly stand out from the granite-coloured temple in the background. Bella's instincts led her to guess that while the portrait itself was old, the artist had drawn their inspiration from somewhere even further back in time, perhaps even from historical myths. The funny thing was, Bella's mum had no idea how she had come by it. "It's a mystery," she would say. "I was just having a sort out, and there it was."

Sometimes, when Bella was really thinking hard about things, it was almost as if the woman whispered advice to her. "Love, learn, forgive and move on," she might say or: "Just keep your big mouth shut for once!"

Bella's tendency to argue and answer back got her into a lot of trouble at school. She seemed to find injustice in so many things. But even if the woman in the portrait never said a word, something about her presence helped Bella calm down and deal with her problems.

"I think she's beautiful," she had told Charlie once while they were having their supper in the attic.

"She looks a bit like you," Charlie had replied, grinning.

"That's because she's a Mayan Indian," Bella had told her proudly. "Just like me."

Taking the time before tea to read as much of her new book as possible, Bella quickly dashed through the first two chapters. Some bits of the story were familiar, like the Golden Jaguar who guarded the treasures of the temple. Jaguars often turned up in Guatemalan myths. They were believed to be intermediaries between the world of the living and the world of the dead, but this was the first time she'd read about one that turned into a fire-breathing beast with three heads! Created by the gods, the mighty Jaguar lay in wait ready to burst into life at the first sign of an intruder. Amongst all the treasures the Golden Jaguar protected, the most spectacular of all was the Itzamna Emerald. Itzamna was the supreme Mayan god. In this modern retelling, the writer had chosen a greedy archaeologist as his villain, who claimed that the priceless stone was "as big as a man's head". The jewel was believed to be the very heart of the Mayan people and had numerous and far-reaching powers. In terms of time and history, the emerald acted like gravity, pulling together and connecting the past, present and the future so that every living thing should know where it came from and where it was going. If it should ever be taken away from Guatemala, the natural balance would change, with chaos and disaster touching every human and animal in the Mayan world.

Later in the book, one of the local villagers told the archaeologist that only the human touched with the spirit of the Mayan god, Itzamna, would ever be allowed to enter the temple and be led to its hidden treasures. This human would have at their command a powerful and precious pendant the like of which no one had ever known before.

"I'm going to be a great explorer when I grow up," Bella told the portrait as she threw down her book, swung herself out of the hammock and bounded over to the chest.

"The power of your will is a tremendous force," came the whispered reply in Bella's head.

Bella looked at the portrait wistfully. It was hard to believe the woman in the portrait could actually speak to her. But one thing was for sure: whoever was responsible for Bella's inner voice thought she was too stubborn for her own good.

Throwing open the chest, Bella dug her hand down to the bottom and fished out a beautiful hand-carved jewellery box. Inside, Bella's treasures included gold and silver earrings and necklaces, bright multi-coloured bracelets, good luck charms of all shapes and sizes and, of course, lots of shiny rings. She wore some of the jewellery when she went to parties but mainly when she just fancied dressing up around the house. Right now she was hoping to find anything that resembled a precious pendant like the one in the story. Tipping the contents out onto the floor, she started to rummage, so engrossed by her search she heard neither her mum's calls for dinner nor her footsteps on the ladder.

"Oh, Bella!" exclaimed her mum, poking her head up through the hatch.

Bella looked up to catch the staunchly disapproving look on her mum's face. Remembering her pledge never to comment on the mess in the attic, Annie bit her lip. "Dinner is on the table, Bella. I don't know what you're up to, but it can at least wait until after dinner."

"But, mum…" Bella pleaded.

"But nothing," said her mum firmly.

And that was the end of it.

Bella and her mum always ate their meals together with the TV off, even if Bella kicked up a fuss and told her mum it wasn't fair. "It's our time," her mum would say. "Our chance to talk about the day."

"Charlie doesn't have to," Bella might protest.

But it never made any difference.

"Did you get any good behaviour stickers today?" Bella's mum asked as they sat down at the table. Good behaviour stickers were an embarrassment to Bella. It was the kind of trick teachers played on the young children to get them to sit and work nicely. Mrs. Sticklan had insisted that as part of Bella's targets for improving her behaviour she too should try and get them. But Mrs. Sticklan knew that this was a no-win situation for Bella: if she got one it made her feel childish, but if she didn't she was in trouble.

"Mum," said Bella, picking up her knife and fork and ignoring the question about stickers, "I've been trying really hard to control my temper."

Her mum smiled. At last, her advice was getting through.

"That's good, dear," she said kindly. "I think those stickers are a silly idea anyway."

Bella loved her mum. She always knew the right thing to say, even if it annoyed Bella to admit it sometimes.

Tucking into her dinner, Bella's appetite for conversation soon disappeared. Her mum, on the other hand, had a list of questions as long as her arm.

"How's it been going with Eugene and Connor?' she asked, determined to get to the bottom of Bella's bad mood.

"Fine," replied Bella. "Mum?" she asked quickly, changing the subject to put to an end to any more questions. "Can I have a pendant for Christmas? I haven't got one."

Suddenly, Bella's mum appeared to have lost her stomach for eating and looked very flustered. Putting down her knife and fork she reached for a napkin.

"Bella, my love," she started slowly, wiping her brow. "You *have* got a pendant."

Bella looked confused. She could see her mum's hand shaking nervously as she reached out for a glass of water.

"Your mother had a pendant," she began. "A most glorious and colourful jewel on a silver chain. It was a wedding gift from your father. She wanted you to have it. The midwife at the orphanage told me that she'd put it into that gorgeous hand-carved jewellery box you keep up in the attic."

"Then where is it?" Bella blurted.

She'd started out just looking for a pendant with which to imagine she could unlock the secrets of The Great Temple of Tikal – and now all she could think about was the fact that somehow her adoptive mum had failed to pass on to her the most precious pendant in the world.

"The midwife told me to look long and hard at the box," stammered Bella's mum. "But Bella, I looked. I just couldn't find it."

Both Bella and her mum had tears in their eyes.

"You lost it!" Bella shouted, banging the ends of her cutlery onto the table.

"Perhaps I shouldn't have said anything," sobbed her mum.

Bella pushed away her chair and ran back upstairs to the attic. Scooping up the jewellery box, she tipped it upside down above her head and stared with misty eyes into the empty wooden casing. "Where is it?" she raged.

She was so angry with her mum. Why hadn't she told her about this before? Giving the box such an almighty shake that she could see stars before her eyes, she then hurled it violently against the wall, stomped across the floorboards and flopped into the hammock. She must have been crying for a good ten minutes before she finally heard the soothing refrain of the voice inside her head. "Look long and hard at the box," it kept repeating.

Bella slowly swung herself out of the hammock, dried her eyes and went across to pick up the box. Examining the damage, she noticed that the tip of one of the top corners had broken off and there was now a small, narrow split on the lid. She felt awful. The jewellery box was part of her mother's gift – a link to her past. If Bella never found the pendant at least she would always have the box.

"The power of your will is a tremendous force," the voice inside Bella's head reminded her, only this time it sounded more like a reprimand than a statement of support.

"I know, I know," Bella acknowledged aloud.

"Be calm and use your head," said the voice gently. "Look carefully at the box."

Bella glanced up to the portrait on the wall. Sometimes, the expression on the portrait's face appeared to change depending on Bella's mood. Right now, it looked like her mum did when she was trying hard not to appear cross. Returning her attention to the box, Bella put one hand on the lid and the other on the base and twisted. There was definitely a hinge because she could feel a small click when she turned it back and forth, but something was stopping it from opening. Taking one of the miniature handles on what she had previously only seen as a fake drawer, Bella turned it and pulled again. Nothing. She tried the other handle, but that too could not be budged. She was just about to give up when she had an idea. She rested the empty jewellery box on the floor and turned both of the drawer handles together. It worked. But surprisingly, she could not pull the drawer out. Again, Bella picked up the box and put one hand on the base and one at the top and twisted. This time it opened to reveal a hidden compartment between the base and the main body.

To Bella's utter excitement and joy, a hidden jewel and chain dropped out of the box onto the palm of her hand. "The pendant!" she stammered.

Raising the silver chain up to the light, she was both dazzled and amazed by the resplendent ruby-red, ochre, amber and emerald-green gems, carefully crafted to form an image of a beautiful bird. "I recognize this creature," thought Bella. "It's like that mysterious parrot I saw this afternoon at the old watchtower."

Standing before the portrait on the wall, she quickly put the pendant on. No sooner had the cold braids of the silver chain touched the hairs on the back of her neck than Bella heard a sharp tapping on the window. She nearly jumped out of her skin.

Someone or something was at the skylight.

CHAPTER THREE

UNEXPECTED VISITOR

Bella looked up into the rafters and peered through the skylight. Whatever was there had little patience, for it was now leaping up and down and making the most tremendous racket. Her heart pounded with expectation as she dragged the old chest across the floor, clambered on it and, standing up on her tiptoes, stretched out to open the window. As she did so, the creature, clearly startled by the movement, was jerked backwards. "Aah!" it screamed.

Bella flinched. She listened to its fading cry as it slid down the roof and crashed into the gutter. She waited for the thud of whatever it was landing on the patio, but it didn't come. A few seconds later she heard it stomping its way back up the roof before it finally poked its beak down through the skylight.

"Do you *mind*?" it squawked. "I could have been killed!"

Bella nearly dropped the window on the bird's head, she was so startled. "What did you say?" she cried, unable to believe her own ears.

"Got a hearing problem, have we?" screeched the bird.

Bella slammed the window shut and pinched her arm as

hard as she could.

"Wake up!" she ordered herself. "This isn't happening."

Through the skylight, Bella could still make out that the bird's head and crest were emerald green with a splattering of yellow highlights. The black and white feathers of its wings cloaked its fiery red body, and as if to set the whole outfit off, the shimmering blues and greens of its tail – which was almost twice as long as its body – looked like the robes of a king. Bella recognized it at once as the colourful bird that had come to her rescue at the old tower. Again, the bird began to peck on the glass.

"Come on," came the muted squawk from outside. "Let me in. It's colder than a penguin's pecker out here."

Filled with a conflict of trepidation and curiosity, Bella reached up and nervously reopened the skylight.

"Fine welcome this is," muttered the angry bird.

Bella timidly got down from the chest to let the bird in. The skylight was small and with so little space to extend its wings the bird crashed, rather unceremoniously, onto the floor.

"Ouch!" it crowed. "For someone with the gift of bird talk you don't show much respect for the higher species." The flustered bird picked itself up, flew up to perch on one of the lower rafters and started to preen its ruffled feathers.

Mesmerized and bemused, Bella took off the pendant to compare its image against the colourful creature before her. Immediately, the Quetzal's command of the English language appeared to desert him as he began to twitter away, making no sense whatsoever. Bella slumped down onto her mum's wooden chest. "What a relief," she thought. "For a moment there, I thought I was actually having a conversation with a bird."

"You were," said a voice inside her head. "Only one girl in the whole world could have worn that pendant and understood what that bird was saying – and that girl is you!"

Bella shot a look at the portrait on the wall.

"Put the pendant back on," the voice concluded.

The second the chain touched her skin, it was as if she'd been plugged back in to the madness of the last minute.

" . . . And that's why I've never liked rude little girls," concluded the Quetzal, stamping his foot.

His rant over, the angry bird stuck his beak under his wing and got on with his preening. Bella flopped onto her back and stared in disbelief into the rafters. What kind of a pendant had her mother left her? Bella could have done with a few minutes of peace to calm her mind, but she didn't get a second.

"And how come it's taken you so long to put it on?" demanded the strange bird, flying down and pecking Bella on the arm. "How was I supposed to find you when you run off halfway around the world and never put the damned thing on?"

"Can you understand everything I say?" gasped Bella, sitting up.

"I can now," he sighed, shaking his head. "Now you've finally decided to put on the pendant and grace us with your hidden talents."

"*My* hidden talents?" stuttered Bella in complete disbelief at the unfolding situation. "You're the one twittering on in fluent English."

"Am I?" snapped the bird.

"Bella, are you alright up there?" Bella's mum called up. "Have the seagulls got in again?"

To her surprise, Bella suddenly realized that neither she nor the bird were speaking in English. They were both chirping away at the top of their lungs. She cleared her throat. "It's OK, mum," she coughed. "It's gone now."

"You shouldn't open the skylight, Bella," shouted her mum. "You'll catch your death of cold."

"Seagull?" queried the bird, clearly offended by her mum's remark.

"Have you escaped from the zoo?" Bella interrupted, totally mystified as to why a talking bird should suddenly drop in through the skylight.

The comment did not go down well.

"Do I *look* like a performing parrot?" he squawked sarcastically.

Here the great bird ruffled up his feathers and raised his beak into the air in a snooty fashion. "We quetzals are a protected species." And as if that wasn't good enough: "Put one of us in a cage with a bag of mouldy old nuts, and you're in *big* trouble."

"I knew you were a quetzal!" exclaimed Bella, hardly able to contain herself. "I've seen pictures of you in holiday magazines, but I couldn't remember your name."

She lifted up her pendant to inspect it more closely. The Quetzal's spectacular emerald green and ruby-red plumage were entirely in keeping with its claim.

"A Guatemalan quetzal?" she asked cautiously.

"There is no other," replied the bird, beginning to relax. "Can you rustle me up a snack? I'm peckish."

Bursting with a hundred questions, Bella slid down the ladder and landed with a thump on the landing. "There's no way I'm letting my mum see *this*," she mumbled to herself, giving the pendant a quick glance before tucking it away beneath her top. " She should have told me about it before." Secretly though, Bella felt a bit mean – especially because her mum had been so upset about losing it.

Sneaking into the kitchen to raid the biscuit tin, Bella was relieved to hear her mum talking on the phone in the living room. "I've got Mrs. Stevens on the line," Bella's mum called, putting her hand over the mouthpiece. "Charlie's just finishing her tea. She'll be here in about half an hour."

As she bounded two steps at a time back up to the landing, clutching a biscuit, Bella could feel her excitement mounting – Charlie was going to love this!

Upon her return, Bella found the Quetzal using his beak to flick through a photo album.

"My mum took most of those pictures," Bella told the Quetzal proudly, tossing the biscuit at the bird's feet. "They're from the orphanage in Quezaltenango where I was born."

The Quetzal screwed up his eyes. The picture he was peering at was of a tall woman with silky black hair. Dressed in a white uniform, the woman stood alongside a grubby old cot, holding a baby wrapped in a shawl.

"Bella Balistica," he mocked, shaking his head from side to side. "Who'd have thought it?"

The Quetzal had his own memory of Bella as a baby in Guatemala, but like many of the pictures in the album, it had faded over time.

"Thinks she's special 'cause she looks a bit different and can speak to the birds," he continued, tutting to himself. "No idea of who she is or where she's going."

"Now look here," snapped Bella, stamping her foot.

The Quetzal was so shocked by Bella's outburst, he took one step back and fell over.

Stirred up by the conceit of her uninvited guest, Bella continued: "I don't know who you are or why you think you can come here and lecture me on things . . . "

"And there's the other thing," interrupted the bird, picking himself up and shaking out his ruffled feathers. "You've no idea how to control your temper. What's the point of having a passion for justice if you fly off the handle at the slightest little thing?"

Bella had been told this a thousand times. She was furious.

"You sound like my mum!" she yelled at the bird.

The Quetzal slammed the book shut. Eleven years of searching for this little girl had eroded just about every drop of patience he had. He had lots to tell her and very little time to do it in.

"I need your help," he yapped, as he nibbled at a biscuit.

"I'm busy," said Bella indignantly, folding her arms.

Curious as she was, Bella had no intention of helping him after he'd been so rude – at least, not without a good argument first.

The angry bird hopped onto the album to give himself a bit more height, but he still only came up to Bella's kneecaps. It was annoying to speak to a young girl who didn't know the extent of her powers. Worse still, a girl who would probably give him a mouthful of abuse as soon as he even tried.

"And anyway," Bella continued, "how can I possibly help you?"

"If you'd let me explain to you about your powers, you'd know," replied the Quetzal.

"Oh yeah," snorted Bella dismissively. "And what powers

are those then? Apart from twittering to pompous, stuck-up, posh birds like you."

Pulling herself up tall to deliver her sharp attack, Bella suddenly checked herself. "Is this really happening to me?" she thought, giving herself another pinch.

"The power to achieve whatever you set your mind to," answered the bird. "The power of your will . . . "

" . . . is a tremendous force," Bella finished his sentence, glancing up at the portrait.

"I'll prove it to you," sighed the bird, as he flew back up to perch on one of the rafters. "I have an idea regarding your problem."

"Not you as well," she groaned. She knew at once that the Quetzal was referring to Eugene Briggs.

Bella's latest gripe with Eugene was that he and his gang had bullied all the girls into agreeing that the football pitch in the main playground was for boys only. The girls could use the small playground or the corners of the main playground by the kitchen and the bins, but basically that was it. Bella loved football. All she wanted was a chance to play in mixed teams on the main pitch. She'd gone to complain to Mrs. Sticklan about it and ended up with a lunchtime detention.

"Challenge the boys to a game of football tomorrow," the Quetzal suggested. "Winner takes all. If the girls win they get to use the pitch whenever they want. If the boys win, the girls do their homework for the rest of the term."

Bella loved the idea but didn't like the odds.

"We'll never win," she protested.

"Wear the pendant," replied the Quetzal. "You'll see."

He fluttered down to devour the remains of the biscuit.

"Not bad," he acknowledged. "But better with chocolate."
Bella couldn't argue with that.

"Bella, Charlie's here," came the call from downstairs.

"Coming, mum!" Bella shouted down the hatch.

"I've got to go," said Bella, turning to the Quetzal.

"Well, that's charming, that is," the bird replied haughtily.
"I haven't finished talking to you yet."

"Can I bring my friend Charlie up to see you?" asked
Bella excitedly.

"Certainly not!" snapped the bird, as an anxious look crossed
his face. "To anyone outside this room, neither me, that pendant,
or any conversation that may or may not have passed between
us, must ever be discussed. Our mission is top secret."

"Our mission?" asked Bella. "You haven't mentioned
any mission."

"You haven't given me a chance!" squawked the irritated
bird.

"Bella, are you coming down?" came the call from
downstairs. "Or shall I send Charlie up?"

"Coming," called Bella as she started for the ladder.

She felt gutted to be running out on the bird just as he
was going to tell her about a top-secret mission – but what
could she do? The Quetzal was beside himself with
frustration. He let out an almighty squawk and stamped
his claw.

"Bella, are you sure that seagull got out safely?" shouted
Bella's mum.

"I'll be back as soon as I can," Bella told the Quetzal,
lifting off the pendant and dropping it back into its secret
compartment. She gave the Quetzal a cautious smile and left.

Bella's mum was showing Charlie the chocolate cake in the kitchen when Bella came down. Like Bella, Charlie was wearing her favourite Charlton Athletic football shirt and navy jeans.

"Look at the pair of you!" Bella's mum exclaimed. "The terrible twins."

Two more unlikely-looking twins you couldn't hope to meet. But it was true: Bella and Charlie had been inseparable since nursery. They chatted so much at school, Mr. Alder refused to let them sit together. What Bella wanted to say was: "Charlie, I found a magic pendant that used to belong to my birth mother in the secret compartment of an old Guatemalan jewellery box – there's a tropical bird called a Quetzal in the attic – and I can understand everything he says!"

"I love your hair," she said instead.

Charlie's long red hair was braided and tied back with colourful ribbons.

"Thanks," said Charlie, smiling happily. "And you've got so many Christmas decorations up! It's like Santa's grotto. I wish I lived here."

Her blue twinkly eyes and brown freckles made her easily the prettiest girl in the class in Bella's view. Charlie's real name was Charlotte, but only her mum and dad were allowed to use it. Her parents ran the trendy hair and beauty salon on Eltham High Street. She was popular with the other girls because she was chatty and friendly and always willing to help them with their schoolwork. Few boys ever took advantage of Charlie's willingness to explain things. They were more interested in who she fancied.

"You can use the dining room table to do your homework

while I put the icing on the cake," said Bella's mum, moving towards the fridge. "What would you like to drink?"

"Apple juice," they both answered together then, turning to each other: "I knew you were going to say that!"

"You two!" said Bella's mum, laughing. "Sometimes I think you've only got one brain between you." She handed them their juice. "Now go on." Saying things at the same time happened a lot.

"I was going to say that!" they were always telling each other.

It was great.

As Bella's mum ushered them into the living room with their drinks, they heard a muffled squawk that appeared to come from the roof.

"I swear we have seagulls in the attic," muttered Bella's mum for the umpteenth time.

Bella didn't give it a second thought. Her head was spinning with thoughts of her magic pendant, the talking Quetzal and the possibility of being involved in a top-secret mission. She was just about to tell Charlie everything that had happened when Charlie, bursting with her own frustrations, blurted: "So what happened with Eugene? Did you get into a fight?"

"I ran," replied Bella, a little startled by the intensity in Charlie's eyes. "Even in my school shoes, he can't catch me."

"Well done," Charlie cheered. "I was worried."

Bella's mind was back in the moment. She too had been anxious about Charlie's fate.

"Did Connor hurt you too?" she asked.

Charlie shook her head.

"And what about getting your bag back?" Bella continued.

Charlie looked embarrassed.

"The stupid boy threw all my books into the wheelie-bin outside the church. By the time I got back, you'd gone."

Bella felt her blood boil. She would get her revenge on Eugene Briggs and his gang if it was the last thing she ever did at Hawksmore Primary.

Usually, Bella's mum made a fuss about her daughter helping her to wash the dishes after dinner, but because Charlie was over, she didn't. While her mum attended to the kitchen, Bella went to get her schoolbag from the hall. As she did, she glanced up the stairs to see the cat strutting its way down with a knowing glint in its eye. Bella pulled a face and growled at it but then thought no more about it.

"Eugene Briggs threw my lunch into the pond," Charlie told Bella, when she returned. "I didn't tell you at lunchtime in case you got into a fight with him. I don't want you getting into trouble because of me."

Bella slammed her books onto the table so hard the Christmas tree lights flickered, and several decorations crashed to the floor. She was furious. There was no point in anyone complaining to the lunchtime supervisors about Eugene. All Mrs. Sticklan would do was call him into her office and talk to him. He was such a sneaky liar he'd have her eating out of the palm of his hand within no time. It was always the other person getting into trouble where Eugene Briggs and Mrs. Sticklan were involved. It wasn't fair. Just because Mrs. Sticklan was friends with his dad!

"What animal are you doing for the project?" Bella asked Charlie, changing the subject. The Year 6 class was doing a project on endangered species.

"The manatee," said Charlie excitedly. "I think they're

great! Let's look on the internet."

Bella went over to the small desk in the corner of the room and logged on to the computer.

"And what about you, Bella?" asked Charlie.

"The Guatemalan quetzal," said Bella proudly.

"Oh, I know those," said Charlie. "They're like parrots."

Bella giggled, as she connected to the internet.

The girls were surprised to discover that the manatee was the largest herbivore in the ocean. They both thought it was comical to look at.

"It's a little bit like a walrus but without the tusks," Charlie laughed, when a picture of one finally downloaded, "but it looks really friendly."

According to the article, sailors of old used to mistake them for mermaids.

"If they looked so much like beautiful woman with flippers, then why did the sailors eat them?" Bella squirmed when she'd finished reading the page.

"They probably taste nice with a side order of fries," replied Charlie cheekily. "It's probably why they're nearly extinct."

"I'd love to see one in the wild," murmured Bella thoughtfully.

"Me too," agreed Charlie. "Let's find out about your parrot," she said, tapping the word 'quetzal' into the search engine.

Even five minutes spent reading about quetzals on the internet when there was one in the attic was too much for Bella. And anyway – what harm could it do?

"Let's take our chocolate cake upstairs," she suggested to Charlie.

"Bella, it's freezing up here," Charlie complained, as she pulled herself up into the attic.

"I left the skylight open," replied Bella, climbing up onto the chest to close it. She looked around, disappointed that the Quetzal was nowhere to be seen.

"Are you collecting feathers?" asked Charlie, spotting a cluster of red and green feathers lying on the floorboards.

Bella was confused. She hadn't remembered so many feathers falling off the bird when he came crashing in. "He must have fallen down again trying to get out," she thought to herself.

"If I were an animal, what would I'd be?" Charlie asked Bella, taking a big bite out of her cake.

"Not this game again," Bella complained. "We played this last week." It had been fun doing their homework together, but now Bella needed to talk.

"Charlie, I want to show you something," Bella interrupted, digging out the jewellery box from her mum's chest.

"It's got a secret compartment," she told her friend. "Hold onto the box and let me show you."

Bella turned the handles on the fake bottom drawers and twisted the lid, to reveal the pendant.

"Wow!" Charlie beamed, holding the pendant up to the florescent light. "It's a quetzal, isn't it? Like the ones we've just been looking at on the internet."

She gazed at it admiringly.

"Put it on," Bella invited.

Charlie put the pendant around her neck and walked over to the mirror to have a closer look.

"It was a present to me from my birth mother," Bella told her friend. "My mum couldn't find it, but somehow I knew where it was. It's the most precious thing in the world to me."

"It's lovely, Bella," sighed Charlie, parading like royalty before the mirror. "Let's see it on you."

"You're breaking your promise to the Quetzal," whispered a voice in Bella's head. She felt a lump come into her throat and turned her back on the portrait. "I better keep my big mouth shut," she thought.

Thinking of the pendant and her birth mother brought Bella's mind back to Eugene's insult.

"Do *you* think I look like a pig?" she asked her friend feebly. "Eugene said my mother gave me away because of my nose."

Charlie took a long look at Bella's worried face. Bella could feel her heart thumping. In truth, her nose was not that different from anyone else's, but Bella was sensitive about how she looked and really didn't know what Charlie was going to say. Toying with Bella as only really good friends can, Charlie walked over until her face was about an inch away from Bella's. Then, without any warning, she stuck her chocolate-covered tongue out at her.

"And what are you two laughing about?" Bella's mum called up. She loved hearing her daughter laugh.

Bella and Charlie were having hysterics. Throwing away their forks, they buried their faces in their cake. They squealed like pigs and scoffed until their faces were completely covered in chocolate and every last morsel had been licked from their plates.

"Now that's what a pig looks like," giggled Charlie, pointing to Bella's face.

Inevitably, as the evening wore on, the conversation returned to Eugene Briggs and the situation regarding the school playground.

"He's nothing but a bully," frowned Charlie. "I hate him."

Both Bella and Charlie were members of the Hawksmore School Council. They'd complained to the headteacher a dozen times about the problem with the playground, but nothing was ever done about it. Bella wanted to tell Charlie more about the pendant and the Quetzal's suggestion, but she didn't want to break her promise.

While Bella's mum called Mr. Stevens to come and pick Charlie up, the two friends jumped into the hammock.

"Where's the cat?" asked Charlie, as the hammock swung violently from side to side.

"That murderer?" growled Bella flatly.

"Bella, you are mean to her," Charlie chastised.

And then it struck Bella. The muted squawk they'd heard earlier, then the cat sneaking down the stairs with that guilty look on her face. And now all those feathers under the skylight. "Oh no!" cried Bella, trying to stand up in the hammock but falling all over her friend. "She's killed him!"

Bella was sobbing.

"What's the matter?" blurted Charlie, disturbed by Bella's dramatic change of mood. But Bella was inconsolable.

Charlie put her arm around her friend and relaxed into the gentle sway of the hammock. "You are kind, Bella," said Charlie, putting two and two together regarding the cat and the feathers. "No wonder there are always so many birds in your garden."

Staring up into the rafters, Charlie noticed something on the skylight. "Someone's been writing on your dirty window," she said, pointing upwards.

Bella had to squint her eyes to read it. The footwork was a little scribbly, but she could just about make it out. The Quetzal had tried to draw a football pitch. At the top he'd written: "Wear the pendant."

Bella couldn't believe it.

"He escaped!" she cheered. "Oh, Charlie. I was so mean." She gave Charlie a big hug. Charlie had no idea what Bella was talking about but was happy that she was no longer upset.

"Don't worry about the football problem," Bella told Charlie. "I've got a plan."

CHAPTER FOUR

THE PLAN

The next morning was Tuesday. Bella got up early and dashed up to the attic in her pyjamas, hoping to find the Quetzal waiting for her by the skylight.

"I should have warned him about the cat," she muttered to herself, as she climbed onto the chest and peered out of the window. "It serves him right for being so bossy!"

But she didn't mean it.

Bella was disappointed that there was no sign of the Quetzal on the roof. "I hope he really is alright," she thought. "And that he kept away from the crows."

She looked up to the portrait of the Mayan woman on the wall. "He'll come," came the whisper. "And when he does – pay attention. He's good."

"He's a cantankerous old nag," groaned Bella out loud, giving the portrait quite a stare. "But don't worry. I'll listen."

She took the pendant from the jewellery box and put it on. That very second, Bella heard a husky squawk from the garden.

"Read all about it!" called the now familiar voice. "Intrepid explorer discovers new clues on the whereabouts of lost tomb."

Hearing her mum singing in the shower, Bella ran downstairs and straight through the the back door out into the garden.

"Shoo!" she shouted at the cat, who was stalking across the patio with a devilish look in her eye. "Get in!" She swung her foot in the cat's general direction and chased her back in through the cat flap.

Bella's slippers made a crisp crunching sound on the lawn. She loved bright, frosty winter mornings when the condensation of her breath hung in the air like smog. Holding onto her pendant, she looked around the garden for any sign of the Quetzal.

"Where are you?" Bella chirped as loudly as she dared. "Stop hiding and come out."

She knew her mum would be furious to find her in the garden before breakfast dressed like this.

"Over here . . . over here . . . over here . . . ," echoed the muffled retort, which appeared to be coming from the old tin watering can by the shed.

Flapping her arms around herself to generate a little heat, Bella walked over. "Quetzal?" she called tentatively.

From over the rusted rim, the Quetzal cautiously poked his quaking beak. "Have those crows gone?" he quivered. "They're not giving me a minute's peace."

Bella scoured the rooftops and garden and found them eerily absent of bird life.

"And where's the cat?" he queried nervously.

"Gone," replied Bella. Then, in a rapid change of tack: "Do you really think we can beat Eugene's gang at football?"

She had hardly been able to sleep, she was so excited.

"Wear the pendant," sighed the Quetzal. "The quicker you're convinced, the sooner we can get on and do what has to be done."

"What do you mean?" asked Bella.

The Quetzal had alluded to some higher purpose than her grudge match with the school bullies, but that was all. It was time to lay his cards on the table. He poked his beak around inside the watering can and popped out with a tattered magazine. "Look at this," he demanded, tossing it at Bella's feet.

Bella bent down and picked up the damp periodical. It was a monthly publication called *Archaeology*. On the front cover, there was a picture of Ted Briggs. His snide grin revealed his yellowy teeth, while his dark shady eyes looked menacing and sly. With his hunched-up shoulders, greying hair and scruffy grey beard, Bella thought he looked like a wolf. She screwed up her face to show her disgust. She wasn't alone in disliking Ted Briggs. The children at Hawksmore Primary saw him not only on prize day but also at Monday assemblies when he was in London, when he'd tell them tiresome stories that were supposed to make them feel small and terrified about the outside world, a place where only people like Ted Briggs dared to go. In the picture, Briggs was dressed as he always was – in a white safari hat and a shabby old khaki suit that didn't fit him because he was so tall.

"He thinks he's some great intrepid explorer," Bella sneered. "But he's just boring. He howls at his own jokes and never listens to anyone but himself. *And* he smells!"

Briggs smoked like a chimney from an old wooden pipe,

which he kept in the top pocket of his jacket. His shoes were always scruffy and worn, and he had a distinctly unpleasant aroma – a combination of sweat and stale tobacco. It was Bella's guess that he hardly ever washed, which was an insult she often used to annoy his son.

"Read the article," ordered the Quetzal. "And hurry up. We haven't got all day."

The article outlined Briggs's latest expedition to the Guatemalan rainforest, where he had made a discovery about a possible entrance to an ancient temple. Briggs believed his discovery would lead him to the final resting place of King Kabah, in whose tomb he hoped to find an infamous emerald. According to legend, the jewel was supposed to be buried alongside the king's sarcophagus so it might be with him when he passed into the underworld. The emerald was thought to have many magical powers, one being that it could see inside human souls. Despite years of archaeological exploration aimed at finding the tomb and the emerald, this famous icon of mythology had remained elusive. Frustratingly for Briggs, the Guatemalan government had refused him permission to excavate and pursue his theory, because they wanted their own archaeological teams to work on it.

"He's getting confused between fact and fiction," Bella decided, dropping the magazine onto the icy path by the shed. "I know that story. It's a Guatemalan myth. Only the human touched with the spirit of the Mayan god, Itzamna, can ever enter the temple and be led to its hidden treasures."

The Quetzal was nodding his beak approvingly.

"According to the legend, there's a jaguar made out of solid gold, with three fire-breathing heads, lurking in the shadows ready to pounce on anyone who tries to raid the tomb," Bella recalled.

She stopped and looked down at the Quetzal.

"What's all that got to do with me?"

The Quetzal was just about to deliver his well-rehearsed speech on the imperative nature of their mission when there was a call from the kitchen: "Bella, where are you?"

"I've got to go," Bella groaned, tucking away her pendant and turning back towards the house. "I'll meet you up in the attic tonight."

The Quetzal lifted his beak and gave out a long screech into the heavens. It was going to be more time-consuming than he had thought to get this girl prepared and up to speed for the task at hand.

Even though Bella told her mum that she was only feeding the birds, she was still in trouble.

"Bella Balistica!" her mum exclaimed, as she caught her sneaking in through the back door. "Get upstairs and get dressed right now!"

It was one of those mornings when everything was a rush. By the time Bella was ready to go, it was ten past eight.

"Have you got any after-school clubs today?" asked her mum, thrusting Bella's schoolbag into her arms as she opened the front door.

"No," Bella grouched. "Football won't start again till next term."

Her mum was giving her a long hard look. Bella knew what was coming next.

"Where's your coat?" her mum asked sternly.

As always, Bella's coat was somewhere other than at hand.

"I think I left it at school," she mumbled, embarrassed that after promising faithfully to bring it home yesterday, she had forgotten it again.

"Bella!" cried her frustrated mum, pointing to the staircase. "Then go and put on another fleece."

So yet again, Bella ran out of the house without her coat on one of the coldest days of the year. For once, she decided to follow her mum's orders and didn't take the shortcut through the woods, just in case Eugene had planned an ambush. As she ran down Shooter's Hill, she considered her team. "Rahina Iqbal is the best striker of the ball," she thought to herself, "and Imogen Meeks must be the tallest girl in school – she'd better be goalkeeper." With Charlie and herself already committed, Bella only had one more player to find.

Bella had already decided that it would be best to challenge the boys to a five-a-side match. That way they could limit the amount of off-the-ball bullying they might get into, and the girls would have more space to use their superior ball skills. When the numbers playing football got too big, it inevitably would become a toe-punting exercise with the big kickers and foulers winning through.

Hawksmore Primary was one of those old Victorian schools with a weather vane on the roof, which had been expanded with a new nursery building and two mobile classrooms where the upper juniors worked. There were some old engraved signs over the entrances, one for the girls and one for the boys, but these days everyone ignored them. Bella met up with her friends in the playground at about eight-forty, just before the morning bell.

"Can I play?" interrupted an excited Melanie Roberts, overhearing Bella talking about the match with Imogen and Rahina. "I'd give anything to teach those boys a lesson."

"Great!" replied Bella quickly, while inside she was thinking: "Is this really a good idea?" Melanie was one of the brightest girls in the school, but she wasn't known for her footballing skills. Still, Bella had a soft spot for her – at least her enthusiasm was infectious.

Surprisingly, none of the girls seemed to mind about the possibility of doing the boys' homework for the next few weeks.

"We won't do it anyway," said Melanie in her typically off-hand manner. "What can they do to us? Things can't get any worse."

"What are you going to do about a ref?" asked Rahina with a little more urgency. "They'll cheat if we don't have one."

Bella hadn't thought of this.

"I say we ask Mr. Alder," suggested Melanie. "The boys all like him because he likes rugby *and* he plays the guitar."

Mr. Alder taught Bella's class, 6TA. Bella liked him because he was really passionate about history and made projects like Ancient Egypt and the Greeks come alive. Because of Bella, he was even going to do the Maya as a topic instead of the Aztecs next term.

"Great idea," Bella agreed and went straight off to the staff room to find him.

Mr. Alder was a tall, awkward-looking man, who walked with a slight stoop, as if he was embarrassed about his height. He tended to wear too much green corduroy and spoke very quietly, and yet the children liked him. Perhaps it was because he played them pop songs on his guitar and told them wonderful stories that everyone, including Bella, would listen to attentively without interrupting. Still, Bella thought it best not to mention the terms of the match.

"It's just a friendly game, Mr. Alder," she told him, as he leant against the staff-room door sipping his mug of tea.

"I didn't think girls liked football," he slurped.

"We love it," snapped Bella, a little annoyed by his tease.

"What time's kick off?" he asked apologetically.

"Twelve-thirty," Bella told him. "Don't be late!"

The morning bell rang, and the children began the usual pushing and shoving towards the cloakrooms.

"Who's going to make the challenge and agree the terms?" called Imogen across the mayhem. "There should be a contract or something."

"Great idea," Bella agreed. "I'll write one up right now and take it straight over to Eugene."

It was Bella's job to take the registers round to all the classrooms in the morning. Mr. Alder and Mrs. Sticklan thought it might keep her out of mischief, but it didn't. She was always getting into trouble for running down the corridor and jumping on the stairs. Mrs. Sticklan had already given her a final warning: any more running and she was going to take her shoes away. "I hope she does," Bella had told Charlie defiantly. "I'll have more chance of staying on my feet."

Bella went to the school office, borrowed a pen and paper from the secretary and then dropped the handwritten contract onto Eugene's table while he was doing his early-morning reading. This was the deal:

We, the undersigned –
Bella Balistica,
Melanie Roberts,
Rahina Iqbal,
Imogen Meeks
and Charlie Stevens
challenge five upper junior boys (yet to be named)
to a five-a-side game of football.
TODAY!
We win –
the pitch is ours (you have to use the small playground)
You win –
we do all your homework (including endangered
species project) until Xmas.

All through literacy hour Bella could hear the boys giggling, as they passed the contract around between themselves. When the bell went for break, Eugene came straight over.

"You're even more stupid than I thought," he scoffed. "Is this your idea or that ginger-nut friend of yours?"

"It's our idea," retorted Bella indignantly. "All of us. We've had enough! Do you agree to the terms?"

"They're perfect," Eugene grinned. "I couldn't have written them better myself."

"Then I want you all to sign," said Bella. "You *can* write your name?"

"You'll have it in writing by noon," he replied. As he turned, he kicked Bella hard in the shin. "That's for squirting apple juice in my face yesterday," he announced. "Last night, you were lucky. Today, you die."

Bella was tempted to answer back but managed to restrain herself as she rubbed her shin. Maybe it was the influence of the Quetzal or the pendant – she didn't know – but somehow she felt different.

The girls met by the bins at break time to discuss tactics.

"What's that you're wearing?" asked Melanie, pointing to the chain around Bella's neck. "You know you're not allowed to wear jewellery in school."

Bella tucked the chain inside her collar and did up her blouse. If Mrs. Sticklan saw it she'd be in big trouble.

"It's just a lucky charm," she said.

It was decided that Imogen was to play in goal, while Charlie and Melanie would play in defence. Bella and Rahina would play up front.

"We'll play the long ball from the back and beat the boys with speed and quality passing," Bella announced.

Numeracy hour seemed to go on forever, but eventually the lunch bell rang. Luckily, the upper juniors were on first sitting. Bella sat with Charlie and the rest of the team to eat their sandwiches. It was Connor Mitchell who strode up to the table and handed them the contract.

"What do you want, Dumbo?" smirked Bella, with her usual cheeky charm. "Don't tell me *you* made the team."

But Connor Mitchell was untouched by the remark. Bella was no good at insults.

"Alright, pig-face," he retorted. "Here's the contract. It's signed by all the boys – me, Ratty, Prakash, Winston and Briggsy. You're doing our homework for the rest of the year." He slammed the signed contract down and walked away. The girls hadn't bargained on doing the boys' homework for the rest of the year, but it was too late to turn back now.

Eugene Biggs had picked a fearsomely good side. Top of the list was Roland "The Rat" Richardson. Roland took no prisoners when it came to tackling. Bella guessed that Eugene would play him as a lone defender. Prakash Malik, the tallest Year 6 boy in the school, had been named as goalkeeper. "His goal coverage is going to be awesome," sighed Melanie, a little dispirited. Bella guessed Eugene's key strategy was attack, playing three out-and-out-strikers: Connor Mitchell, positioned to the right of midfield, and Winston Geoffrey on the left, with Eugene playing down the middle.

"This could be really humiliating," Imogen lamented.

"No it won't!" Rahina contradicted. "We're going to win."

"Yeah," said Bella, packing away the remains of her lunch. "Let's show them!"

CHAPTER FIVE

THE MATCH

By twelve-thirty Tuesday lunchtime, the word had got around. All the lower juniors who had managed to devour their sandwiches at break were sitting along the touchline with the upper juniors, waiting for the match to begin. Mr. Alder had put on his trainers and got himself a ball, four cones and a whistle from the PE cupboard. Using toe-to-toe footsteps to measure out the goals, he marked their position on the tarmac with a piece of chalk to make sure there was no cheating before he put down the cones. The rest of the goalmouth, the vertical line of the posts, and the height of the crossbar would be left to his discretion.

"I'd like to see the team captains for the toss-up," he announced. Bella and Eugene stepped up. "I want to see a good clean game," he told them. "Ten minutes each way. Any arguing with the ref, it's the red card. Understood?"

They both nodded. Eugene and Bella stared directly into each other's eyes. The second Mr. Alder turned his attention to finding a coin in his pocket, Eugene grinned arrogantly at Bella and raised his fist to her face. But Bella didn't even flinch. When Mr. Alder flicked the coin into the air, she simply smiled and without turning her eyes away from Eugene's glare, called: "Heads."

"Tails!" shouted Mr. Alder.

Eugene chose to kick downhill towards the playing fields. It was going to be an uphill struggle all the way for the girls.

"Take your positions," Mr. Alder ordered as he stood with his foot on the ball and checked his watch.

The noise from the upper junior boys who were watching was ear-splitting.

"Come on, girls!" Bella shouted to all the girls in the crowd.

That's all it took. The responding cheer was amazing. The news that a victory for the girls meant the upper junior boys would move their daily matches away from the main playground was proving popular even amongst lower junior boys.

"Come on, girls!" they shouted.

"Boooo," roared the upper junior boys.

"Boooo," countered the girls.

Then, without any warning, Mr. Alder blew his whistle, and the boys kicked off.

Eugene immediately pushed the ball out to Connor Mitchell on the right wing. Charlie was quickly on to him, blocking his first attempt at a cross and then keeping pace with his run, so that he ended up by the drain marking the right corner flag. Unfortunately, there was no protecting herself from Connor's elbow challenge, as he pushed his way through on the inside.

"Foul!" shouted Bella, raising her hand up from the halfway line. But Mr. Alder, unable to see because Roland had decided to make his way up to the halfway line and stand right in front of him, waved play on. Connor put a devastating cross into the box, and before they knew it – wham! Eugene's powerful header had the girls 1–0 down.

The cheers and jeers around the playground had got the attention of the staff-room upstairs, where nearly all the teachers were now watching from the window. This was bigger than sports day. In the relative tranquillity of her office, Mrs. Sticklan slammed down the document on child exclusions she was enjoying and considered going out to see what all the fuss was about. "Damn those children!" she growled.

"Stay calm," Bella told Imogen, taking the ball from her dejected goalkeeper. "We've got another nineteen minutes. The game's hardly started."

"Exactly," sighed Imogen. "And we're already one–nil down."

The girls, though, were impressed with Bella's command of the situation. Instead of shouting at the referee and pleading against a decision that was never going to be changed, she simply threw him the ball.

"Bella seems so calm and focused," Rahina whispered to Charlie as they moped back to their starting positions. "Normally she goes ballistic when this kind of thing happens."

All Bella's team sensed that there was definitely something different about her today. Just before kick-off, Bella reached under her blouse to feel the pendant. "Come on, Bella," she urged herself. "Stay focused." But her confidence had taken a knock.

For the next nine minutes Bella's playing was inspirational. She made several darting runs around Roland Richardson, but each time her final pass or shot was thwarted by Eugene Briggs, as he rushed back to help his one-man defence. With less than thirty seconds of the first half left on the clock, Bella was making a blinding run down the wing when she was fouled by

Roland. Mr. Alder was checking his watch and missed the incident, much to the irritation of the supporting fans. The ball was taken up by Winston Geoffrey, who cut inside Charlie and from ten metres out shot the ball right over the imaginary crossbar into the playing fields.

"Goal!" shouted Mr. Alder.

"No!" shouted the angry fans.

"Yes!" shouted Eugene Briggs and his euphoric team mates.

A long blow from Mr. Alder's whistle signalled the end of the first half. Bella could hardly gather the energy to get to her feet, she felt so deflated.

"On your knees already?" sneered Connor Mitchell as the teams swapped ends over the half-time break. "You're so dead."

"What's the matter, Bella?" asked Charlie, running over to see if Bella was alright after her fall.

"It's not fair!" Bella complained. "I was fouled, and that shot was miles over the crossbar."

"It doesn't matter," Charlie urged her friend. "We're playing well. If we can get an early second-half goal, we're right back in it."

Bella felt so depressed. The pendant appeared to be as good as useless.

Although Bella was finding it difficult to get into the game, the second half got off to a good start for the girls. Twice Charlie shot from long range, forcing Prakash Malik into diving saves. Rahina too had a short-range shot kicked off the line. But, as they knew, playing well and scoring goals don't always go together. With three minutes left on the clock the girls were still 2–0 down. Bella felt under her blouse for the pendant.

"I thought you were supposed to be magic," she mumbled, her confidence and faith in its powers all but gone.

A loud squawk from the roof of the bicycle sheds alerted Bella to the colourful bird perched on the gutter. "Believe," chirped the Quetzal. "The pendant only works if you have faith in it and yourself. Now come on!"

"Two more minutes!" shouted Mr. Alder, checking his watch.

Eugene Briggs took a long-range shot that rebounded off Imogen's legs and came to Charlie. She played a perfectly weighted through-ball to Bella who turned and volleyed – thud! The ball went flying through the goal. The crowd went wild.

"Come on, girls!" they shouted.

"Boooo," howled the upper junior boys.

"Two–one to the boys," announced Mr. Alder. "One minute plus injury time remaining."

"What injury time?" complained Connor Mitchell to Eugene Briggs. "I ain't injured no one. Yet."

But the boys were looking tired. And the girls had the downhill advantage now.

"Right," Bella called to her team mates, "gather round." Her confidence was returning. "They're going to be defending this all the way to the final whistle. I want no long shots or toe-punts up the field. I want short passes to the feet and don't shoot until you're in an unmissable position."

"What's going on over there?" asked Melanie, pointing to the flock of screeching crows on the bicycle shed roof.

Bella's heart skipped a beat as she turned to see the Quetzal scramble his way free from his attackers and soar into the sky.

"Go, Quetzal – go!" went Bella's silent cheer.

"Believe," called the departing bird.

"It's a parrot," exclaimed Imogen.

"It looks like a Guatemalan quetzal," corrected Charlie. "Me and Bella were reading about them last night on the internet. But there couldn't be one here!"

Mr. Alder blew his whistle.

Bella took the ball and passed it to Rahina, who played it to Charlie's feet.

"Believe," Bella reminded herself, pulling out the pendant and rubbing it between her fingers. A blast of energy shot through her body. "Come on!" she yelled to her team-mates.

Turning and beating Winston Geoffrey for pace and skill, Charlie chipped the ball over Roland Richardson's lunging tackle right into Bella's path and – whack!

"Two all!" cheered Mr. Alder.

The noise from the crowed was deafening.

"We'll now play golden goal," Mr. Alder shouted through the bedlam. "First team to score, wins."

Bella tucked the pendant away and looked up into the heavens. There, circling the match from high in the sky, she could just about make out the colourful coat of her friend.

"I believe," she said to herself.

By now the bell for the end of playtime had gone, but none of the children were making a move. There was to be only five minutes extra time, so Mr. Alder told them they'd have to start with a drop-ball. To the shock of all the teachers watching from the staff-room, Mrs. Sticklan made an unexpected appearance at the doorway. Sensing a feeling of frivolity alongside the usual lunchtime chaos, she marched up to the window to see what all the fuss was about. Instantly furious that Mr. Alder was keeping the children out late, she thrust her head out of the window. "Stop!" she bellowed at the top of her lungs.

Her voice reverberated around the playground like an exploding bomb, while a cold shiver shot through everyone within earshot. The children in the playground looked up, waiting in trepidation for the short sharp attack of her tongue. Even from a distance, Mrs. Sticklan's angular face and glistening white teeth gave her the appearance of a shark.

"Perhaps you didn't hear the bell, Mr. Alder," she snapped.

"But this is too important," asserted Mr. Alder as best he could. "The children are playing some truly inspired football."

Annoyed beyond words, Mrs. Sticklan bit her tongue and sent her mind into overdrive. "Very well, Mr. Alder," she thundered snootily, "but five minutes only."

She'd have him up before Ted Briggs and the governors for this.

Eugene Briggs made absolutely no attempt to play the drop-ball and instead kicked Bella hard on the shin. Without any hesitation at all, Mr. Alder got out his red card, and Eugene was off.

"No!" shouted Mrs. Sticklan from the window, suddenly interested in the game. "That wasn't a sending-off offence."

Slamming the window shut, Mrs. Sticklan stomped toward the staff-room door. The other teachers in the room, desperately trying to finish their photocopying and gobble up their sandwiches in time for the afternoon session, visibly cowered as she passed.

"I'm not standing for this," she snarled, slamming the door.

Mrs. Sticklan was a terrifying woman when she was on the warpath.

Eugene was outraged by the sending-off decision and the fact that the girls in the crowd were cheering as if they had already won.

"Stay focused," Bella shouted to her team-mates, raising her fist in defiance of the enemy.

Bella took the free kick, passing the ball to Charlie, who was now playing as an attacking full-back. It was then that the crippling challenge occurred. Bella saw Connor Mitchell setting off to tackle Charlie with only one aim in mind – to push her over. Bella felt a sudden rush of power and energy emanating throughout her body. As Charlie returned the ball and was hit by Conner Mitchell, Bella struck the ball with the outside of her right foot. It looked like it was missing the goal by a mile, but the heavy slice Bella had put on the ball was causing it to bend. The whole thing appeared to happen in slow motion. Charlie, tumbling sideways to the ground, stuck out her right hand to break her fall just as Bella's shot clearly dipped under the left-hand corner of the imaginary crossbar.

"Goal!" shouted Mr. Alder. "The girls win!"

The deafening cheers were soon subdued by the presence of the grey-haired Mrs. Sticklan marching out to the centre of the playground. At six foot two, in her black heels and grey pinstriped suit, few would have dared to confront her as she blew her whistle and decreed in a shrill voice: "That shot was over the crossbar, Mr. Alder – and you know it! Now come on everyone, back to lessons. There's been enough trivial nonsense for one playtime."

But Bella was in no mood to comply. She went straight over to her friend.

"Charlie, are you alright?" she asked calmly through the

chatter of the dispersing crowd. But Charlie was in too much pain to talk. She was lying on her back, clutching her right wrist.

"I think it's broken," she grimaced in pain.

"Come here!" screeched Mrs. Sticklan, striding purposefully towards them. "Inside, now!"

Ignoring her, Bella bent down and gently put her hand on Charlie's wrist and felt the movement of the broken bone. "Use the power of the pendant," whispered a voice inside her head. She reached hesitantly for her pendant and rubbed it lightly over Charlie's injury. Then, for the first time in her life, Bella felt the rush of an awesome power. It was like a thousand volts of electricity were shooting round her body, through the pendant and on into Charlie's broken bone. For a moment she felt too dizzy to see.

"That feels good," Charlie sighed. "Wow!"

But Mrs. Sticklan was approaching too quickly. Bella tucked the pendant away just in time. Grabbing Bella by her ear, Mrs. Sticklan pulled her up.

"My office – now!" she shouted.

"But *Miss*," Bella pleaded. "I was only looking after my friend. I think she's broken her . . . "

It was here that Bella had to stop talking because Mr. Alder was helping Charlie up by her injured wrist. She seemed to be in no pain whatsoever.

Bella was spellbound. What had she done?

CHAPTER SIX

REPERCUSSIONS

Mrs. Sticklan was sitting at her desk, talking on the phone. She was feeling both triumphant and vindicated, having just visited the upper junior classrooms to pass judgement on the match.

"Ted, hi there, it's Margaret – Margaret Sticklan. Where are you, the signal is awful – Guatemala? No, don't worry, it's the school phone – I was just calling to update you on our problem. This time, I think we've got her. I'll text you on the school mobile after I've spoken to the education authority and her mum."

She hung up.

Bella had a miserable afternoon. She had to miss registration and go sit outside Mrs. Sticklan's office, while she toured the school to investigate lunchtime events. Bella wasn't even allowed to take a book. Instead, she just stared at the cracks in the wallpaper and kicked the legs of her chair. It was a routine she knew by heart. The crimes could be anything, from shouting out and answering back to teachers in class to crawling under the mobile classrooms for balls during lesson time, but at least they were varied. Some children only got to see Mrs. Sticklan when they did *good* work.

"Stop swinging your legs!" shouted Mrs. Sticklan from the comfort of her office chair later that afternoon.

Bella heard her get up and clomp her way to the door.

"I've been looking through your discipline record," she snapped stiffly, stepping into the corridor. "It's not good. And what with the riot you caused at lunchtime, I'm going to have to consult with the governors about what steps I can take with you."

Bella was too devastated to speak. For weeks now, she'd been doing her best to collect those stupid good behaviour stickers. If she got five in a week she was awarded a special certificate in the Friday afternoon good-work assemblies. Last month she almost managed it, but one of her stickers was taken away when she'd shouted at the lunchtime supervisors for letting the Year 6 boys push in for second helpings.

"Sit still," Mrs. Sticklan ordered, disappearing back into her office. "If I hear you swinging your legs just once more, I'll take the chair away."

"Yes, Miss," Bella mumbled sullenly.

Left to her thoughts, Bella tried to rationalize the afternoon's events. 'At least we won the match.' she thought. But Bella was worried about Charlie and the incident with the wrist. For one thing, the shot of energy she'd experienced as she held the pendant against Charlie's wrist was not only spooky, it was downright scary. To compound things even further, it appeared to have actually healed Charlie's broken bones.

"I must be going dippy," Bella thought. She wondered

about the magical powers of her mother's gift. Perhaps the pendant, the Quetzal and her birth mother were connected to each other in some way.

"I'm trying to get hold of your mother," barked Mrs. Sticklan, poking her head around the door just before three. "They say she's too busy to come to the phone." Mrs. Sticklan spent most of her life shaking her head and moaning about something. "Well, it's not good enough. You're just going to have to wait here until I reach her," she concluded.

Bella felt her sense of injustice starting to rise. "It's not easy getting to the phone when you're delivering a baby," she was thinking. Unusually for Bella, she kept her mouth shut.

To Bella's relief, Charlie came straight round to the office after the home-time bell.

"Charlie," Bella beamed. "Are you alright? How's your wrist?"

Charlie too was happy to see her friend. She held out her right hand. "I don't know what you did, Bella," she said, smiling. "But your massage with that lucky trinket seemed to do the trick." Bella had felt the bone – it had most definitely been broken.

"It's fine now – look!" Charlie smiled, revolving her wrist to prove her agility.

Bella could feel a warm tingly sensation around her neck. She wanted to get the pendant out and look at it but decided to keep it tucked safely away. Something very weird was going on.

Charlie crouched down to whisper into Bella's ear. "The boys are saying that we lost the match."

Bella could feel her body tense.

"Eugene Briggs said that Mrs. Sticklan was in a much better position to see your final shot. Because she disputed your last goal, it doesn't count."

"But it was two–two at full-time!" Bella cried, raising her voice.

"Not when you disallow your last second-half goal for off-side," whispered Charlie sadly. "Mrs. Sticklan said you were at least a metre in front of Richardson and Mitchell when the ball was passed."

"But we don't play off-side in five-a-side football," Bella pleaded, a little too loudly for comfort.

"I know!" Charlie hushed, putting her finger to her lips. "But that's what Mrs Stricklen says. And her decision is final."

Bella felt more depressed than ever.

"And there's more," added Charlie, as quietly as she could. "Mrs. Sticklan has told all the upper junior classes that no one is to speak with you after school."

"That's right, Charlotte Stevens," snarled Mrs. Sticklan, opening her office door. "You can come and see me at lunchtime tomorrow."

"Yes, Mrs. Sticklan," said Charlie despondently, standing up quickly and lowering her head. "Sorry."

"Go," Mrs. Sticklan ordered.

Charlie turned and walked slowly away down the corridor.

Eventually, Mrs. Sticklan called Bella into her office and handed her a brown envelope. "Since I can't get your mother on the phone, I've had no choice but to write her a letter. I've spoken to Mr. Briggs, and we've decided to exclude you for three days."

Bella felt her legs wobble. There had been low points

during her time at Hawksmore Primary, but since the governors had got rid of the last headteacher and appointed Mrs. Sticklan, Bella had been free-falling into disaster.

"You can appeal to the governors, but I don't advise it. Mr. Briggs and I are running a pretty tight ship here. The three days start from tomorrow, so we won't be having the pleasure of your charming company again until Monday morning next week. Go on. Be off with you."

Bella took the letter with trembling hands and left. Her mum was going to be heartbroken.

CHAPTER SEVEN

REPRISALS

Eugene Briggs had been furious with his defenders after the match. "Toe-punters, all of them," he grumbled to Connor Mitchell, as they sloped off back to the classroom. "From now on, it's just you and me. And as for that Mr. Alder, he's on a two-year contract that I just can't see being renewed somehow," he chuckled. "Not when my dad gets to hear about this."

"And what about Bella Balistica?" asked Connor. "We're not going to let her and that ginger goody-goody get away with this, are we?"

"We'll follow them home," sneered Eugene. "Tonight, they're both getting it."

By the time Bella got to the school gates, even the habitual stragglers had gone. Feeling as if things couldn't possibly get any worse, she decided to cut through the woods. It was a mistake.

"She's coming," Connor Mitchell whispered from his hiding place behind the tree.

"Excellent," Eugene hissed. "Have you got the string and the scissors?"

Connor nodded.

"Now remember," Eugene hushed, "first, hit the back of her knees. I'll put the sack over her head. You tie her arms."

"I know, I know," Connor grunted, picking up his stick. "We've already done this once tonight, remember?"

Eugene smiled to himself. His father was going to love hearing about this.

Dejected by her exclusion from school and having the result of the match overturned, Bella had ripped off her pendant and was considering whether or not to hurl it into the bushes. "Some power I have," she moaned. "It doesn't matter what I do – I can't win."

She was just about to throw the pendant when she was distracted by a rustling in the bushes. Terrified that it might be an ambush, Bella started to run but was whacked with a stick behind the knees before she could get into her stride. As she fell, she stuck her arms out to break her fall and managed to roll away just in time to avoid Connor's boot. Before the boys could capitalize on their strategic advantage, Bella was up.

"Quick, again!" She recognized the voice of Connor Mitchell and knew right away what they were up to.

"They're not pinning me down and torturing me with stinging nettles and hawthorns *today*," Bella muttered through gritted teeth. She thrust the pendant into her pocket and lunged at her attackers.

Eugene Briggs hadn't been expecting Bella to stay on her feet. Holding up the sack meant that his hands were full, making it easy for Bella to knock him down with her charge.

"Ouch!" he cried when his elbow hit the path. "Right on my funny bone!"

But he too was quickly up.

"After her!" he shouted. "She's not getting away again."

Bella had already put the pendant back on and was now sprinting away through the woods. "I wish I could fly," Bella thought as she jumped over icy hollows and woodland debris. "What's the good of having a pendant that makes you talk like a bird if you can't fly like one?"

Bella skidded into a glade. A recent storm had uprooted a large tree, which had crashed to the ground and now blocked her path. At first glance, the trunk was too high – still, her instinct said: "Jump!" Holding her breath, Bella closed her eyes and leapt. To her amazement, she glided straight over it and landed ten metres clear on the other side.

"What the . . . ?" she heard Eugene Briggs cry, as he stopped to clamber over the obstacle. But he was gaining – and fast!

Bewildered by her short flight, Bella didn't know which way to turn. "What's going on?" she was thinking. "First Charlie's wrist, and now this!"

Bella's instincts were in disarray. Her mortal body was telling her to run, and yet something deep inside made her stop and look up. In a flash of inspiration she seemed to understand the unthinkable. Focusing all her energies on the higher branches of the tallest oak tree she could see, Bella bent her knees, opened her arms and jumped.

In terms of aviation, nothing about that first flight was commendable, other than the fact that having crashed through the tree with the grace of a bumbling baboon, she somehow managed to cling onto a branch. "Did I really just fly up here?" she panicked, as the branch began to bow under her weight. Bella was completely baffled. She'd banged her knees into the trunk, poked her right eye and was so preoccupied trying to avoid scratching her legs, as they dangled in the branches below, she almost forgot about her pursuers.

"I don't believe that girl!" Bella heard Connor exclaim.

Suddenly, Bella realized a new danger: "What if they saw that jump?" she gasped. "They'll call me a freak."

The thudding sound of Eugene's and Connor's boots as they approached was sluggish compared with the racing tempo of Bella's heartbeat. From her precarious position in the upper branches, she wiped her weeping eye on the sleeve of her jumper and squinted down to watch her dismayed pursuers pass by. It was lucky she didn't have a problem with heights.

"Where's she gone?" Connor wheezed.

Bella watched in trepidation, as the boys doubled back and started to zigzag through the trees, but they weren't even warm. When she was sure she couldn't be seen, she pulled herself up onto the strong arm of the main branch to catch her breath. When she finally managed to open both her eyes fully, the enormity of what she'd just done struck her. She'd found it hard enough to jump over the hurdles at last summer's sport day, and yet she'd just jumped twenty metres at least. This was something supernatural, way beyond anything she'd ever experienced before. "It's the pendant," she thought. "It summoned the Quetzal and now it's doing all this."

Bella had a feeling her life was never going to be the same again.

"It must have something to do with my mother and the fact I'm Guatemalan," she mused. "But what exactly?"

When her heart finally stopped pounding, Bella pulled herself up again and hesitantly shuffled herself over to the trunk. In truth, she had no idea how she was going to climb down. The choices were bleak: she could either stay where she was and call for help, which might mean alerting Eugene and Connor to her whereabouts, or she would have to experiment with the unthinkable. Deciding on the latter, Bella put the pendant into her mouth and took a quantum leap in faith. She opened her arms and began to flap them up and down as fast as she could. Immediately, she banged her head on the branch above her. A voice in her head said: "Idiot! Look where you're going."

The next attempt was even less graceful than the first. Choosing the nearest tree she could see, Bella bent her trembling knees, opened her arms and jumped. As she tumbled down through the thickest part of the tree, she just managed to grab onto a small cluster of branches, saving herself from a nasty fall. "Believe," she told herself. "Stop thinking you're going to fail before you even try."

Battered and bruised, she regained her footing and went for it again, then again, each time gaining more confidence and dexterity in the air.

Taking short tentative flights from tree to tree, Bella continued to explore her newly-discovered skill until she was right by the Shooters Hill entrance to the woods. Jumping down from the lower branches, she tore her brown and orange school skirt, but she didn't care. Then as fast as her legs could take her, she ran home. Thrusting her key into the lock, she threw open the front door. The cat squealed in horror and shot through her legs out into the front garden.

"Mum, where are you?" she called.

Even when her mum was on a day shift at the hospital,

it was quite unusual for Bella to be home before her.

"Mum!"

Bella was desperate to talk to her. She rushed through to the kitchen. On the table there was a note.

Hi Bella,

Managed to get away from the hospital early.
Charlie called round after school. She says she's
OK, but I'm taking her home. I won't be long.

Love,
Mum
xx

Bella felt her heart sink. Something terrible must have happened.

CHAPTER EIGHT

INQUISITION

Bella burst out of the house into Birdcage Crescent. The sound of the door slamming could be heard even above the heavy commuter traffic from the main road, and several neighbours were drawn to their windows to peer at the girl in the ragged school uniform sprinting towards Shooters Hill. "Going out without her coat again," the neighbour opposite reported to her husband. "I don't know what her mother can be thinking."

The streetlights were already on, but there were still a few creepy gaps on the way to Charlie's house. In these places, the eerie sound of creaking trees and distant footsteps gave Bella the unsettling feeling of being followed. She felt nervous and reached for her pendant for a tingle of reassurance as she ran. Normally she wouldn't go out on her own after dark.

Taking a sharp left by the traffic lights on Shooter's Hill, Bella skidded into the grass verge, picked herself up and sprinted on towards the Well Hall Roundabout. Charlie's parents owned a large semi-detached house on Harrison Road. Bella loved sleeping over. Mr. and Mrs. Stevens had a cleaner three days a week to do the housework and a professional landscaper for the front and back gardens. Consequently, the house was always spotless. Not that this in itself was appealing to a girl like Bella Balistica, who could trash a tidy worktop before she'd even kicked off her shoes and dropped her jumper to the floor. It was more the fact that playing over at Charlie's house was different from the chaos of her own home.

Bella knocked loudly on the front door. "Come on," she muttered impatiently. She guessed her mum must have called Mrs. Stevens at work. "What have they done to you, Charlie?" she was thinking to herself.

Mrs. Stevens opened the front door. It always amazed Bella how tanned and healthy Charlie's mum looked. Today, as ever, she looked petite and chic in the trendy black outfit she wore at the salon.

"Hi, Bella," Mrs. Stevens smiled kindly.

"What happened?" Bella spurted.

But Mrs. Stevens was too full of tears to speak. She simply gestured to Bella to come in.

Bella ran to the stairs but bumped straight into her own mum who, having heard Bella's voice, had come out to greet her. Usually, Bella's mum would have refrained from making a comment about her daughter's appearance – but tonight, she couldn't.

"Bella!" she cried, holding the little ruffian at arm's length and staring down in disbelief. "What *have* you been doing?"

In truth, Annie had been worried sick that Bella had met the same fate as Charlie. She was just finishing her tea and was anxious to return home, when Bella knocked on the door.

Along with the torn skirt, scuffed shoes, filthy hands and face and the weeping red eye, Bella's hair was stained with bark and the residue of rotting leaves.

"I've been playing in the woods," said Bella, who often skated around the truth but never told barefaced lies.

"I can see that, you little monkey. Now where's your coat?" asked her mum, relieved that she was otherwise unscathed. She caught a glimpse of the chain around Bella's neck and could hardly contain her delight. "Bella . . . !" she exclaimed.

Bella rolled her shoulders and wriggled her neck, hoping to hide the pendant. Tactfully, her mum decided not to pass comment.

"I want to see Charlie," Bella demanded.

Bella's mum refused to let her go and see Charlie until she had washed her hands and face and had her eye attended to. Secretly, she liked the idea that her daughter was happy climbing trees and exploring the woods, just so long as she didn't go there after dark and without her coat.

"Charlie's been badly bullied," she whispered in the downstairs bathroom, as she wiped Bella's eye with cotton wool. "She came straight over to our house after the attack." She paused. Bella could see her mum was as upset as Mrs. Stevens. "They did some pretty mean things to her," she concluded.

Bella couldn't help herself. She started to cry. She knew only too well the kind of mean tricks that Eugene and Connor could play. Her mum crouched down to give her daughter a good long hug. "Bella . . . ," her mum stumbled. "Are you and Charlie being bullied?"

She pushed Bella away to arm's length so that she could

scrutinize her face with an eagle eye. Bella tensed. Her mum felt the first drops of tears form in her own eyes, as Bella bit her lip, furrowed her brow and violently shook her head. There was nothing else to do but hug. "You're not alone, Bella," Annie whispered into her daughter's ear.

Neither of them spoke for a full minute.

"Can I go and see her now, mum?" sniffed Bella at last. "Please, mum."

"Yes," snuffled her mum. "But wipe away your tears. Charlie doesn't want to see you crying. And be prepared," she said gently. "Her face is badly bruised and . . . ," she was finding it difficult to speak, " . . . they didn't leave her with very much hair."

Charlie was sitting up in bed, when Bella walked in. Bella was shocked to see just how brutally her beautiful red hair had been chopped. Mr. Stevens was sitting rather uncomfortably on a small chair by the bed with his notepad in hand, trying to work out what to do with his long legs. His long face told its own story. He'd been trying to follow Charlie's explanation of events, but things just weren't adding up.

"Bella," Charlie beamed, pushing back her pillow to sit up a little straighter. "You were quick."

Bella came round to the side of the bed to give her friend a hug. As she did so, Charlie whispered: "Please don't tell them." Bella could see that Charlie had several bruises on her face and arms.

"I fell over," said Charlie optimistically.

"Bella, we're hoping you can help us," said Mr. Stevens kindly, pushing away the chair and perching himself at the end of the bed. "Charlie says she doesn't know who did this to her.

Have you any idea?"

Bella felt obliged to make up answers to Mr. Stevens's questions about the bullies, who apart from cutting Charlie's hair and covering her in stinging nettle rashes and bruises, had also ripped up her homework. It was a frustrating experience for Bella, who saw no reason at all to hide the truth. But it was Charlie's wish, and Bella would never betray her friend. Later, when Mr. Stevens went downstairs for his tea, they had a quiet moment to discuss the issue.

"Charlie, why can't we tell him?" Bella pleaded. "We could get them excluded."

"But they would come back," Charlie argued. "And then it would be worse."

They sat in silence for a few minutes before Bella said: "Maybe it would. But it's not right to protect a bully by not telling on them."

Charlie lowered her head. She knew Bella was right.

It was eight o'clock by the time Bella and her mum got home with takeaway pizzas. No sooner had they opened the front door than Bella was making a dash for the stairs.

"Whatever you're doing, don't be long," called Annie, "otherwise your pizza will be cold."

Bella rushed up to the attic expecting to find the Quetzal, but he was nowhere to be seen. Looking up to the skylight, she realized that she had forgotten to leave it open. "You're late," scolded a voice inside her head as she stared around the room. "You didn't really expect him to hang around on the roof all night, did you?"

She gave the portrait on the wall a long hard stare, then got onto the chest to prop open the skylight. Putting her pendant safely back in its secret compartment, she went downstairs.

After their pizza, Bella's mum let her stay up late to watch TV. They sat cosily together on the sofa, while Annie gently brushed the knots out of Bella's hair. "I need to speak to the Quetzal," thought Bella. Not only was there her flying experience to talk about, but there was that mindboggling moment when she touched Charlie's wrist with the pendant and cured her broken bone. But these weren't the only things on Bella's mind. Right now, there was the small matter of her three-day exclusion from school to deal with. Her mum was going to be devastated when she found out.

"Mum, I've got something to show you," said Bella, pulling away from her mum's careful brushing to get the letter from her bag.

"Is it that beautiful pendant I saw you wearing this afternoon?" asked her mum tentatively. "You know Mrs. Sticklan will confiscate it if she ever catches you wearing it." Bella flinched, embarrassed that her little secret had been discovered so soon. "Well?" said her mum. But Bella was too upset about the letter she was about to show her to cope with anything else.

"I'm sorry, mum," she began to sob. "I've got some bad news."

"Don't worry about that," her mum smiled gently, as Bella sat down beside her on the sofa. "I played Mrs. Sticklan's messages when I got in."

"You know?" gasped Bella, taken aback.

"I know that you will tell me all about it when you are ready," her mum replied. "If you talk about this problem with the bullies, we might be able to do something about it." She had tried many times to get Bella to open up about these things, but it was impossible.

"You look out for everyone but yourself," she scolded.

Bella snuggled back into the warm nest of her mum's arms.

"I guess this means you'll be losing your part in the Christmas concert," her mum surmised, running a hand soothingly through Bella's long dark hair, "but it's not the end of the world. Maybe Mr. Alder will ask Rahina to take your place. You'd prefer that, wouldn't you?"

Bella nodded and buried her head into her mum's cuddle to try to hide her tears.

By the time Bella got into bed she was exhausted, but she still wanted a story. "Tell me about your trip to Guatemala when you found me in the orphanage," she insisted, sliding cautiously under the cold duvet.

Annie had told her daughter this story a million times.

"Wouldn't you rather have more of that Guatemalan book you're reading?" she suggested. "The one with the fire-breathing jaguar?"

"No,' snapped Bella. "It's stupid." She kicked the underside of the duvet with her foot to demonstrate her displeasure. In truth, Bella loved a good adventure story, especially one which involved a quest for hidden treasures, but it was much more reassuring to hear an old yarn she knew inside-out just before she went to sleep.

And so, for the umpteenth time, Bella's mum told her daughter about the day she volunteered as a midwife at the orphanage of Santa Maria in Quezaltenango. She described its shabby whitewashed facade and the battered old sign that hung above the door. She told Bella about the friendly midwife who had shown her around the ward and how the babies stopped crying the instant she picked them up. What Bella was really waiting for, however, was the bit in the story where her mum saw the beautiful baby with jet-black hair and fiery eyes for the very first time. "That was me!" Bella would shout when she was younger. These days she just asked more and more questions about every detail of the story.

"Oh, Bella, do you *really* want to know about that?" her mum would sigh to whatever Bella asked. Secretly though, she was always happy to tell her – even if she had to make it up. Bella always wanted to hear about the lovely Guatemalan midwife who'd looked after her when she was born and who took care of her sick mother before she died.

"What did she say about my mother?" Bella would ask her adoptive mum.

"She said that she was kind and gentle and that she loved you more than life itself," her mum would answer. "Apparently she used to sit by the orphanage window and sing to the birds, a bit like you do."

Best of all though, was the bit of the story where her adoptive mum picked Bella out of her cot without her nappy on and Bella weed all over her. "I knew you were trouble," her mum would tease, as she affectionately rubbed noses with her daughter or ruffled her hair. "But I just couldn't resist you."

Tonight, Annie was too tired to answer Bella's questions. "You know the rest," she yawned sleepily. "Goodnight."

She kissed her daughter on the cheek and got up to leave. "I'll take the day off work tomorrow, and we can go and visit

Charlie. I can't see her going back to school this week until this incident has been sorted out. If she's feeling well enough, maybe we can all go to the café in Greenwich Park for ice cream."

Her mum was so wonderful sometimes, Bella almost felt like crying.

"Mum," she just about managed to blurt out. "Something very strange happened to me today." Then thinking about it some more: "Two things actually."

Her mum sat back down on the edge of the bed and smoothed her soft warm hand over Bella's brow.

Bella wanted to tell her mum about finding the pendant, but there was so much on her mind. "I'm confused," Bella went on. "I don't know what's happening to me."

It was rare to hear such things from Bella.

"Talk to me," murmured her mum gently.

But Bella couldn't keep her eyelids open another second. She had the vague feeling that she should have been doing something else, but she was too tired to remember.

"I love you," said Bella's mum as she bent over to give her one final kiss and tuck her in.

But Bella was already asleep.

Bella was awoken by a creaking noise in the attic. She sat bolt upright in bed. "The Quetzal!" she thought. "I was supposed to meet him in the attic last night."

The alarm clock by the orange bus on her bedside table was showing that it was two in the morning, long past her mum's bedtime. Bella shivered when she recalled that she had been dreaming about the Golden Jaguar with three fire-breathing heads. It had crept its way towards her through a dark tomb while she stood in her pyjamas frozen to the spot with fear. Thankfully, her mum had remembered to leave the hall light on, otherwise she might have screamed. Bella hated the dark with a vengeance. She always panicked and thought that strange creatures were lurking under the bed. Suddenly wide awake, she jumped out of bed. Feeling a draught, she put on her bright-red dressing gown and tiptoed out onto the landing. As she climbed the ladder up into the attic, Bella heard the gentle flapping of wings and the chattering of a very cold beak.

As soon as she popped her head through the hatch, she saw the half-frozen Quetzal hopping around on the timbers trying to get his circulation going. She went over and put her warm hands around him, but got a sharp peck on the knuckles and a mouthful of incoherent chirps. Realizing at once that she wasn't wearing her mother's pendant, she went to get it.

"About time," quivered the angry Quetzal the second she put it on. "We had an arrangement, remember?"

Bella felt awful. She'd asked for a pizza when she should have come straight home. "I'm sorry I was late last night," she apologized, crouching down to twitter as quietly as she could. "I had a really bad day."

"*You* had a bad day?" screeched the Quetzal. "You should have had the day I had. Attacked by a cat, hen-pecked by a brood of chickens, bullied by a mob of crows and snorted at by a snoring old owl who couldn't keep to his own side of the nest. Not to mention . . . ," and here he paused to let out an almighty sneeze, " . . . that someone who was supposed to be my friend forgot all about our pre-arranged meeting and locked me out for the night. How are we going to get ourselves prepared for this mission if you don't keep better time?"

"I thought that's all done with," sighed Bella. "We lost – even with the pendant."

The Quetzal looked pityingly at Bella.

"You're sad," he told her, all his powers of diplomacy deserting him. "That wasn't the *real* mission. That was just a way of letting you get a feel for your potential. You're starting to believe – and that's good. But you're going to need a little coaching." He paused and looked Bella up and down as if measuring her for the task at hand.

"But what does this mission involve?" Bella snarled, annoyed by the Quetzal's attitude. "And why are you keeping everything such a big secret?"

"We'll start with *who* this mission involves," replied the Quetzal grimly. "Besides you and me, that is."

"Good idea," said Bella, as patiently as she could. "Go on . . . "

"Come with me," ordered the Quetzal, flying up to perch by the open skylight. "Tonight, Bella Balistica," he announced, "we're going on a reconnaissance mission to 48 Eltham Gardens."

Bella was totally unimpressed.

"That's the Briggs's pet shop," she replied haughtily. Secretly, Bella had always wondered what it was like inside Eugene's house at the back of the shop. No one ever went back there for tea or after-school parties.

"Well, are you coming or not?" the Quetzal squawked.

"Now?" exclaimed Bella. "Wouldn't you prefer a mug of hot chocolate?"

The Quetzal stared at her reproachfully.

"OK," sighed Bella. "If we must." She made her way to the hatch.

"I'll go and get my slippers."

CHAPTER NINE

ANIMAL RESCUE

The Quetzal was already up on the roof by the time Bella returned with her slippers. Standing on the Guatemalan chest, Bella reached up, gripped onto the outer edge of the skylight and pulled herself up.

"Why don't you use the pendant?" asked the Quetzal as he watched Bella's slow and lumbering effort to get onto the roof.

She felt like giving the bird a piece of her mind but decided to keep her mouth shut.

"A little bird told me you did a bit of flying today," chirped the Quetzal, a little too mockingly for Bella's liking. "How did you find it?"

"It made me dizzy," Bella moaned. "And I poked my eye on a branch."

The Quetzal laughed. His apprentice looked anything but happy to be hanging around on an icy slate roof.

"I can't get a grip in these slippers," Bella complained. "I don't like it. I'm going back in." She bent down as if to do just that.

"Come on," demanded the Quetzal, tugging at Bella's

dressing gown until she finally relented and stood up. "We've got work to do!"

The resplendent bird opened his wings ready for flight.

"This is just what she needs," the Quetzal muttered to himself. "Hopefully, by the end of the night she'll have a little more idea about what she can achieve if she focuses." He could tell her the extent of their mission then – when she was feeling a bit more confident about her powers.

"Focus your mind on what you want to achieve and just do it!" the Quetzal ordered. "And for goodness' sake, hurry up!"

And with that, he was off.

Bella closed her eyes and gathered all her strength. "I can fly," she said to herself as she clenched her fists and tensed her body.

"Believe!" screeched the Quetzal from above. "Just try to believe a little bit quicker, will you? It'll be Christmas before we get anywhere if you don't hurry up."

Bella raised herself up so that she was balancing on the edge of the angled skylight, opened out her arms, bent her knees and slipped. Falling flat on her bottom, she missed crashing through the skylight by a hair's whisker. She slammed down the palms of her hands to try to stop herself from sliding. It didn't work.

"Help!" she screamed, "I'm going to fall!"

She was petrified. As she slid down the roof towards the broken gutter on a one-way ticket for the patio, Bella thought it was the end.

"Come on," groaned the Quetzal. "Open your arms and jump. You're not a dodo!"

"Oh, shut up!" Bella howled as she disappeared over the gutter to take in a bird's-eye view of the terrace. Her pendant swung before her face as she opened her arms and felt a sudden rush of cold air around her ears. Suddenly, her course changed from the terrace to the bird table and then, by some miracle, to the hedge.

The sharp edges of the leafy partition brushed Bella's knees, as she swept over the bottom of the garden and upwards into the star-studded sky.

"Wow!" she called out to the Quetzal. "This is fantastic!"

Bella had occasionally had flying dreams that made her wake up feeling happy – but this! This was something out of this world. Far more exciting than any ride she'd ever experienced – even at the Southend funfair. She started to use her legs like a rudder and her arms as wings, while the cold December wind gathered her up and whisked her onwards into the night sky after her impatient instructor.

"Faster," ordered the bird.

But Bella's mind was focused on taking in the moment. There was no way she would be rushed by the Quetzal's hectic schedule.

Higher and higher they climbed, until the lights of Shooters Hill were nothing but twinkling dots on the ground.

"Keep your head up," the Quetzal chided. "You're flying like a goose."

But Bella was more interested in looking down at the distant streetlights than where she was going. "So many things look smaller from up here," she gasped. "But somehow the city looks even bigger than I thought it was."

As far as the eye could see, the sparkling lights of London stretched out into the horizon around them. A little to the north, she could see the flashing Christmas lights on the skyscrapers around Canary Wharf, set amongst the snake-like bends of the River Thames.

"Follow me," instructed the Quetzal in a very businesslike manner. "As you know, Mr. Briggs is away on an expedition. Mrs. Briggs sleeps sounder than a hibernating bear, and Eugene is out causing trouble in the woods."

"At this time of night?" cried Bella, appalled.

The Quetzal was shaking his head sorrowfully yet again.

"That boy is going to get his comeuppance," the Quetzal warned. "You mark my words."

Bella and the Quetzal winged their way down to the roof of the pet shop at 48 Eltham Gardens. Here they had an excellent view of the aviary at the bottom of the back garden. Unknown to the two intruders, the whole property was protected by carefully hidden surveillance cameras and alarms. Luckily for them, Eugene had turned off the alarm when he sneaked out of the house about half an hour before.

"We'll deal with the birds later," chirped the Quetzel. "First let's sort out the animals inside the shop. We can't save the tropical fish, but we must do what we can for the rest."

"But how are we going to get in?" asked Bella, who had no experience of breaking and entering but knew that it was bad.

"The same way as that little brat, Eugene, got out," sneered the Quetzal. "Through the bedroom window."

Bella and the Quetzal flew down to Eugene's window ledge. From the open window they could see a long rope dangling down to the kitchen roof. Peering into the bedroom, they saw that the end was attached to the leg of Eugene's bed. He'd obviously used this to climb down to the kitchen roof, from where he must have descended the drainpipe to get to the ground.

"How often does he do this?" Bella gasped.

"According to the prisoners watching from the aviary, about two or three times a week if you include weekends."

Bella saw the bitterness in the Quetzal's eyes. If it was difficult for her thinking about caged birds, it must have been twice as hard for him.

Hopping down into Eugene's bedroom, Bella wasn't surprised to find that the room was a mess and that the walls were covered with posters of war and sci-fi films. She was, however, taken aback by the viscous-looking animal traps strewn all over the floor.

"You wouldn't want to get your foot caught in one of these – believe me!" warned the Quetzal, as he pottered through onto the landing. "And if you *are* going to revert to your human form, watch where you're putting your big feet. Mrs. Briggs is a deep sleeper, but there *is* a limit."

"What are you talking about?" replied Bella, looking down at her slippers. As far as she was concerned, she'd never been anything but herself.

It was soon very clear to Bella that Eugene's house wasn't that much bigger than her own. "You can hardly move in here for all the stuff," Bella complained under her breath. "And it smells so musty."

The décor and furnishings on the impressively spacious landing looked seriously antiquated, more like an exhibition than a home. As well as all the fractured pots and slabs of hieroglyphics on display, there were a number of effigies and creepy sculptures.

"This place gives me the jitters," Bella shuddered. "It's like the thought of being inside the British Museum at night with all those Egyptian mummies." Under Bella's slippers, every creak in the floorboards sounded like the grinding joints of a slowly awakening skeleton.

"Mr. Briggs is a fortune hunter," the Quetzal whispered, as they tiptoed down the stairs. "He travels the world in search of historical treasures. So far, he's stolen artefacts of only minor importance, but I fear he's on the brink of a major discovery that's going to make him either very rich or very famous – possibly both."

"How do you know so much about historical treasures?" Bella asked suspiciously.

"I'm a quetzal, stupid," snapped the bird, too loudly for Bella's liking. "We know everything."

They could hear Mrs. Briggs snoring all the way from the downstairs hall. Bella glanced up to the tiny red laser light high on the ceiling. If it was an alarm, they were as good as caught. It didn't occur to her that it might possibly be a small CCTV camera.

At the bottom of the stairs, something outside, most likely a cat, set off the porch light, casting a bright beam into the hall.

"Aaaaah!" Bella squealed, jumping back.

Her nervous yelp ripped through the eerie hush of the house. There before them was the huge life-size portrait of a tall bearded man in a khaki suit and safari hat. A much younger-looking Ted Briggs, his hair more blond than grey, was posing with a pickaxe by the Sphinx in Egypt. Bella could just about make out the imprint made by the wooden pipe in his top jacket pocket. The inscription at the bottom of the picture read: *Professor Edward Briggs – City University, London, 1989.*

"So he *was* a professor," Bella hushed, trying to steady her nerves.

"Until he was disgraced," snorted the bird.

As the two intruders waited anxiously for Mrs. Briggs's intensified snores to relax back into their monotonous rhythm, Bella cowered beneath the glare of Ted Briggs's eyes. The lines on his forehead were furrowed in a way that made him look scholarly and important – a man on a mission whom no one should cross. He looked a formidable enemy.

"What did he do?" Bella whispered.

"It's what he didn't do," replied the Quetzal gravely. "He developed a bad habit of *not* declaring his historical findings. – except to very rich collectors. He took university funds to go on extravagant expeditions and used them for his own ends. Look around you." The Quetzal was getting madder by the second. "The man's a kleptomaniac!"

"Shh," Bella ordered, grabbing his beak. "*We're* the ones breaking the law here, remember?" she hushed sternly.

"The university sacked him," mumbled the Quetzal, when Bella finally released her grip.

Bella was shocked to realize that with less than two weeks to go before Christmas, there were still no decorations up. "No wonder Eugene's such a sourpuss," she thought to herself. "It's like Christmas doesn't even exist in this house." Then she checked herself. There must be millions of children all over the world for whom Christmas was nothing more than just a rumour. "I must try and be more forgiving of Eugene," she thought – but it wasn't going to be easy.

The way into the shop was through a red velvet curtain at the back of the living room.

"Is that a real tiger skin?" Bella gasped, staring at the rug by the fireplace. It looked like someone had run over a Bengal tiger with an industrial steamroller. With tears in her eyes, she ran over and began to stroke it. It must have been a beautiful majestic animal.

"Awful, isn't it?" tutted the Quetzal. "Briggs's men smuggle the skins into the country, and he sells them on."

Bella choked back her tears, as her blood began to boil.

"Come on," sighed the Quetzal. "Let's keep to the mission at hand."

Considering there were about fifty species of animals in the shop, it was eerily quiet. The only thing making much of a noise was the budgie, chirping away in a small cage by the curtain cord.

"Good morning," it twittered in English.

"For goodness' sake, speak properly," cried the Quetzal.

The poor thing fell off its perch.

"Sorry," apologized the budgie in common bird talk, shaking the sawdust from its wings. "I thought you were the boy."

Bella had only been in the pet shop once before. That time, she'd come in by the front door. She'd thought she wanted a guinea pig, but when she saw it in its cage, she wanted to cry. "It's OK," her mum had tried to reassure her. "They don't mind it as long as you take care of them properly. But remember, any pet we buy today is for you, not me. I've got enough to do going to work and looking after you."

Bella knew that many of her friends at school had guinea pigs and hamsters, and hardly any of them did anything to help their parents look after them. This thought made her even sadder for the poor animals. She hated the shop then, and she hated it now. To make things worse, the smell here was even more disgusting than in the house.

"Most of them are so depressed they hardly know they're alive," mourned the Quetzal. "I doubt if more than a handful could even be bothered to run, but we've got to give them a chance."

"But some of these animals come from different countries. We can't release them here," Bella warned. "They'll affect the ecosystem. They'll either kill or be killed."

The Quetzal stared mockingly at Bella.

"Right," he said, having been practically pecked to death himself by the jealous crows. "But I'm putting my foot down with the birds," he went on. "A cage is no place for a creature with wings and a beak. At least some of them can migrate," he mused. "Show a bird the sun and it will find its way home from anywhere."

Bella walked around the cages. It was worse than the zoo for seeing depressed-looking animals. There were chinchillas, sugar gliders, wallabies, skunks, even pythons and scorpions.

"Start with the ducks and mice," ordered the Quetzal. "They're all indigenous, and they need a head start on the kittens and ferrets. And for goodness' sake, if you do get any philanthropic urges to invigorate the local ecology, leave the snakes and tarantulas till last."

Bella had no problem with the bossy bird over this last order. She could have left them alone, period!

As quickly as she could, Bella opened the cages and ushered the animals out.

"What now?" muttered a dozy bunny. "I was trying to sleep."

Bella opened her mouth in astonishment. "Excuse me?" she tried to utter. "What did you say?" But instead of her words coming out in plain English, she produced a strange snuffly noise, rather like a rabbit.

"You're starting to remember some of your hidden skills," remarked the Quetzal. "You're not as dumb as you look. Wearing that pendant is turning out to be an even better idea than I originally thought. It's been a while since I heard a human speaking Rabbit." He paused to consider his final verdict. "But you need to work on your accent."

Bella was gobsmacked. Her mum was always telling her that she should learn another language, and here she was, speaking fluent Rabbit, albeit with a London accent. She undid all the bolts on the shop door and opened it up. About half of the animals, given the chance, decided to make a dash for it.

"Thank you, Miss Bella. Thank you, Mr. Quetzal," quacked the ducklings, as they waddled after their mother. "Be sure to come and visit us at the park."

"We will," Bella choked, finding Duck-talk much harder to grasp than Rabbit.

Holding the containers housing the snakes and spiders at arm's length, Bella squirmed, as she peered in.

"Promise me you won't kill anything on legs or scare any children," she ordered. "Or I'll tell the crows and owls to track you down."

"We promis-sssss-e," they hissed.

She lowered the containers slowly to the floor and gently tipped them out. Leaving the shop door open to allow the streets around Eltham Gardens to slowly fill up with a diverse assortment of scurrying creatures, Bella and the Quetzal turned their attention to the aviary.

"We need to find the key, and there isn't much time," twittered the Quetzal, getting into a flap. "It must be here somewhere."

He pointed his beak toward the drawers behind the counter. Bella tried to open them one by one, but all of them were locked. They looked everywhere – under the counter, up on the shelves with all the pet food, inside the plastic filing boxes on the counter – but they found nothing. They were just about to give up all hope, when, in a high sleepy voice they heard: "Under the straw in the budgie cage."

"Thanks," said the Quetzal to the racoon. "Much obliged to you."

"You're welcome," replied the racoon politely, snuggling up in his straw. "You couldn't close the door, could you? It's awfully drafty."

Bella closed the pet shop door and went through to the living room.

"You might have said," she reprimanded the budgie as she opened the cage and picked out the aviary key.

"You made me fall off my perch," protested the little bird.

"You're going to have to stay, I'm afraid," Bella told the budgie sternly. "There are too many jealous crows around. You're better off here."

"Suits me," said the budgie, "but I wouldn't mind some more nuts."

Bella fetched him a handful of peanuts from a dish on the dining-room table.

Access to the back garden was through the kitchen, and luckily for Bella and the Quetzal, Mrs. Briggs had left the key in the back door. Within seconds, Bella had run down to the aviary and unlocked it. The excited squawks of twenty species of bird pierced the tranquillity of the night. Parakeets, pelicans, parrots (the list was longer than a toucan's beak), raced each other to the escape hatch in an excited flurry of activity.

"South, south, south," came the cry. "Head for the south."

"Shhh," hushed Bella. "You'll wake the whole neighbourhood making this racket."

But her complaint fell on deaf ears. There were simply too many birds in too much of a rush to get away.

"We need to get going," chirped the Quetzal, spreading his wings.

"Where to now?" asked Bella, flustered by the sudden rush.

"Oxleas Wood."

It was only a short flight from Briggs's pet shop to the woods. They came down to land at the foot of the oak tree by the old watchtower.

"I was here the other day," said Bella.

"I know," replied the Quetzal sarcastically. "*I* was here too. Remember?"

Bella nodded appreciatively. Without the Quetzal's intervention, she may well have fallen prey to Eugene Briggs and his gang.

"I'm not sure if you've ever really expressed any gratitude for that yet," the Quetzal chided.

"Sorry," said Bella reluctantly. "You were great."

The Quetzal was such a cantankerous old know-it-all, having to say thank you rather grated with Bella.

"Now, come on," he ordered. "We haven't got much time.

Close your eyes, filter out all extraneous senses and focus on your ears," he told her.

Bella did as she was told. At first, all she could hear was the gentle hum of distant traffic.

"What are we listening for?" she asked impatiently.

"Concentrate on the higher frequencies. Animals use a higher tone level than humans. It's one of the reasons people think we can't talk," the Quetzal explained.

As soon as she was given this advice, Bella understood what the bird meant. She didn't need her eyes. All around her she could hear the tiny voices of a hundred animals whispering in the wind. But that wasn't all. Nature itself was alive and communicating. The lament of the creaking trees, as they gently rocked in the wind, the last breath of a falling leaf as it fell into the rotting vegetation – all these Bella could hear, creating a soundscape unknown to her before.

"What's that scampering noise?" she asked at last. "It sounds like the pitter-patter of furry paws."

"Badgers," said the Quetzal. "And they're in great danger."

It was then that they heard a sudden crash and a groan of an animal in pain.

"Quick," whispered the Quetzal. "That was the trap. Fly low but don't let your slippers drag through the fallen leaves."

The Quetzal knew that Bella had yet to understand the form her flying body took.

"We need the element of surprise," he concluded.

They glided through the darkness until they saw the silhouettes of two human figures jumping up and down with joy.

"Got him!" one of them was shouting. "Fetch me a stick, and let's see how he moves when we poke him."

Bella recognized the voice at once and had no problem guessing who he was talking to. It wasn't enough that they tortured and tormented children – they had to pick on animals, too. Bella knew that Eugene and Connor had been setting traps for animals since they were in Year 3. Eugene's collection of animal skin and bones was renowned, but somehow, whenever the animal protection agency, the RSPCA, turned up at the house, they could never find any evidence.

"Right," said the Quetzal, "here's the plan."

It was decided that the Quetzal was going to swoop into the clearing, making as much noise as he could, while Bella screamed at the top of her lungs. Hopefully the boys would scarper, and Bella would free the badger.

"Murderers!" yowled Bella, as the Quetzal dived at Eugene Briggs's head. "Badger killers!"

Eugene and Connor nearly jumped out of their skins. While the Quetzal chased them away, diving at their heads and dropping stones, Bella rushed to the badger's rescue.

"Thanks very much, Miss," winced the courteous creature, as she freed him. "Serves me right for being a nosey old badger, I suppose. I just can't resist the smell of human cakes."

Bella looked into the badger trap. Eugene had used a piece of pecan pie to bait him.

"Have you got time to pop by the sett for some fruit and nuts?" snuffled the badger.

"Another time," smiled Bella, who had a fondness for the furry creatures of the woods. "I need to get home before the sun comes up."

"I know what you mean," said the badger.

Bella and the Quetzal were reunited back on the roof of 14 Birdcage Crescent.

"What a night," gasped Bella, as she sat herself down on the ledge of the skylight. "I've never experienced anything like it."

"You'll get used to it," said the Quetzal.

Bella wasn't sure if she really wanted to get used to it. She liked the excitement and the thrill of flying, but she didn't want people thinking she was a freak.

"Can I just fly when I really need to but still be a normal girl?" asked Bella.

"You're normal, alright," snapped the fractious old bird. "You're the most normal girl around these parts."

"To *you*, maybe," said Bella, irritated. "But how many girls my age do you see shivering on the roof in their dressing gown and slippers chattering to a tropical bird?"

"Exactly," retorted the Quetzal. "Normal. At least you haven't forgotten your heritage. You *do* know, don't you, that every human in the world has an animal twin?"

"Yes," shouted Bella indignantly.

"Well, I'm yours!" replied the bird. "We share the same birthday."

"Well, don't expect a card!" grumbled Bella, as she grabbed hold of the window ledge and lowered herself down into the attic. The Quetzal was being too patronizing for words. On top of that, she had the feeling she wasn't being told the whole truth about his visit. Tempted as she was to slam the skylight in his face, Bella let the Quetzal follow her down.

The Quetzal was rather hoping Bella might have been in a better mood. He still had lots of things to tell her and so little time in which to do it.

Bella's mum had bought a stack of books from The Quetzal shop in Greenwich over the years. Consequently, Bella knew a great deal about Guatemala and the culture of the Mayan Indians who lived there. She was aware that according to Mayan belief, every human had an animal twin. The animal was born at the exact same moment as the human, who would then take on its characteristics. A child with a sloth as an animal twin for example, would be sleepy and slow, while a child born with a lion twin would be fierce and proud.

Bella had rather hoped that if all the twin stuff was going to be true, she could be twinned with a jaguar – at least something a bit more fiery and flashy than a pompous old bird!

"I suppose you would like a mug of hot chocolate before you go?" Bella guessed.

Somehow, she knew it was going to be a long night.

CHAPTER TEN

WE'RE ALL CONNECTED

After their reconnaissance mission to 48 Eltham Gardens and the incident in the woods, Bella and the Quetzal stayed up all night chatting in the attic. For the first time in their brief and frenetic relationship, Bella felt an underlying affection for the strange bird. In truth, they were more alike than she cared to admit. During the conversation so many strange and wonderful new discoveries emerged, Bella's head was spinning. Needless to say, she had more questions than the bird had time to answer.

"The trouble is," sighed the Quetzal, "most humans forget that we're all connected. That's why there are so many endangered species. Either you kill the animals for their fur, eat them or lock them up in zoos. At least in places like Africa and South America, the animals can still slip into the cities and villages at night to make sure their human twins are OK."

"But what about the fish?" Bella asked, throwing up her arms at the wonder of it all. "Who do they look after?"

"Think about it," said the Quetzal. "Who takes care of the fishermen? Who guides the boats and looks out for all the swimmers and surfers in the world? And what about all those people living in remote places that need fish to survive?"

"You mean the fish *let* people catch them?" Bella gasped.

The Quetzal stared at Bella in disbelief.

"You don't know anything, do you?" he cried. "At least animals *know* they'll be born again as soon as they die. You lot can't seem to remember anything!"

The Quetzal began to lecture her about the characteristics of certain species: who to trust; who not to trust; which animals you could turn to in times of trouble; which ones were good at problem solving and so on and so on. There were so many things he wanted to tell her before he revealed the challenges that lay before them. The problem was, he was waffling. In the end, Bella, who was still trying to work out the connection between the Quetzal, her mother's pendant and Ted Briggs, just had to interrupt.

"Why did you come here?" she asked bluntly, clearly bored by the Quetzal's long-winded monologues. The bird slowly lifted up his beak and looked her straight in the eye.

"No patience," he sighed, shaking his head. "I knew you were trouble the day I set eyes on you." He gave himself a good shake-out and pulled himself up. "I've come to help you unlock the secret of who you are and why you're here," he proclaimed.

"But I know who I am!" Bella grouched. "My name is Bella Balistica. I live at 14 Birdcage Crescent, London. Stop trying to confuse me!"

The Quetzal had half a mind to peck her on the nose, he felt so tired and crabby. There was still so much more to tell about her powers before he could unveil his plan. The trouble was Bella could hardly keep her eyes open. Still, the Quetzal decided to go for it.

"It's like this, Bella. Many centuries ago . . . "

It was then that Bella heard her mum's alarm clock going off. Before the Quetzal could even finish his sentence, Bella was at the ladder. "I've got to go," she yawned. "My mum will kill me if she finds me up here."

The Quetzal was annoyed beyond belief. He'd had all night to brief her, and he still hadn't got down to the nitty-gritty.

"But this is important!" he pleaded, stamping his right claw.

"So is this," said Bella. "See you."

Bella had no idea whether the Quetzal stayed in the attic or if he had somehow managed to push open the skylight and go. In truth, she'd been so worn out and frustrated by the conversation, she didn't care.

"What was the point of it all?" she said to herself, as she tiptoed down the hall to her bedroom. She'd wanted to ask the bird more about Ted Briggs and his latest trip to Guatemala, but he'd twittered on so long about twins they'd run out of time. As she slipped into bed, it wasn't just the cold duvet that made her shiver – she could already hear her mum's footsteps on the landing. Rolling over, she shut her eyes and felt for her pendant. Fingers crossed, she'd got away with it.

Bella's mum poked her head around the bedroom door and took a long, bleary-eyed look at her daughter. "She looks exhausted," she thought to herself, as she quietly pulled the door to. "This incident at school has really upset her. She needs a good long lie-in."

Squinting through half-closed eyes at her alarm clock while

her mum stood in the doorway, Bella discovered to her horror that it was 6:30 a.m. She moved her attention to the little orange bus that she kept on her bedside table and peered at the small figure of the driver, as he waved to her from the cabin. "I'd love to meet the kid who made it," she thought to herself. That was the last thing Bella remembered before she fell into a deep sleep.

Bella's mum had already decided that she wouldn't get her daughter up until lunchtime. With any luck the lead midwife at Greenwich Hospital would find someone to cover her shifts for the next few days so she could spend some time with her daughter.

"I'll try," her boss had told her, "but you might have to be on call if there's an emergency."

It was hard being a single mum with a demanding job, but Annie was an excellent juggler of time. How she managed to coordinate being a full-time midwife and mum, as well as fitting in yoga, photography and Spanish classes, was a wonder.

When Bella finally woke up around midday Wednesday morning, it was to the sound of driving rain against her window. She'd been dreaming of a journey on an orange bus with lots of Guatemalan children. The driver at the wheel had been permanently glazed in the one waving position for the entire trip, and yet somehow the journey had passed without any serious collisions. She put on her red dressing gown, made sure the pendant was well tucked inside her pyjamas and went downstairs to find her mum cooking.

"Good morning, Bella. Are you ready for some lunch?" her mum asked cheerfully. "You wouldn't believe what I saw this morning when I popped out to the shops."

"What?" mumbled Bella, still fuzzy in the head from the

effects of her late night.

"A pelican," proclaimed her mum with a look of wonder. Bella's eyes widened.

"There he was, as large as life, standing on the red postbox at the end of the road. I mean, it was as if he was expecting to pick up a delivery or something. I called the RSPCA, and they said they'd been absolutely inundated with calls. Apparently, there are animals everywhere. Mrs. Stevens says there's a toucan on Eltham High Street who won't come down from the lamp-post outside the barbers. It's a zoo out there!"

Bella kept her head down. "So much for migrating birds," she thought to herself. "What's for lunch, mum?" she asked rubbing her eyes. "I'm starving."

As they tucked into a delicious pasta lunch, Bella and her mum talked.

"What shall we do with our afternoon off?" her mum asked. "We could go to The Quetzal shop in Greenwich and look at the lovely Guatemalan things. Or, if you're really feeling energetic, we could get in the car and go to Southend for the day."

Bella loved going to both these places. She could spend hours in the aircraft simulator at the Southend funfair. Her mum joked that she'd had so much practice she could probably fly herself to Guatemala if she had a plane. But the coast was for sunny days, and Bella didn't fancy going out in the rain, even to her favourite shop.

"Let's stay in," Bella garbled, with a mouthful of pasta. "Maybe you could help me with my endangered species project."

Bella was still in her pyjamas and dressing gown, searching

the internet for quetzals, when the mobile rang.

"But I can't work today," Annie complained. "I need to be with my daughter." Bella examined the sadness in her mum's face, as she went quiet for a moment and then said: "OK. But then I'm coming straight home." She hung up.

"Bella, I'm really sorry," she said dejectedly, slowly getting up from her chair and giving Bella a big hug from behind.

Bella didn't mind. She was proud of her mum. Delivering babies was a very important job.

"There's a problem at the hospital," explained her mum, giving Bella a big kiss on the back of the head. "Two premature labours on top of the three deliveries already scheduled. I better give Charlie's mum a call."

Bella really wanted to stay home by herself, but she knew her mum wouldn't let her if she could help it.

When Mrs. Stevens finally answered her mobile, they found that she'd already taken Charlie to the doctors in Eltham and that they were now doing their Christmas shopping in Central London.

"She's nearly finished," said Bella's mum after she'd hung up. "Then she and Charlie are coming straight over to pick you up. Just carry on with your project work until they get here."

Her mum was now in a real fluster to get changed and out of the house. "Don't forget to feed the cat," she shouted down from upstairs.

Bella got out her project notes, while her mum whizzed around, gathering up her things.

"I'm off now, Bella," she called finally.

Bella rushed into the hall to kiss her goodbye – and then she was gone, leaving her mobile on the table.

The second her mum left the house, Mrs. Stevens was on the phone again. She'd misplaced her handbag in Debenhams and was going to be late. The sound of muted screeches started just as Bella put down the phone.

"Help! Bella – I'm caught in the window. Hurry!"

Bella recognized the voice of the Quetzal at once and rushed to the attic as quickly as she could. She guessed right away what had happened. Her mum had probably noticed the draught from the skylight and gone up to close it. Finding it shut, the poor bird had tried to open it with his beak and somehow managed get his head stuck in it. It was an excellent guess.

"No wonder you're an endangered species," Bella laughed, climbing onto the chest. "And you sound like a duck."

Bella's flippant attitude didn't please the bird.

"How about a bit of respect for your animal twin," he croaked while still trying to push back the window.

Reaching up, Bella pushed the skylight open and helped the Quetzal down.

She sat on the chest and rested the Quetzal onto her lap, while she tried to smooth out his ruffled feathers. It didn't take him long to get down to business.

"Glad to see you're still wearing the pendant," he announced, giving himself a good shake.

Bella sensed the urgency in the Quetzal's jumpy and distracted manner.

"We've got to go," he told her, pecking Bella's knee with rather more force than he should.

"But I'm working on my project," Bella insisted, returning the gesture with a glare. "I've started making notes on . . . "

"I know," interrupted the bird. "That's why I'm here," he

lied, hopping from foot to foot.

The Quetzal had decided: ready or not, there was no more time to waste.

"I don't understand," said Bella, her arms flopping to her sides. "How can you help me?"

The Quetzal was taking a chance. If he told her too much about the mission Bella might tell him to get lost. He decided to use subversive tactics.

"What do you say we go and visit some endangered species?" he suggested tactfully.

Bella thought the bird was looking a bit shifty. He had the kind of twinkle in his eyes that she imagined herself having when trying to get her own way with her mum.

"Where?" she asked suspiciously.

"I could take you to a place that's just a short flight from here," said the Quetzal. "We might even be able to talk with some endangered species along the way."

Bella was confused by the Quetzal's sketchy plan, but the temptation for adventure was hard to resist.

"OK," she said. "I'll come. As long as we're not too long."

The Quetzal had guessed this strategy would work. He could unveil his real plan later, when there was no turning back.

"But how are we travelling?" Bella asked. "I can't be seen flying during the day."

"Time for another lesson," sighed the beleaguered Quetzal.

It was hard enough for Bella to accept that she could fly like a bird and talk to the animals. On top of that, she'd discovered that she could heal broken limbs just by touching them. To think that she might have even more feathers to her cap was too much.

"What now?" Bella complained. "Don't tell me – I can make myself invisible."

The Quetzal screeched with laughter. "You may have spiritual and mystical powers, Bella Balistica, but you're no wizard," he hollered.

This came as a great relief to Bella. One Harry Potter in the world was enough for anyone.

"Take a look in the mirror," the Quetzal told her.

He flew up to one of the lower rafters to allow her to get up.

Bella went over to the mirror and stared at her reflection. "Eek," she squirmed. "Horrible."

"Windswept, I grant you," chuckled the Quetzal, hardly able to speak for laughing.

Bella thought she looked awful. She hadn't had a wash or brushed her hair since returning from last night's trip. The Quetzal was still having a laughing fit.

"Oh, shut up!" she shouted at him, using her hands to flatten her hair.

"You're not looking at yourself properly," squawked the hysterical Quetzal. "You're still thinking in human. Try to think 'bird' for a moment. Remember that feeling you had last night when you were flying over Oxleas Wood."

Bella remembered the feeling well. She'd felt as free as a . . . That was it – that's what the Quetzal was talking about – she'd felt as free as a bird. Bella embraced the memory of that feeling and looked again into the mirror. To her complete disbelief, she saw the reflection of a rather large and resplendent quetzal.

"What are you doing there?" she exclaimed, looking up to the Quetzal. But the bird was too far away to be caught in the reflection. It suddenly struck Bella that *she* was the quetzal in the mirror. The bird flew down from the rafters and stood beside her. Sure enough, despite the fact that Bella was much bigger than her animal twin, there they were – two quetzals together. In place of Bella's jet-black hair, there were yellow and white feathers, a rich red plumage over her chest, and long emerald-green wings where her arms had once been. Her sparkling eyes were still there, but there was now a beak in place of her nose.

"This is awful!" Bella squawked. "Turn me back, now!"

But the Quetzal was too busy rolling around the floor in hysterics.

"I knew you hadn't noticed," he chirped with glee. "You don't think you fly as a human, do you? Every time your feet leave the ground, you become your animal twin."

Bella looked down to the floor to examine the space her human feet had once occupied, but all she could see were six scrawny claws.

"To be honest," sniggered the Quetzal. "That's how I see you, even when you're not flying. It just depends which way I choose to look at you."

Staring directly into the face of her own reflection, Bella searched for any sign of her human form. At first glance, there was none, other than the fact that her feathers were much more ruffled and scruffier than the real Quetzal's, and her beak was a bit smaller at the end. But the more Bella stared in disbelief at her reflection, the more of her real self she could see. There was a roundness about her face and a fiery glint in her eyes that was reassuringly familiar. In truth, she looked exactly like the quetzal she would have been had she been born a bird.

"How come I look like this when I'm not even flying?" she squawked.

When the Quetzal finally managed to control his giggles, he tried to explain. "It's like this," he said, as if speaking to a very small chick. "Because humans are not programmed to see the supernatural, they don't. The second you start to use your powers to fly, they see you as a bird. It's only animals and people with special powers who can see you in both your forms at the same time. I'm just teaching you to look at yourself in a new way. Now come on – we've got lots to do in the handful of hours left before your mum comes home. I can play *some* tricks with time, but I can't stop it indefinitely!"

CHAPTER ELEVEN

THE JOURNEY

Bella didn't even have time to change. Picking up her camera and throwing the carry strap over her head, she soon found herself flying south over the outskirts of London and onwards across the English countryside. She was getting used to the fact that as soon as she started to fly, her body took on the form of her animal twin. What was weird was that, if she looked really hard, she could still see the translucent image of herself as a human girl, appearing like an outer garment over her quetzal exterior. By playing games with the way she chose to look at herself, she could almost make the two images interchangeable.

"This is fun," Bella giggled, looking up to her friend. "Now you see me – now you don't."

After half an hour or so, the refreshing breeze that Bella had enjoyed while flying over the countryside was starting to be replaced by a stiff oncoming wind.

"It's too cold," Bella complained. "And I can't seem to get any speed up."

She looked out towards the ocean. It looked grey and bleak.

"We need to fly higher," said the Quetzal with a sense of urgency. "Follow me."

Bella flew after the Quetzal as fast as her wings would carry her. Once they were above the clouds, the strong headwinds began to give way to a comforting warm current.

"Wow!" Bella sang. "It's like a summer's day up here."

The fluffy white clouds were bathed in bright sunlight. To her left and right she could see the distant images of aeroplanes soaring through the sky.

"Are we nearly there yet?" she asked, expecting to be interviewing rare animals already.

"Patience," tutted the Quetzal. "It's further than you think. Try not to talk so much."

"But you said it was a short flight," Bella protested.

The Quetzal sighed. Dealing with humans was much more frustrating than he had expected.

"If you put a bit more effort into it, we'd be there already," he lied.

Bella didn't want the Quetzal to think that she was sluggish, so she flapped her wings as fast as she could and picked up speed. Despite the distance, she was getting excited about the prospect of seeing a blue whale in the ocean. Then, thinking about her friend: "I suppose I ought to look out for a manatee for Charlie."

"Anything else?" cried the sarcastic Quetzal. "A unicorn, perhaps?"

They travelled for many hours. Bella tried to put out of her mind the fact that she should have been at home working on her endangered species project. "This is field work after all," she consoled herself.

With her studies in mind, Bella convinced the Quetzal to fly low over the ocean to allow her to scour the sea for signs of aquatic life.

"I can see for miles." she called up to the Quetzal. "And I love this salty smell!"

The sheer expanse of the ocean was daunting – but the thrill! Bella was so exhilarated, she swooped down, stuck out her feet and tried to surf. Rather than skimming across the water like a delicate flat stone, she hit the waves like a brick and only just managed to flap her way out of trouble.

"Watch out!" squealed the Quetzal as a huge explosion of water fired out of the ocean, spraying Bella's feathers with bracing cold water.

"What's that?" she called out, her heart pounding with excitement and fear.

"It's just a submarine," replied the irritable bird hurriedly, choosing not to turn. "Come on."

"Are you sure?" Bella queried, doubling back to get a closer look.

The Quetzal reluctantly changed course to swoop around and circle the area. He was going to have to own up.

"Well, I never," he sighed grudgingly. "If it's not a blue whale. Listen."

Sure enough, from the depths of the ocean, Bella could hear a distant rumbling. As she circled, she became aware of a humongous shadow below the surface that was rapidly getting bigger.

"He's coming! He's coming!" she shouted, starting to feel a little nervous.

She tried to get hold of her camera, but as soon as she did, her wings turned to arms and she started to plummet towards the ocean.

"How irritating!" she exclaimed, regaining her hovering stance above the expanding shadow.

"How you see yourself and what you can physically do in your different forms are two different things," the Quetzal told her.

Then it happened. With an almighty blast, the ocean opened up, forcing a huge wake of cascading waves to break out in every direction. Bella quickly snapped a photograph.

"Wings!" yelled the Quetzal, as Bella started to nosedive headfirst towards the waves.

But Bella was quick. She let go of the camera, opened her wings and was soon hovering above the long flat head of the whale, as it crashed back into the ocean. The upshot of spray this time was even higher than the last.

"Brrr," Bella shivered, immediately soaked to the skin.

"You better watch out," warned the Quetzal. "He's . . . "

Even before the Quetzal had finished his warning, the whale reappeared with another flourish of water.

"Look at that blowhole!" Bella screamed in delight.

She was getting a bird's-eye view of one of the real wonders of nature. The scale of the whale's shiny blue and grey back stretching out across the ocean was unbelievable. She flew up and took another nosediving photograph, before gliding across the full length of its back.

"His skin looks so smooth," she called out to the Quetzal. "Do you think we could stand on his head and ask him some questions?"

"I'd rather stand on your head and . . . "

"What was that?" asked Bella, straining to hear the Quetzal through the roar of exploding water.

Bella's proclivity for engaging with endangered species was causing delays that could jeopardize the whole mission.

"I said, 'we don't stand a chance,'" sighed the Quetzal with some relief, as the whale lowered his head into the deep and left them with a majestic flick of his impressive tail.

Aided by a strong tailwind, they travelled for many miles with the weather gradually getting sunnier and warmer. The turquoise-blue water all around them made Bella feel like she was on holiday. "Charlie and mum would love this," she thought to herself and then: "I hope Mrs. Stevens hasn't come over yet. Mum's going to kill me, if she finds out I wasn't in." Thinking of Charlie awoke Bella to her worries about her friend. "I hope she's told her mum what Eugene and Connor did to her," she thought. "When I get back, I'm going to help her tell her mum."

"Do you think we ought to be getting back?" she asked the Quetzal.

"Plenty of time yet," replied the bird.

Bella had lost all track of time. She got so tired during the next part of the journey that her mind drifted off into sleepy thoughts of how she and Charlie could plot their revenge on Eugene Briggs. She could have sworn that she'd been asleep when the Quetzal shouted: "Land ahoy!"

At the sight of sun-drenched beaches and gently swaying palm trees unfolding before them, both travellers felt a huge sense of relief.

"We're in the Caribbean," the Quetzal yawned, slowly coming round from his own daydreams. "Are you hungry?"

"Ravenous," replied Bella.

"Then let's fly around and find a good place to peck for bananas," he suggested.

On one side of the island, Bella could see that there were lots of holidaymakers enjoying the beaches, but on the far side there was a deserted bay.

"It's much rockier over on that side," explained the Quetzal, leading the way. "The tourists don't like it."

They glided down to rest on an outcrop of rock in the middle of a bay. As soon as they landed, Bella relaxed into her human form, took off her slippers and dangled her feet into the refreshingly cool waters.

"Look at all these multi-coloured fish!" she exclaimed, directing the Quetzal's nonchalant gaze with her right foot. The waters were so clear, Bella could see right down to the colourful coral at the bottom. It was a wonderful feeling to be so close to nature in such a beautiful place. With the sun warming her back and the gentle sound of lapping water relaxing her mind, Bella felt as if she hadn't a care in the world.

As she looked across the glistening waters, Bella noticed a strange-looking animal in the distance, flicking up water with its short flattened tail.

"Is it a manatee?" she cried excitedly, kicking her legs in the sea so hard she made a frothy wake. "I'm sure they have tails like that."

"Not again," the Quetzal muttered to himself. "I suppose it might be," he reluctantly conceded. "I don't suppose we'll ever find out for sure."

"Let's go and visit him," cheered Bella, standing up. "Charlie would be so excited!"

The Quetzal was starting to feel resigned to diversions.

"I suppose it's only to be expected," he grumbled to himself. "If I'm inquisitive, she's bound to be. It's the curse of being her twin I suppose." Still, the Quetzal tried to put Bella off.

"You might think manatees are friendly, plant-eating mammals," he told Bella. "But so many of them have been caught up in human fishing nets and killed by speedboats they don't take too kindly to humans. We'd better go."

Bella felt awful. It was embarrassing being a human sometimes.

"Do you know him? Can you talk to him?" she pleaded, reluctant to leave. "I'd like to apologize."

"It's a female," the Quetzal informed her. "And no – I've never seen her before in my life." He glanced shiftily in the manatee's direction. "And anyway, she looks like one of the really angry ones."

"Yoo-hoo! Hello there, Quetzal," called the cheerful manatee, gently gliding towards them. "I haven't seen you for ages. How are you, my good chap?"

The Quetzal blushed with embarrassment.

"She doesn't seem *that* angry," said Bella, looking suspiciously at the Quetzal.

"You seem to be in the company of a very rare creature indeed," said the manatee, as she gracefully slid through the water.

"Does she mean me?" gasped Bella quickly, clapping her hands.

"I can see you for what you are," butted in the manatee, scratching her itchy back against the outcrop of rock where Bella and the Quetzal were standing. "If I'm not mistaken,

118

you're still wearing your pyjamas."

Bella looked down. All she could see was wet plumage, a dangling pendant and a camera.

"This is confusing," she moaned.

"Like you, animals can see you in both your forms at the same time," the Quetzal explained to Bella. "Only they're much better at it than humans. They've had more practice."

"I must say, this is a rare honour," the manatee interjected. "The human being in touch with its animal nature is the most endangered species on the planet."

Bella slapped herself across the face just to check she was awake then snapped a photograph of the manatee for Charlie's project.

"What can we humans do to help you?" Bella asked.

"You can stop polluting the oceans, if you don't mind," said the manatee flatly. "They get more full of chemicals and rubbish by the day."

Bella knew what the manatee meant. Last year there were no tadpoles or sticklebacks at all in the school pond because of litter. "But what can *I* do?" sighed Bella, feeling helpless. "It's a huge problem."

"Be practical," said the manatee, rolling onto her back. "Start by warning your friends about the dangers of synthetic packaging and take it from there. Humans can achieve so much when they feel passionate about things and work together."

"I promise I'll try," said Bella.

"See you again, I hope," waved the manatee, beginning to roll. "Goodbye."

They watched as the manatee completed her turn and gracefully swam away. Bella turned quizzically to the Quetzal.

"I take it that's the first time you two have met?" she asked sarcastically.

The Quetzal knew she'd seen through him.

"Terrible memory," he muttered. "Sorry."

"I wonder who else we're going to meet to make me feel bad about being a human?" Bella pondered.

The Quetzal nodded sympathetically.

"It's not easy, is it?" he acknowledged. "Seeing how interconnected we all are."

"Especially when you're *this* hungry," Bella reminded him.

"Follow me," said the bird. "I know a great place for a snack."

Surprisingly, this turned out to be a field of sugarcane a short island-hop away. The Quetzal showed Bella how to peck her way through to the sweet juice.

"It's like lemonade," slurped Bella gleefully, "only even more delicious."

To satisfy Bella's nagging, the Quetzal agreed that they could island-hop and explore the forests of the Caribbean for half an hour. They sat in coconut and banana trees and spoke with many toucans and parakeets as well as the parrots. Using her human form to work the camera, Bella got some lovely photographs. Feeling refreshed, they set off for the last time.

"Where to now?" asked Bella.

"Home," said the Quetzal.

What he didn't tell her was which home.

They flew across the Caribbean Sea for quite some time, following the Central American coastline before turning inland.

"This doesn't look like England," said Bella suspiciously.

"There's too much sunshine and jungle."

"We're flying over Belize to get to Guatemala," said the Quetzal with a sideways glance.

"But Mrs. Stevens is coming over to pick me up!" Bella wailed. "Everyone's going to be worried if I'm not there."

"Relax!" snapped the Quetzal, rather more aggressively than he'd intended. "I've got all that under control."

"Relax?" cried Bella. "You don't know my mum. If she finds out I left the house, first she'll go ballistic and then she'll cancel Christmas!"

But she was shouting into the skies to no one but herself. The Quetzal had picked up speed and was already some way ahead.

"Wait for me!" Bella yelled while flapping her wings like mad to catch him up.

Guatemala from the air was beautiful. Instead of cities and motorways, there were mangroves and deciduous forests, savannah, spectacular highlands and, most impressive of all, the tropical rainforests.

"What do you think?" called the Quetzal.

Bella could tell that he was feeling proud because the red feathers on his breast were all puffed up.

"It's amazing," she cheered, genuinely impressed. "I thought most of the great rainforests had been cut down."

"And they have," replied the Quetzal sadly. "Even here, the government is chopping down huge areas of rainforest and selling the wood."

Bella looked down to see a small area of rainforest to the west that had been recently cut down. But the forest was so vast it hardly seemed to make any difference.

"It's just the start of it," the Quetzal told Bella. "They've already used all the wood from the tropical rainforest in the far north."

Apart from feeling sad about the trees, Bella was enjoying every second of her flight across the rainforest.

"Mr. Alder's a good teacher, but this is the best Geography lesson ever!" she told the bird.

The noise from the lower canopies was unbelievable. A cacophony of growling jaguars, screeching monkeys and croaking frogs almost drowned out the ear-piercing racket made by the tropical birds. Some of the roars sounded like they belonged to large ferocious beasts on the rampage, but when Bella came down to land in the trees close by, she found that they were made by a troop of fruit-eating monkeys having a laugh. The spider monkeys leaping through the canopies below them seemed to defy gravity, while above them a black-collared hawk soared the skies in silence searching for his prey.

"Are we safe here?" Bella asked nervously.

"Yes, but we need to stay on our guard," warned the Quetzal. "Hawks, I can handle."

Something about the way he said this struck Bella as distracted and unconvincing. She followed his gaze. The Quetzal seemed to be focusing his attention on a large, ominous-looking bird hovering high in the sky to the east.

"What's that?" she asked, pointing towards the black and white bird.

"That?" snapped the Quetzal, as if abruptly waking up from a hideous nightmare. "That's nothing you need to be worrying about. Come on. Let me show you around."

Bella felt strangely at home in the rainforest. It was an awe-inspiring place. The lushness of the upper canopies and the clear blue skies were the perfect backdrop to photograph the spectacular bird life. Then suddenly, as if out of nowhere, Bella saw the ruins of a magnificent temple towering above the trees. Surrounded by so much greenery, it looked completely out of place. As she got closer, the sheer scale of the ruins became much clearer.

"It's bigger than a skyscraper!" Bella exclaimed, comparing the enormous pyramid below to the imposing towers at Canary Wharf. Overawed, Bella followed the Quetzal.

"The one you can see above the trees may be the biggest," said the Quetzal, trying to give Bella an idea of the context and scale of the whole area. "But look at these."

He flew with Bella across the whole site, where she counted five big temples surrounded by a scattering of smaller structures. The closer she got to the main temple, the more intimidating it appeared. She could also see that it was a huge square-based pyramid.

"What are all those people doing down there?" she asked.

"They're tourists," replied the Quetzal. "You tell me. They climb up and down the temple, take a photograph, buy an ice cream and go home. Madness, if you ask me!"

Bella quite liked the idea of an ice cream but thought it best not to ask.

"What's the temple made from?" she asked.

"Granite," replied the Quetzal. "And you should know that!"

Bella hated being spoken to like an idiot but decided not to answer back. If this was anything like as interesting as studying the Ancient Egyptians, she couldn't wait to find out more.

Bella could see that all the temples had deeply-cut steps on all four sides, leading up to an impressive dome at the summit. All around these buildings, for as far as the eye could see, there was nothing but rainforest.

"What do they call the main temple?" Bella finally gasped as they flew directly over it.

"The Great Temple of Tikal," replied the Quetzal in his most serious voice. "Built by the Maya."

"I'm Mayan," Bella chirped excitedly.

Then it came to her – the book with the three-headed jaguar she was reading. That had been set at the Great Temple of Tikal. According to the legend, only the human touched with the spirit of Itzamna could enter the temple and be led to its hidden treasures.

"It was our forefathers and mothers who designed and built these structures,' proclaimed the proud bird. "*This* is your spiritual home."

"You mean it's like a church," Bella inquired, "where the Mayan people used to worship?"

The Quetzal nodded. How these amazing temples ever came to be built in such a remote part of the world was mystifying to Bella.

The moment she landed on the summit of the temple, her arms fell to her sides like dead weights. The Quetzal too was tired. Burdened further by the knowledge of the task in hand, he decided to make a clean breast of things.

"Our greatest challenge is still ahead of us," he told her, wondering how quickly he could get to the point without upsetting her. But Bella was distracted.

"Where are all those people going?" she blurted, gazing down at the multitude of tourists descending the temple towards the awaiting buses.

"They're in a rush to get back to their campsites before nightfall," snapped the frustrated Quetzal. "No one without special permission is allowed to be here after dark. Now, have you finished?"

She took another picture while the Quetzal cleared his throat.

"Many moons ago," he continued, "during the centuries in which our own mythologies were first formed, it was foretold that a human girl with exceptional powers would be born."

"Is this story going to take long?" Bella interrupted. "Because I need to be home in time to finish my homework and set the table for tea."

The Quetzal took a deep breath and soldiered on. "She would live amongst her own kind, but her ability to communicate with the animal world would form a new bond between species. Together, we would fight a great battle, the outcome of which would become destiny itself and the start of all mythologies to come."

"I haven't heard that one," said Bella with a little more interest. "But it sounds like a good story."

The Quetzal continued: "Eleven years ago, the cry of a newborn baby was caught by the wind. The cry was carried hundreds of miles, deep into the rainforest. It was heard by a mosquito, who whispered his discovery to an old armadillo who in turn passed it on to a young jaguar cub. The whispers turned into rumours. 'She's arrived,' they said. 'The human child is amongst us at last.' "

"I'm glad it's going to be a girl," said Bella excitedly. "I'm sick of boys getting all the good bits in these stories."

"For goodness' sake," shouted the Quetzal. "Can't you

listen without butting in?"

"Sorry," said Bella, making a gesture to zip up her mouth.

"I tracked down the source of these rumours to an old dilapidated building in the heart of Quezaltenango," the Quetzal informed her.

"That's where I was born," Bella interjected, unable to keep her mouth closed with so much excitement bursting up inside her.

The Quetzal stopped and glared at her. He held his stare for a full five seconds before he said: "I know, Bella."

Bella felt a cold shiver run down her spine. The Quetzal wasn't telling a story. He was trying to tell her about something real.

"What happened to the baby?" she asked nervously. Her voice was quivering so much, even she could hardly make out what she was saying.

"She was taken from us," replied the Quetzal with tears in his eyes. "One minute I was singing lullabies to a mother and her sleeping baby, the next they were gone."

"And where is the baby now?" hushed Bella through the sound of the Quetzal's uncontrollable sobs.

The Quetzal lifted up his head and squawked: "Right under my beak!"

Bella felt faint.

"And if you think that after eleven years of scouring every neighbourhood between here and Timbuktu, I'm taking her home to finish her homework and scoff chicken nuggets and fries, you've got another think coming!"

By now the Quetzal was in floods of tears. He may have given the impression of being a bossy old so and so, but at heart he was as big a softy as Bella was.

Bella stared listlessly down at the temple and the departing tourists while trying to take in the enormity of the Quetzal's story. It upset her to think of herself as an orphan and made her heart ache for her real mother and father. If this bird was a link to understanding the past and learning more about herself, there was sure to be more pain. She turned to the Quetzal with a hundred questions forming in her mind.

"No time," announced the Quetzal, wiping his eyes on his wings. "Now pay attention."

The situation was critical. "The hidden riches of Tikal are under imminent threat from Ted Briggs and his band of looters," the Quetzal went on. "Even as we speak, he's planning to break into the labyrinth of tunnels that run throughout this historic site and steal our treasures. Even if some of it does end up in museums, one thing *is* for sure – we'll never see them again. And if he ever gets his hands on the Itzamna Emerald . . . "

The Quetzal was so choked up, he could hardly speak. What he was about to say was too unbearable to even contemplate. "The emerald is the bedrock of our very existence," he went on, "the life-force of everything, past, present and future. Without it, we are lost."

It was one thing to learn such things in books or on the radio at home, but quite another to be told them by a talking Quetzal while sitting on the summit of an historical monument in the middle of the Guatemalan rainforest. To top it all: Bella was in her pyjamas, dressing gown and slippers.

"But what can I do?" she murmured. "I'm only eleven."

"You can start by waking up to the fact that we're in big

trouble," shouted the Quetzal, staring with terror into the skies.

Bella's eyes shot to the heavens, where to her horror she saw the enormous black and white bird hovering over their heads.

"It's a harpy eagle!" yelled the Quetzal.

Bella shivered. The eagle had a menacing look. Its sharp claws looked like they could tear the Quetzal to pieces at whim.

"It's as big as I am!" shrieked Bella. "What if he attacks?"

A shadow fell across them as the eagle swooped in for the kill.

CHAPTER TWELVE

VIPERS

As he reached for his old trusted pipe in the top pocket of his jacket, Ted Briggs stared dejectedly at the archaeological plan of the temple. It lay unfurled on the bonnet of his Land Rover alongside an astrological chart. "As good as useless," he muttered while filling his pipe with tobacco.

Last night's expedition probing into the area of vegetation around the eastern side of the temple had uncovered the remains of an ancient jaguar statue. Briggs was convinced that the statue served the same symbolic role as the Sphinx guarding the pyramids in Egypt. It made complete sense to him that the Mayans would have worshipped the sun as it rose in the east in the same way as the Ancient Egyptians had. All his cross-referencing and calculations with astrological charts pointed to an entrance here. Last night his undercover team had used only trowels and shovels. Tonight he was taking more drastic measures.

"I want the dynamite ready for detonation as soon as the sun goes down and the tourists have gone," he told his men.

It had taken Briggs a great deal of time and energy to

organize his ten-man team, most of whom he'd been forced to hire off the streets of the capital city so as not to alert the authorities. While these poor souls were being paid next to nothing for their endeavours, Briggs had splashed out on hiring a helicopter and pilot. But then a speedy exit was going to be essential.

For the second time in the last hour, Briggs's mobile phone went off. He reached into his inside pocket and pulled it out. It was a text message from England: "Bella Balistica excluded. Getting closer to a permanent solution. M.S."

Ted Briggs smiled to himself. Hawksmore Primary felt a long way away, but it was always pleasing to receive good news. "Nice work," he said to himself, as he returned the phone to his pocket. Margaret Sticklan was turning out to be an excellent appointment.

Meanwhile, back at the top of the temple, the harpy eagle dived to attack the Quetzal.

"Stay in your human form!" shouted the Quetzal. "It's your only hope." With that he lunged off the summit. But the eagle was quick. With its huge grasping claws it swooped to grab the Quetzal's tail. Bella had to turn away as the flapping wings of the attacker brushed violently against her back.

"Run!" yelled the Quetzal, just managing to swerve away in time.

As quickly as she could, Bella started the long descent. Her mind was in chaos. "Stop. Fight. Run. I want my mum. Stay focused. What am I doing . . . ?"

Half a dozen times she stopped and started to climb back up, but it was too late. The Quetzal and the harpy eagle were already airborne.

"Go, Quetzal, go!" she yelled into the flurry of activity.

Birds were screeching, monkeys howling – it seemed as if every animal in the rainforest was joining the chorus of support for the Quetzal.

Through all the fear and turmoil, Bella's instinct was for survival. Down the temple she went. Each step was four or five times the height of the stairs at home, and in the fading light they were difficult to judge. Twice, she nearly lost her balance and fell as she turned to check on the fleeing Quetzal.

"Wait for me!" she cried out to the tourists.

But no one could hear her through the din of the rainforest and the revving of engines. The light was quickly fading, and all the Land Rovers at the foot of the temple were swiftly departing. By the time she reached the bottom, there would be nothing but bats and vipers.

To make things worse, her legs felt like jelly, and the temperature was rapidly falling. "What am I going to do?" she panicked. She looked up into the heavens for any sign of her friend, but there was nothing. "What if that horrible eagle got him?" she thought to herself, tears rolling down her face.

Apart from the residents of the K'iche' village two kilometres away, trespassers around the Great Temple were arrested on sight. The government was fearful of looters – the lost treasures of Tikal were one of the great mysteries of modern archaeology. If Bella were to be found here after dark, she would have a great deal of explaining to do.

The sound of the rainforest at night was deafening. Bella didn't need her special gifts to hear the monkeys and frogs competing against each other to make the most nauseating din. Despite this, she could still make out what the mosquitoes were saying, as they buzzed around her head. "She looks tasty," they were whining to each other, but when Bella told them off in their own language, they soon backed off. But for all her angry words, Bella was scared. Her slippers squelched and disappeared into the mud with each step, while the incessant dripping of rainwater soaked through her night clothes and chilled her to the bone. In the twilight, she could sense movements in the tall grass.

"Hiss," lisped the voices. Bella didn't hang around to see what was making these spine-chilling sounds but trudged on as quickly as she could, deeper and deeper into the jungle.

Suddenly, through a moonlit chink in the trees, she saw the silhouette of a large slinky cat. Peering closer, Bella could just about make out the black and white markings on its coat. "A jaguar," she trembled. "I'm dead." She crouched in the tall grass. The jaguar stopped abruptly and let out a long deep growl. Slowly taking the pendant, Bella put it into her mouth and bent her knees ready for take-off. "Don't let me down now," she whispered as she opened up her arms and jumped in an attempt to fly.

The sound of breaking branches alerted the jaguar to Bella's desperate lunge. Bella had been so consumed by fear, she hadn't even cleared the nearest bush. Suddenly, flying, which had seemed like second nature only half an hour before, felt impossible. Instinctively, the jaguar turned and started to creep towards her. Hidden by the thick undergrowth, Bella prayed. "Just turn around and go," she chanted to herself, as she rubbed the pendant between her fingers and willed the beast to retreat. She was too scared even to breathe.

Her senses alert, Bella listened intently for the jaguar's

footsteps through the cacophony of the rainforest. Amongst all the other sounds she could hear, the ominous slithering of scaly skin as it brushed against the grass filled her with dread. She squinted her eyes and stared into the undergrowth, searching for signs.

"We can ssseee you," hissed the approaching voices, getting louder by the second. Whatever they were, they were close by.

The jaguar's ears pricked up. He let out an almighty roar, and then, for no apparent reason, turned and bounded away into the rainforest. Bella's relief was fleeting. There was something slithering around her ankle. She jumped up, her heart pounding, to see a viper wrapping itself around her feet.

"Hissssssss," whispered the hidden chorus.

She tried to run but the snake had already got her in its grip.

"A human child in the jungle? Why are you here?" spat another, much larger viper, raising itself up before her.

She stared in terror at the narrow slitty eyes that made it look so devious and cruel. It reminded her of Eugene Briggs.

Before she knew it, there were vipers everywhere. Their bright yellow scales were as dazzling as they were repellent. If Bella had known that these vipers were Golden Eyelash Vipers whose active venom would kill her within a minute, she might well have fainted.

"Get away!" she screamed, trying in vain to kick herself free. Her efforts sent her crashing headfirst into the undergrowth.

"Come with usss," they hissed into her ears. "If you try to escape, we'll fill your veins with poison."

The viper at her feet unwound itself. Feeling as if she had no choice, Bella gathered up her wet slippers and trudged on after them, heading even deeper into the jungle. She sensed a trap.

"Are you taking me to see humans?" she trembled, her hand on her pendant.

"Yesss," they hissed. "Hu-man-sss. You'll be quite sssafe."

The residue of evaporating water fell from the trees like incessant rain, dampening any hope that she was ever going home.

"Why are you letting me down now?" Bella growled at the pendant tucked safely away beneath her pyjamas. Her confidence and faith in it had taken a real battering after her disastrous flight from the jaguar. It was puzzling how, for all the pendant's power for language and flight, it could do nothing just when she needed it the most.

Eventually, they came out into a clearing. Bella could see at once that it was being used as a campsite.

"Our friendsss," the vipers hissed. "They'll be happy to sss-eee you."

In the middle, two men were cooking over an open log fire. Both were wearing khaki shorts and walking boots, but that's where any similarity ended. The tall thin man with the dark hair and tanned complexion was wearing a smart white shirt rather like those worn by aircraft pilots. The other man was wearing a black T-shirt and was much scruffier. He was shorter and chubbier with big baggy eyes and saggy cheeks. Bella thought he looked like a bloodhound.

"Your own kind," whispered the vipers. The vipers didn't seem to want to go any nearer to the flames and slipped away into the rainforest. "Go on," they called. "You're quite sssafe."

Crouching down in the tall grass, Bella surveyed the scene. While the tall tanned man turned a large skinned animal on a skewer, the short flabby one stoked the fire. Behind them there were three large tents where about a dozen or so men, most of them with holsters and handguns, were busy unloading spades and sacks from the back of three Land Rovers. Through the murky yellow light of the kerosene lamps, Bella's eye was drawn to a tall skinny white man in a crumpled khaki suit. His unkempt mop of shaggy grey hair was unnervingly familiar.

"I don't believe it," she murmured to herself. "I know that man. It's Eugene Briggs's dad."

Just then, the vipers, bored of waiting for Bella to reveal herself, darted up behind her. Thrusting themselves up onto the tips of their tails to display their venomous fangs, they made ready to spit their poison.

"Aaaah!" Bella screamed.

The two men looked up. "Another scavenging kid from the village," said the short chubby one. "We should give her a good beating and send her on her way." With that they picked up sticks and started running straight for her.

There was no escape. Before Bella could even think about flying, the vipers had tripped her. The taller of the two men grabbed her around the waist.

"Get your hands off me!" Bella squealed, kicking her legs and digging her nails into his arms.

"Why, you little rat," cried the short man, wiping his sniffly nose before grabbing hold of Bella's feet. He spoke in Spanish, but Bella instantly understood.

"She curses in English," spat the tall man. "We'd better take her straight to Mr. Briggs."

Before Bella knew it, the two men had turned her over and tied her hands behind her back with vines. A crowd of sweaty men quickly assembled, and Bella was made to kneel before them. She knew she was in trouble even before she recognized the dank aroma wafting towards her. Stepping forward from the ranks, the tall figure of Ted Briggs towered over her.

"Bella Balistica," he growled in disbelief.

Ted Briggs may have appeared to be calm, but in truth he was shocked. It made no sense that Bella Balistica was here. He could only think that Mrs. Sticklan had lied to him about her expulsion and that Bella and her mum were even now on some hell-bent witch-hunt to bring him down. Ever since that phone call he'd made to Bella's mum to complain about her daughter's outburst during one of his assemblies, they'd been out to get him. Another official complaint to the local education authority, and his reign as chair of governors at Hawksmore Primary would be over. He reached for his pipe.

"You look ridiculous in that quetzal costume," he jeered. It hadn't occurred to Bella that her green pyjamas and bright red dressing gown actually made her look like a quetzal, even as a human.

"I'm on to you, Mr. Briggs!" Bella shouted passionately.

Ted Briggs got out his tobacco case and started to refill his pipe. If Annie Balistica and her troublesome daughter had dragged themselves halfway round the world to expose his expedition, they had another think coming.

"And I'm on to your horrid little son," Bella went on. "I caught Eugene trapping badgers in the woods. I'm going to report him to the RSPCA."

Ted Briggs smiled contentedly at the thought of his son's antics. But Bella wasn't finished.

"*And* I've seen inside your house. Don't tell *me* you came by those artefacts legally. No wonder Eugene doesn't have any friends over to play except that spineless wimp, Connor Mitchell. You've got too much to hide."

Ted Briggs felt bemused by Bella's rant. If, by admitting to all this, she thought she was going to get one over on him, she was even more stupid than he thought. There was no way he was going to let her get away from him now.

"And don't get me started on the birds," Bella continued, adding yet another nail to her coffin. "I released the lot of them!"

Inside, Ted Briggs was seething. With this little girl seeming to know so much about his dubiously acquired collection of historical artefacts, he couldn't possibly allow her to discover the truth about this expedition. In fact, it would be much better if he never saw her wretched little face ever again.

"Chuck her in a sack," he ordered his minions. "I have plans for Bella Balistica."

CHAPTER THIRTEEN

TRAPPED

It smelt musty inside the sack, like having your nose wedged under someone's armpit on a hot sticky day. Unfortunately, this was exactly the kind of day it was. With her hands still tied, Bella lost her balance when her captors started to drag the sack. Thorns from the undergrowth ripped through and cut into her knees as she fell.

"Ow!" she cried, her eyes welling up with tears. The pain was excruciating. "Don't think that you're going to get away with this," came the muffled shout from inside the sack. But despite her rage, Bella was sounding braver than she felt. She wanted her mum.

The two men dumped Bella in her sack down by the Land Rovers and returned to the group for a wild pig and tortilla supper. As they were walking away, they heard the flapping of wings and saw a flickering light cross right before them.

"That was one *big* firefly," said the tall one, ducking to get out of the way.

"That was no firefly," sniffed the other. "If I'm not

mistaken, that was a quetzal." They thought nothing more of it.

Seeing Ted Briggs at school was one thing. There at least, Bella could speak her mind, knowing the worst he could do was get her excluded for a few days. Here, in the middle of the Guatemalan rainforest, the stakes were much higher. It didn't take much to work out what he was up to. Bella felt the depressing weight of her responsibilities bearing down on her. She knew that if he managed to achieve his ambition and take the Itzamna Emerald out of the temple and then out of the country, the Mayan world would be tossed into turmoil and disorder. She had to act quickly.

Despite the discomfort of her imprisonment, Bella wiggled herself upright and tried to get focused. Through the distant rumble of thunder, she could just about make out some of the things the men were talking about while they ate.

"The dynamite is in place. As soon as the thunder and lightning is overhead, we'll start detonating." Bella recognized Ted Briggs's voice. "What about the guards?" he went on. "Are they drugged?"

"They're sleeping like babies, boss," someone snuffled.

Briggs howled with laugher. "Once the artefacts are on the helicopter, I'll take them to Quezaltenango," he told his men. "We'll meet there as arranged for payment."

Bella felt her heart skip a beat. She'd been born in Quezaltenango.

"And what's our guarantee that you won't just get on a plane to England and leave us stranded?" one of the men asked suspiciously.

"You have my word," said Briggs.

A chorus of mutterings followed.

The vines around Bella's wrist were bound so painfully tight, she could hardly feel her fingers. Using her feet, she started to explore the rips in the sack caused by the thorns and found that one tear was wide enough to stick a foot through. As quietly as she could, she used her right foot to slowly make the hole bigger and bigger. Through all this, she listened carefully to the conversation of the men. Every time they laughed or the discussion became heated, she used the opportunity to rip the sack a little more. It was a risky business – sometimes the tears seemed to make such a noise she was sure she was going to be discovered. The final splitting of the material arrested the attention of Ted Briggs himself. He watched Bella pull herself out of the sack and start to run towards the trees.

"Leave her to me," he smiled ominously, putting away his pipe. "She can't get far with her hands tied."

Ted Briggs watched his prey dart through the undergrowth like a bewildered chicken. For a millisecond he almost thought he felt a little pity for the helpless creature. But he dismissed the idea immediately. "She's got it coming to her," he mumbled to himself, as he strode through the tall grass towards Bella. He was just thinking about what he was going to do when he got his hands on her, when the roar of jaguars stopped him dead in his tracks.

"Perfect," he exclaimed. There was no need to do a thing. Bella Balistica would either be eaten by jaguars or poisoned by snakes long before she could ever make it to the tourist camp at Flores. He watched her stumbling off into the trees and was just about to turn back with this optimistic thought in mind when he saw a long furry arm reach down from a tree and pull her up. Bella gasped as her legs left the ground.

"Ow! You're squeezing too tight," she shouted, astonished that anyone could be so rude. "And stop tickling my neck." To her amazement she found herself swinging through the trees while the thumping heart of the hairy beast holding her reverberated like jungle drums in her ears. On and on they swung, from vine to vine and tree to tree, away from the spellbound Ted Briggs.

The sound of howling laughter that Bella had heard in the distance when she'd first landed in Tikal was rapidly getting louder. "What now?" Bella was thinking as the mysterious creature started to slow down. Whatever it was that had saved her from Briggs was too big and hairy to be human. Its five-fingered hands and long arms were so powerful, Bella feared it could crack her head open as if it were a nut. Warning bells were ringing in her head even before the animal dropped her. "This is it," she thought as she crashed through the trees towards the forest floor.

Bella had fallen off her bike many times and even once from the shed roof, but never from the higher canopies of a tropical rainforest.

"Aah!" she screamed at the top of her lungs.

"Aah!" mimicked the strange creature, who was free-falling in unison with her.

Just as she was about to hit the ground, the creature grabbed her with its long tail and used its arms and feet to break their fall. Bella tumbled safely into the vegetation to the obvious delight of everyone around.

A troop of monkeys, larger than any she had ever seen on television, surrounded her. Most of them were as black as coal although some of the smaller ones looked browner in colour.

Their wide-set nostrils would have made them look tough if their black penetrating eyes didn't have such a friendly glow about them. "You can tell a lot by looking into someone's eyes," Bella's mum would say.

Bella stared into the eyes of the monkeys and put her hand over her pendant in an attempt to summon up courage. "So, are you going to eat me or what?" she demanded. Again the monkeys howled with laugher. "What's so funny?" Bella shouted. "And do you have to howl *so* loud when you laugh?"

This only made the animals holler even more.

"We're vegetarians," said one of the small browner ones. "And we howl because we're Howler Monkeys." The little monkey became hysterical following his triumphant play on words.

"Oh," said Bella indignantly. "And I *suppose* you think I should thank you."

"That's right," chirped a familiar voice.

Bella looked up and couldn't believe what she saw. The Quetzal was perched on a nearby branch. He looked battered and somewhat dishevelled but otherwise fine.

"You escaped!" cried Bella in absolute glee. "I thought you were dead."

"You weren't the only one," twittered the beleaguered bird. "Deceived as you might be by my obvious maturity and regal good looks, I can still duck and dive like a young whippersnapper."

"Just as pompous as ever," sighed Bella, with more affection than she expected. In truth, she'd never been so pleased to see anybody.

"I tried to get back to you," said the Quetzal, "but the

eagle was waiting for me at every turn. It's thanks to the diversions of these kind monkeys that I finally got away."

He turned towards the howler monkeys, who immediately bowed their heads. "You did well," he told them. "Now you know what we're dealing with here," the Quetzal told Bella solemnly. "We must move quickly."

Watching the whole scene from his hiding place in the bushes, Ted Briggs was trying to catch his breath without giving himself away. He could hardly believe his eyes. Beating a path through the rainforest to catch up with the monkeys, he'd actually lost them – until their unmistakable laughter had given them away. While he couldn't understand anything that was being said, it looked like Bella was actually *talking* to the animals. There was no way he was going to let her out of his sight now. This was far too interesting.

The Quetzal pecked through the vines binding Bella's wrists. "You look a little queasy," he told her. "I think we better organize you a ride."

Bella climbed onto the back of one of the larger howler monkeys. "And no swinging," she ordered the monkey. "Just keep to the forest floor."

The obedient monkey scampered through the undergrowth towards the Great Temple, followed by the Quetzal and the troop. All Bella could think about was holding onto the monkey, but the animals had other things on their mind. If Bella wasn't the one, then all their years of searching had come to nothing. If Briggs's expedition managed to gain entry into the temple and find the tomb of King Kabah, they were *all* in trouble.

"If this doesn't work," said one of the monkeys to his wife, "the balance of our world will be tipped. There'll be nothing but earthquakes and floods for a century."

With all this going on in the minds of the animals, it was perhaps no wonder then that no one noticed the man in the crumpled safari suit following their tracks by the light of the full moon.

The Quetzal landed at the foot of the great monument just as Bella was dropped off by the obliging howler monkey. Surveying the area, he caught sight of a family of armadillos snuffling in the undergrowth nearby. "I'm looking for the animal entrance," he told them bluntly. "I command you to tell me where it is."

Bella looked at the Quetzal quizzically. Her mum would have sent her to bed without any supper if she'd spoken to anyone like that.

As if reading her mind, the Quetzal turned to her: "You're forgetting that I'm king of the higher canopies," he reminded her with an air of put-on nobility. "Quetzals are the national symbol of Guatemala. A certain manner is expected of me, even when addressing land animals." And then, as if trying to pump himself up for a showdown: "And don't you forget it!"

The armadillos bowed before the Quetzal. "We won't forget," they mumbled shyly.

Bella and the Quetzal followed the armour-plated armadillos a few metres back into the jungle, where they started to use their long snouts to clear a small area in the vegetation. As she watched, Bella was aware of a strange stirring in the rainforest and had the sense that they were being watched. She shivered as she scoured the dark undergrowth for movement before turning back to watch the armadillos.

"It's here," snorted the armadillos in unison. "But we can't open it."

"Do they always speak at the same time like that?" asked Bella.

"Strange creatures," whispered the Quetzal. "They hardly ever speak because they always seem to know what the other is thinking. Consequently, when they do speak, they often say the same thing at the same time. It makes talking rather pointless."

"It's like me and Charlie," laughed Bella excitedly. "We can do that."

Using her hands to pull back the bushes, Bella slowly became aware of a large flat stone. Brushing away the soil she could see some red, cartoon-like markings of people. "Look!" she exclaimed. "Hieroglyphics."

At the sight of the inscription the Quetzal turned to the on-looking animals. "Leave us," he ordered.

"But we want to help," complained the chattering monkeys.

"Go!" ordered the Quetzal. "For now, your work is done."

All around them, a mind-boggling array of mammals began to reveal themselves from their hiding places.

"I had a feeling we were being watched," said Bella, stepping back in wonder as pumas, crocodiles, alligators, sloths, monkeys, tapirs, ocelots, deer, even some of the cows and bulls from the local village, along with a hundred animals Bella couldn't even name, stepped into the open.

"Why should we go?" snapped one of the alligators.

The Quetzal opened his wings as wide as he could to accentuate his command of the situation.

"Why?" he repeated nervously. "Because . . . " For a moment the cocky bird seemed at a loss for words. "Because she's got the hopes and expectations of the whole Mayan world bearing down on her." The Quetzal's confidence was growing. "The least you all can do is give her the peace and quiet she needs to think straight!"

Reluctantly, the animals began to disperse back into the rainforest. "I'm not so sure," Bella heard one of the anteaters say to a porcupine. "I think she's going to need all the help she can get." The seriousness of her tone gave Bella the jitters.

Secretly, the Quetzal liked the reassuring presence of other animals, but he was scared in case any of the less trustworthy beasts got to hear things that they shouldn't. Unfortunately for the Quetzal, the most untrustworthy beast in the vicinity was already in earshot.

Ted Briggs threw himself into the undergrowth. He was panting like a wolf. "What on earth are all these crocodiles and alligators doing so far away from the river?" he thought as he gazed through the trees onto the scene. Seeing the pumas and jaguars sent him scampering up the nearest tree. How he got away without being seen was a miracle. But then, the animals were unusually distracted.

"Recognize the writing?" whispered the Quetzal, returning his attention to the hieroglyphic figures on the large flat stone. He quickly checked that there was no one around. The coast appeared to be clear.

Bella stared hard. Something about the images was vaguely familiar.

"It's the ancient language of the K'iche' Indians," the Quetzal informed her. "Your forefathers wrote in this language and created some of the finest literature ever written. Much better than the rubbish people write today."

"Can you read it?" asked Bella.

"I can," retorted the Quetzal. "The question is, can you? According to legend, only the human touched with the spirit of Itzamna can open this entrance and be led to the treasure within."

"Then why are you worried about Ted Briggs?" asked Bella, irritated by the Quetzal's lack of human logic. "He's not touched by anything but greed."

"Prophesies and legends are one thing," sighed the Quetzal sadly. "Explosives are another. He'll simply destroy the place, as he rips it apart to find the Emerald."

This was so typical of a Briggs, Bella thought. Eugene would sooner burn down the school hall than have to be in one of Mr. Alder's drama productions. He nearly did last year too, and *still* he didn't get excluded!

Bella squinted her eyes to study the writing in detail. Absentmindedly, she reached for her pendant. Rubbing it against her fingers, she focused all her energies on the ancient script, as her understanding slowly began to unfold. For each letter of the alphabet there was a picture. The sentences ran from right to left and from the bottom to the top. Bella didn't know how, but she could read it. Slowly raising her eyes to the Quetzal, she nodded. Then, in a deep and steadfast whisper she started to chant: "Harak, karadak, lopatos, almanos."

For a moment nothing happened. It was as if the world needed time to wake up to the mystical forces unfolding. Then, from the very centre of the earth, there was a long disquieting rumble and from all corners of the rainforest they could hear the sound of terrified animals scattering in all directions.

"Stand back!" squawked the Quetzal. His glittering eyes

looked like they were going to explode in wonder.

Bella dived into the tall grass, as the whole earth quaked beneath them again. She closed her eyes, expecting the temple to be shaken to its very foundations, but when she turned around, all she could see was the upturned rock. The granite stood erect in the ground like an enormous tombstone.

Ted Briggs had fallen from the tree during the first quake. Lifting himself up and brushing himself down, he found himself gawping in disbelief at the miracle that had unfolded before him. "This is it!" he thought. "The break I've been waiting for." He quickly hid himself back down in the tall grass.

"The Earth favours you, Bella," trembled the Quetzal, unaware of anything but Bella and the upturned rock. "But be warned. The Earth's a fiery beast, and her mood can change very quickly."

Bella understood only too well how erratic passionate people could be.

"You are the gatekeeper now," warned the Quetzal. "Forget the words inscribed on this door at your peril."

"Harak, karadak, lopatos, almanos," Bella chanted to herself again and again. How she understood their meaning, she had no idea. "Love, learn, forgive and move on," she said to herself. It was the same advice as she got from the voice in the attic, only for the first time Bella realized that these voices in her head had always been in this ancient language.

With her heart pounding in anticipation, Bella walked gingerly up to the opening beneath the upturned rock and looked down. By the light of the moonlit skies, she could see that there was a steep stone staircase that descended into the bleak abyss. She was shaking, over-awed by a sense of her emerging power and yet terrified of taking the next step into the dark unknown. "I don't suppose you brought a light," she trembled through chattering teeth.

The Quetzal flew up into the trees and came back down with a kerosene lamp hanging awkwardly in his beak. He laid it down carefully on the floor. "I took it from the human camp," he confessed proudly. "I turned the light down low so they wouldn't see me."

Bella turned up the wick by using a small round knob on the side of the lamp. Immediately, the lamp lit up. The Quetzal flew up onto her shoulder. "Let's go," he cheered as best he could. "And watch your step."

But Bella wasn't going anywhere. The biggest furriest spider she had ever seen in her life had just scuttled over the lip of the entrance and was heading right for her.

"Aaaah!" she screamed, jumping from foot to foot. "Do something . . . do something." The spider was so big, Bella could even see its mouth and look into its black beady eyes.

"Ouch!" shouted the spider, covering its ears as best it could. "You *are* loud."

"Please excuse her," the Quetzal warbled, doing his best not to fall off Bella's shoulder. "She's got a phobia."

"Me too," huffed the spider. "Squeamish girls." The spider shrugged its shoulders and went scuttling on. "You're going to love it down there," chuntered the spider mockingly.

"*That*," snapped the Quetzal after the spider had gone, "was embarrassing. Now come on." Bella rubbed her fingers over the pendant for courage and took her first tentative steps into the temple.

From his hiding place in the undergrowth, Briggs watched

in amazement, as Bella and the bird disappeared down the hole. Keeping his voice down to a whisper, he tried to use his mobile phone to rally his team back at the camp.

"Damn these stupid things!" he muttered, as yet again the "no signal" message appeared on the screen. He tossed it into his jacket pocket and tried the radio clipped to the collar of his jacket.

"Alright there, boss?" came the distorted reply. "Where are you? The signal's awful."

"I need backup, now!" Briggs hissed as loudly as he dared. "I'm entering the Great Temple via an upturned rock on the south-west side of the quadrant." He turned the reciever volume to low, slipped quietly through the tall grass and slithered down the stairs after them.

The underground staircase was covered in moss and vines, which got tangled around Bella's slippers and made it difficult for her to lift her feet. "I feel all itchy," Bella moaned, scratching her head. She raised the lamp up through the long dangly cobwebs that draped around her head. The lamp cast yellowy shadows onto the grimy walls, while its movement dislodged spiders from their webs with every move.

"What's that?" she cried, feeling the tickle of bristly feet scampering through her hair. She tried to brush them away but only succeeded in knocking more spiders onto her face and shoulders. "Aaaah!" she screamed.

They listened to the piercing echo, as it faded into oblivion. The Quetzal tried to pick the scurrying creatures out of her hair with his beak, but there were so many he gave up.

"They're gone," he lied.

Bella tried to block out her fear by focusing on her footing, but it was impossible with all the draping cobwebs and the thought of so many spiders. "Don't think about it," she kept chanting to herself.

But she did.

The deeper they went, the more humid it became, and it wasn't long before Bella was drenched in sweat. There was a stale smell within the temple that reminded her of Ted Briggs's foul aroma.

"Look at the walls," gasped the Quetzal. "I haven't seen writing like this for centuries."

Bella raised the lamp and peered at the drawings. Then, just as she was about to lower the lamp and move on, she saw a face staring out at her from behind the grimy veneer. Using her spare hand to brush away thousands of years of dust and grunge, she started to unearth the image in full. "I know this woman," cried Bella, excited by her discovery. "I have a portrait of her in the attic at home."

The Quetzal peered at the painting. "She looks a bit like you," he commented.

The more Bella stared at the face, the more she couldn't believe her eyes. The black hair and those fiery dark eyes: in so many ways it was identical to the portrait at home. The colour of the woman's garments had faded over time, but the resemblance was remarkable.

"Bella," said the Quetzal in his most serious voice. Bella had the feeling that what she was about to hear would change her life forever. "This is Itzamna in her female form," the bird told her. "You are her direct descendent. You have powers beyond your wildest dreams. You, and only you, could have opened that door."

Bella looked into the eyes of her animal twin. The Quetzal

knew more about her than she did herself. "I'm scared," she said quietly. "You won't leave me, will you?" Her pendant was ice-cold.

Ted Briggs was about twenty steps behind them. He hadn't been able to hear any of the conversation between Bella and the Quetzal, but the result of their endeavours was opening up a whole new world. None of his archaeological maps or astrological charts had predicted this opening. The possibility of a complex underground labyrinth of tunnels running beneath the well-documented passages of the main structure was exciting. All that stood between him and his life's ambition was this wretched little girl. If she got a chance to tell the authorities about his plan, he was done for.

"It's not my fault she broke into my house," he rationalized. Reminding himself of the day she left him standing like an idiot before the whole school, he felt the sweet sense of revenge beckon. "And it's not my fault she's here." He was starting to form his plan. "And surely I couldn't be blamed if she should have an unexpected accident – especially as her mother has clearly neglected her parental obligations." A contented grin started to form on Briggs's face. It's not that Ted Briggs was intrinsically evil. Inspired by greed, he just took choices that took him closer and closer to evil's source.

Closing in on his victim, he reached out and grabbed the Quetzal. Bella, realizing the danger too late, went to swing the lamp into the face of their attacker, but Briggs was quick. Before she could even turn her head, he gave her an almighty push down the staircase.

"Whoops," he exclaimed sarcastically.

Bella could hear the howl of his cruel laughter echoing

through the chambers, as she tumbled into the depths of the earth.

"Hold on, Bella!" squawked the Quetzal. "Remember who you are." His voice was shrill, constrained by Briggs's forceful grip around his neck. They were the last words Bella heard from the Quetzal. As he headed back towards the light, Briggs was already tying the poor bird's beak with vines.

For some reason, Bella held onto the lamp for dear life. It had gone out as soon as she'd started to fall and kerosene was flying everywhere. About twenty steps down, she crashed onto the dusty plateau that marked the beginning of a long horizontal passage.

"That was lucky," she thought. From the opening at the surface, long beams of moonlight faintly defined her surroundings. But Bella's luck, if that was what it was, was only fleeting.

"Quetzal!" she cried, looking up and thrusting her foot onto the first step of the staircase in an attempt to run to his rescue. In a huge explosion of dust, the floor beneath her suddenly gave way and, Bella found herself free-falling into an abyss. "Aaaah . . . !" Instinctively, Bella focused on the power of the pendant and flung out her arms. As if she'd just opened a parachute, there was an abrupt jolt and a dramatic deceleration in her fall, but she still made an unhealthy thump when she hit the bottom. "Ow!" she screamed in pain and distress. "My arm!" Her cry reverberated through the darkness and faded away to stony silence.

Alone in the pitch dark and shaking with fear, Bella curled herself up into a little ball and sobbed. This was her worst nightmare.

CHAPTER FOURTEEN

RAIDERS

Ted Briggs couldn't believe his luck. He'd had no idea that there was an entrance to the temple on this side of the quadrant – this was going to save him a fortune in dynamite. With that meddlesome girl out of the way, there was no one to stand between him and his life's ambition. The British Museum would pay the earth to display the artefacts from this archaeological expedition. But Ted Briggs was not going to share his discoveries with the nation. He knew that the sky was the limit when it came to the price he could command for such artefacts from private collectors in London and New York. But when it came to the Itzamna Emerald, Briggs had no intention of selling. It would be for his eyes only, the very centrepiece of his own private collection.

Climbing a good way up the exterior staircase of the temple, Ted Briggs eventually got a signal on his radio. "Where the hell are you?" he demanded when he finally got to speak with his pilot. "I want the helicopter and the whole team."

He looked up into the face of the half-hidden moon, at the height of its ascendancy and besieged by gathering clouds. The storm, ideal for masking detonating dynamite, might yet end up being a curse. "Bring the pulleys, ropes and all our halogen lighting equipment," he howled down the phone. "Now!!!"

Storm or no storm, they had only eight hours before the tourist buses would start to return. To be caught excavating without a permit was a serious offence in Guatemala.

The pain in Bella's right arm was excruciating. She tried to move it but found she could hardly lift it at all. In different surroundings she might have been quicker to consider using the pendant to ease the throbbing, but the distant sound of rolling thunder reverberating through the temple was too much of a distraction. All her irrational fears were becoming a reality. "I want my mum," she kept thinking. And she was worried sick about the Quetzal.

"Briggs!" she blurted out loud. "That's what I could smell." Bella had no doubt who had grabbed the Quetzal and kicked her down the steps. "The poor thing will probably end up in a zoo," she thought, "or worse, stuffed and mounted inside a glass case in that hideous house of his."

Pulling herself up with her left arm, Bella rubbed her eyes and waved her hands before her face. She couldn't see a thing. As she used her senses to try to orient herself to her invisible surroundings, she felt something run across her foot. "Rats!" she cried out.

And there were – hundreds of them. But they weren't the only creatures of the underworld Bella was about to encounter. There were bats all around her too. She could hear their high-pitched squeaks as they flapped around her head. "Get off!" she shouted, manically waving her arms in the air.

She tried to fly but couldn't lift herself up because of the sprain in her arm. Gathering all her powers of concentration, she took the pendant and held it against her wound. "Come on," she mumbled. "It worked on Charlie."

She rubbed the pendant gently over her bruises and felt a light tingling sensation running through them, nothing like the explosion of energy she'd experienced when she'd so unwittingly healed Charlie's wrists. Perhaps that had been beginner's luck, but one thing was for sure – there was to be no quick fix this time. Feeling less than confident, Bella tried again but failed miserably. Utterly dispirited, she flopped back down to the floor.

After a time, and heightened by her lack of vision, Bella's ears were becoming more sensitized to her surroundings. In the distance, she could hear the noise of Briggs's men working on the surface. The teachers at Hawksmore Primary were always telling her she was a poor listener, but they were wrong. It was only when they were being boring that she talked in class. She remembered the night when she and the Quetzal saved the badger from Eugene's trap. "Close your eyes, filter out all extraneous sense and focus on your ears," he'd told her.

That night she'd been able to hear a soundscape unknown to her before. Perhaps if she did the same thing now and focused on her eyes she might be able to see. Holding the pendant firmly in her left hand and blocking all other sense out of her mind, Bella opened her eyes as wide as she could and tried to see the world in a new way. It didn't take long. Slowly, as if someone had turned on some very weak Christmas lights, she became aware of small and very dim fluorescent dots appearing before her eyes. "I'm delirious," she panicked. "I'm losing blood, and I'm going to die."

Breathing quickly to compensate for the thin air, Bella tried to keep herself conscious. It took a full minute for the reality of this unusual lighting to become clear. "Glow-worms?" she asked, cautiously.

"Yes," said something with a very squeaky voice.

Bella wasn't sure where it came from but could see that a number of creatures that looked like rats were nibbling on her slippers. "Get off!" she shouted angrily, kicking one away.

Vaguely aware of light-footed tickles all over her body, Bella brushed herself down and quickly scanned her surroundings. Things were becoming clearer by the second. She was standing in the middle of a rocky tomb about the same size as her living room at home. As her eyes became accustomed to the dim light, she noticed a dark shadowy figure as big as her hand, crouched inside a crack in the far wall. The hairy animal was staring right at her. Bella gulped. She couldn't count the legs, but she could see that they were long and spiky with red tips that looked a bit like bristles.

"Oh no," she shuddered. "A tarantula."

Bella gasped in horror, as the tarantula shot out its front legs, seized a passing fly and popped it straight into its mouth. The crispy insect made for a loud snack. "I suppose she does look a bit like her," the tarantula pondered aloud as she crunched.

Bella's teeth were chattering so loudly, it was difficult to hear anything else. Frozen to the spot with fear and disgust, she peered down to the floor and tried to make out who the spider was talking to. To her horror, she saw that she was covered from head to toe in hairy spiders. Worse still, they were on the move, scuttling this way and that across her dressing gown and pyjamas. She was just about to let out the biggest scream of her life when the tarantula shouted: "Don't move!" The spiders running up and down Bella suddenly froze. A quiet stillness filled the air.

"I think she might have a problem with spiders," hushed the tarantula.

"You're damned right I do," Bella shivered.

As she peered around the room, Bella saw an assembly of insects that ran all across the floor, up the walls and over the ceiling. This was the last place on earth for anyone with a phobia of dark, spider-cluttered places to be. She clutched her pendant tightly and tried to stop her knees wobbling.

"Can she understand what we're saying?" squeaked a red ant.

"Of course I can understand," squealed Bella in indignation. "Are you going to help me or what?"

Shocked by her outburst, the tarantula leant back on its haunches and raised its head and legs, as if to attack. Bella shuddered to see its long curved fangs. She'd always thought her fear of spiders was irrational, but standing here, completely covered in them, staring straight into the face of a larger-than-life tarantula, her fears seemed entirely justified.

"Alright, alright," she cried, fighting back her alarm. "Stop showing off."

"It is," squeaked the rats. "It's Itzamna."

It never took Bella long to say what was on her mind. "My name's Bella, if you don't mind. The old relation of mine you're referring to is dead. Although, as you can see, I do seem to have inherited some of her talents." She peered around at the assembled animal life. "Like talking to you lot!"

A thousand insects all took a step back. Bella was getting heated now. "There are thieves up there planning to steal everything they can get their hands on, including the Itzamna Emerald."

The sharp intake of breath made by so many animals was startling. Amongst a cacophony of "How does she know?" exclamations, Bella composed herself and waited for the silence to return. When she was sure she had the attention of every living thing in earshot, she started.

"The first thing I'd like to request," she said, trying to stay calm – "is that all the spiders – especially those with big hairy feet – GET OFF!!!" she shouted at the top of her lungs.

A hundred terrified spiders scuttled down Bella's pyjama legs and made for cover.

"The next request," Bella went on, brushing away the slowcoaches with the back of her hand and checking she was spider-free, "is that we work together to stop these impostors."

Far above them, Bella and the animals could hear the noise of the human invasion. There was the clank of heavy metal and the shouts of men trying to communicate in the storm. It didn't take long for the murmurings to begin again.

"It's happened before," Bella heard the mosquitoes drone, "in the smaller temples."

"The humans will take everything," the spiders muttered.

"It will bring bad luck," whined the rats. "To humans and animals."

Up on the surface, Ted Briggs was busy tying the Quetzal's wings and packing him away inside a box. "You're going straight into my aviary when I get home," he snarled at the bird, as he slapped on the lid. "Stay in touch on the mobile," he shouted to the pilot. "I'll need containers. And whatever you do, make sure these people handle anything that comes up with care."

Briggs's crew were tired and soaked to the skin. Most of them were so fed up they were ready to quit. "It's not worth it," sniffed the short chubby man who'd helped catch Bella. He was talking to a small group of six men. "Not for the money he's paying us."

"I don't like this storm," said another. "I think the gods are brewing up another earthquake."

"They don't want us to go into the temple," said another. "We'll be cursed, the lot of us."

The lashing rain was forming itself into drainage channels and flooding through the entrance and down the temple steps like a waterfall. It was much too treacherous underfoot to enter without a rope and harness. Drenched and wearing a bright-yellow hardhat with a powerful torch on its rim, Ted Briggs attached himself to the harness. Once he was underground, the hydraulic pulley system would be his lifeline to the outside world.

"How much cable have we got?" Briggs demanded.

"About half a mile," replied the operator.

"Excellent," said Briggs. "Lower me in."

Taking a torch and pickaxe from one of his men, he descended into the temple.

About twenty metres down, at the point where he had kicked Bella into the darkness, Ted Briggs noticed a small gap in the roof of the tunnel. Being a tall man, he was able to reach up and strike it with his pickaxe. "Damn!" he cursed as the dust fell into eyes.

It didn't take long for him to make the hole big enough to throw up a climbing anchor, pull himself up and peer through. Shining his torch into the room, Briggs was excited to see a sarcophagus and immediately started examining the tomb for any sign of the emerald. He imagined that it might have its own case at the head of the sarcophagus. To his frustration, it was difficult to make things out through the cobwebs and shadows from his uncomfortable and restricted vantage point.

"I need help to break down this wall and get into this tomb," he shouted up to his men. "A man with a pickaxe."

It took another hour's digging to get Briggs and his disgruntled helper into the tomb.

"Looks like a bit of a red herring this one, boss," sniffed Briggs's stout assistant, rummaging through a box of antiquated tools. "My guess is, this tomb was the final resting place of the architect who designed the temple." As proof, he held up a stone tablet with a diagram of the temple and sneezed all over it.

"Damn and blast it!" Ted Briggs shouted, rubbing his eyes and choking through a cloud of dust. He picked up a pot and smashed it against the wall, just missing his assistant's head. The Ancient Egyptians had also built 'decoy' tombs like this within the pyramids, designed to make thieves think that they had discovered the real treasure. This tomb was full of Mayan pots, many of them decorated with painted images of richly-dressed men in headdresses. He'd seen these figures before in early Mayan ceramics and was quite familiar with the value collectors put on them. The artefacts were of historical interest, but compared with a large, three-headed jaguar cast in solid gold and an emerald the size of a man's head, they were relatively worthless. "I'm going to need more time," Briggs snarled loudly, aggravated to be so close and yet so far away from achieving his quest.

Despite his frustration, there were still several bowls that caught Briggs's eye. One of these was a delicate ceramic bowl which had an ornate hummingbird perched on the rim. "Take this and wrap it up," he ordered, thrusting it into the arms of his wheezy assistant.

Tipping out one of the storage pots, Briggs found that it was full of ancient coins, some of which, when he wiped away the dirt, were silver.

"It's not *all* bad, boss," remarked the assistant. "These coins are worth a small fortune."

Other pots contained simple necklaces carved out of wood, seeds and fish vertebrae. Briggs knew that he could sell many of these on the black market to raise some quick cash, but he wanted more. To the best of his knowledge, no one had yet discovered any passages leading to an underground network of tunnels and chambers. Expeditions to date had all focused on the premise that the Itzamna Emerald was hidden inside the main frame of the temple as it was perceived from the ground. "But they're wrong," Briggs had said a hundred times. "*They* wouldn't be so obvious."

He knew instinctively that the devious architect who designed this temple would have other ideas. The tomb of King Kabah that housed the infamous emerald and its mythical three-headed, fire-breathing protector would be somewhere *much* deeper. As the first archaeologist to discover tangible evidence of an underground network of passages and tombs, Briggs felt that he was closer than any other explorer before him to finding the Itzamna Emerald.

"Right," he told his assistant. "I'll call for reinforcements. Get all this stuff into boxes and up into the helicopter. I'm going to explore the tunnels that lead under the temple."

He tried in vain to get a signal on his radio to talk to the man operating the pulley. Instead, he just stuck his head out into the cobweb-ridden corridor and shouted: "I want another three men down here now!" His shouts bounced around the temple, causing a small landslide of ricocheting debris.

There was a moment's silence, then the distant cries of: "Alright, boss."

"Give me a little slack," Briggs called. "I'm going further in. Any sudden jerks – hold me steady. When I tug three times on the rope, pull me up. Not before. Is that understood? . . . understood . . . understood . . . ?"

Briggs got himself back to the staircase and lowered himself down until he reached the bottom. There, to his wonder, the floor had fractured to give way to a vertical shaft into which Bella must have fallen. He stood for a moment to search his emotions for guilt, but there was none. He peered down into the tunnel. "It looks like some sort of trapdoor," Briggs pondered to himself, "an entrance to the lower levels."

The Ancient Mayans had demonstrated an impressive capacity to carve labyrinths of incredible mathematical complexity. All Briggs had to do was to break the code. Needless to say, many an ill-equipped looter had met their death attempting such a challenge. But Ted Briggs wasn't your average thief. He had a backup team and the hydraulic pulley to help him.

Briggs turned the light on the brim of his hat down to half-beam to conserve battery power. Pulling his harness taught, he found his footing and started to lower himself into the darkness. "It looks like this tunnel could lead to the very centre of the earth," he thought, as the hairs on the back of his neck pricked up with trepidation and excitement.

Meanwhile, somewhere much closer to the pit of the earth, Bella was passionately telling her story to the assembling crowd of rodents, insects and spiders: " . . . and that's when Ted Briggs pushed me down the staircase and kidnapped the Quetzal," Bella concluded. "So you see, it's a matter of the utmost importance that you help."

"Stand clear," ordered the tarantula, as she made her way across the rocky floor. Bella followed her with her eyes and for the first time became aware of the small opening in the wall behind the spider. She wondered if the gap was big enough to squeeze through.

"Now here's what I think we should do to help Bella," said the tarantula, who seemed to have taken it upon herself to be team leader. The other animals listened intently to her plan. "Judging by Miss Bella's size, we're not going to be able to take any shortcuts. We'll have to use the ancient burial route. Has anyone here been that way in recent times?"

One of the larger rats raised his tail.

The tarantula had already sent two of the smaller rodents off on a mission to steal matches from the humans. There was just enough kerosene in the lamp to make it worthwhile.

"Even with our guide *and* with the lamp," the tarantula went on, "we're going to need as many rats as possible to carry the glow-worms so we can all see where we're going . . . "

In their rush to get organized, no one had noticed the dim artificial light, emanating from the man steadily lowering himself towards them. Even if they had, they might have thought it was nothing more than a harmless glow-worm.

Upon the successful return of the resourceful rodents, Bella lit the lamp. For the first time, she became aware of the faded carvings and the strangely familiar hieroglyphics on the walls. She was sure the images told stories of immense significance to the humans and animals of the Mayan world.

"No time to read them now," chivvied the tarantula. "Follow that rat."

Bella followed the rat to the narrow gap she'd seen in the wall. It was a tight squeeze, but when she turned her body to meet it in profile and ducked her head down to the widest section in the middle, she just managed to push herself through. Almost immediately however, the height of the passage that lay beyond it diminished. Deeper and deeper into the subterranean labyrinth Bella crawled, surrounded by a large number of excited animals.

"The air down here is so thin," Bella wheezed.

"Then save your breath," advised the tarantula, scuttling up the wall to avoid the thick layer of dust on the floor.

Her lead was quickly followed by many of the other insects and spiders. Unfortunately for Bella, she had to pull herself through on her stomach using her sprained arm while at least a dozen rats got a free ride on her back. She tried in vain to visualize where she was within the temple but was too disorientated by the obscure route.

"Why do we keep taking alternate left turns that always take us down?" she spat, noticing at certain junctions how the tunnels parted into tributaries that extended in all directions.

"I thought you were trying to get me out!"

"I'm going to show you the *real* treasures of Tikal," replied the tarantula with pride. "You need to know how important your mission is."

It was then that one of the rats riding on Bella's back saw the approaching figure which appeared to have a large glow-worm attached to his head.

"We're being followed," he squealed. "By a human!"

But Bella didn't hear, and no one else took any notice. They were all too busy clinging onto Bella's dressing gown.

Not a moment too soon, the tunnel opened up, and Bella found herself crawling into what she envisaged to be an enormous crypt. She got to her feet and brushed the dust from her hair and face. Then, with a jittery hand, she turned up the wick on her lamp.

"Wow!" she trembled, as the light cast long dim shadows around the spooky tomb. "It's like being inside a huge stone grave, deep in the underworld."

Despite the lamp and the best efforts of the glow-worms, it was hard to take everything in. The animals too gaped in wonder, speechless at the treasures before them. Huge granite pillars carved out of the rock supported the roof under which a whole host of dusty gold and silver sculptures stood to attention, as if guarding something of immense importance.

"This crypt contains some of the best examples of work by the early Mayan gold- and silversmiths," whispered the tarantula, as if she were in a church. "They knew how to weld gold with silver and to plate copper with gold centuries before your own culture."

Around the burial chamber, colourful masks dripping in golden jewellery adorned the walls.

"We try to keep it clean," squeaked one of the rats, "but it's like fighting a losing battle."

"That's what my mum says about my bedroom," said Bella quietly, secretly feeling a little homesick.

Bella was still thinking of home, when she noticed a faded painting on the wall.

"What's that?" she asked, pointing to the image of four skeletons carrying an ornate chest like the one in her attic.

"It symbolizes the Festival of the Dead," hushed the spider.

Bella grimaced and decided that she would keep the chest at home permanently covered. The thought that it might have been used for such a festival was too spine-chilling for words. All around her she could see small mosaic masks glaring out at her though the dusky light.

"Funeral masks," the spider informed her, as she scurried up a cobweb and disappeared into an eye socket.

The idea of an all-seeing eye gave Bella the strangest feeling that they were being watched.

"The sooner we get out of here the better," she mumbled.

All around the tomb there were ornate ceramics and large silver chests, presumably full to the brim with treasures beyond anyone's wildest dreams.

"Nearly all the great works of Mayan literature are here," explained the spider, as if giving a guided tour. "The parchments have been well protected in these stone cases for thousands of years, and the rats haven't nibbled on any of them."

There were universal squeaks of agreement from the rodents who were now scampering around the place trying to tidy up as best they could.

"All the great religious leaders, the philosophers, the astrologers, you name it; they all have their works here,' the spider continued. 'When the Mayans first heard about Christopher Columbus, they had the collections brought here for safety."

Bella knew all about the Spanish Conquistadors who had invaded these countries. They stole what they liked and killed whoever got in their way. Columbus and the man who followed him, Hernando Cortez, were supposed to be the biggest pirates of them all. The thought that even one piece of this treasure might have eluded these crooks only to end up in Ted Briggs's private collection was too much to bear. Funnily enough, Ted Briggs was thinking about such acquisitions himself, as he crawled along the last few metres of corridor that would lead him into the tomb.

Bella had been unaware of the larger-than-life glow-worm following them through the underground tunnels. Nevertheless, as she moved further into the crypt, her sixth sense continued to tell her she was not alone.

"Watch your back," whispered a voice inside her head.

Just then, a huge crack of thunder reverberated through the temple. It seemed as if the earth itself was quaking with anger. Bella fell to the ground and covered her head with her hands, terrified that the whole temple was about to be rocked to its foundations. Up on the surface, Ted Briggs's men stopped packing the artefacts onto the helicopter and started to panic.

"We need to get him out of there," shouted the pilot. "This expedition is bringing bad luck. The gods themselves are telling us to keep away."

The trembling earth and the din of heavy rain and thunder was deafening.

"But he hasn't given us the order," yelled the man operating Briggs's harness. "And I can't get a signal on the radio."

Some of the men were already starting to leave their posts, as the first cracks in the earth started to appear. In less than a minute, all but the pilot and the harness operator dropped what they were doing, got into the Land Rovers and drove away.

"Cowards!" shouted the pilot.

But even he made sure the helicopter propellers were turning.

All around her, Bella could hear the sound of crashing pots and falling rocks, while animals everywhere scampered for cover. She waited for the dust to settle then slowly raised the lamp. Wiping the glass with the sleeve of her dressing gown to produce maximum light, she raised it above her head and peered around. There, just through the crack in the floor through which she'd entered the tomb, she saw a dim light. She was just about to explore further, when she was distracted by another earth tremor. The second wave of cascading dust again made it impossible to see anything.

"What was that all about?" cried Bella, clearing her throat.

The taste of dirt was disgusting. She crouched down to gently wipe away the thick grime around her feet, to see if the spider was still there.

"Where are you?" she spluttered, the inside of her mouth as dry as a bone.

Again she lifted her lamp and wiped the dusty glass.

"Be careful," coughed the tarantula.

Bella looked up to see her guide clinging to the side of what looked like a large pillar.

"Best not to make any sudden movements," the tarantula warned.

Bella examined the base.

"These look like claws," she whispered to the tarantula and the large crowd of insects gathering around her slippers.

"They are," replied the tarantula. "Now whatever you do – stay calm."

Something about the spider's tone struck Bella as worrying. She raised the lamp until it was hanging over her head. This was no pillar.

Gawping up in wonder, Bella found herself in the presence of a beast the size of a Tyrannosaurus Rex. A cold shiver shot down her spine. Despite the dimness of the light, she could see that it had a ferocious look of intent upon its face. But there was more. If Bella's lamp had been a little brighter she would have seen with absolute terror the other two heads lurking in its shadow.

"Its legs mark out the four corners of the sarcophagus," announced the well-informed tarantula.

Bella looked for the sarcophagus. Lowering her lamp, she watched as the rats brushed away the cobwebs and dust to reveal the gold casing of the coffin, raised several feet above the floor by a buffer of four solid gold slabs. Embedded into the casing were rubies and emeralds the size of her hand, as well as thousands of tiny diamonds. "This is unbelievable!'" gasped Bella. "Whose burial chamber is this?"

"This is the tomb of King Kabah the Great," the spider announced solemnly.

Bella felt her knees starting to shake – she had to go and lean against one of the statue's legs just to stay on her feet.

According to the Guatemalan folktale she was reading at home, this was the very tomb in which they thought the Itzamna Emerald was hidden.

"Then, isn't this the place where a giant, three-headed jaguar breathes fireballs on anyone who tries to get near it?' she stammered.

It was at that very moment that Ted Briggs finally managed to pull himself into the tomb. He gazed with amazement at what was unfolding before his eyes. Bella was too awestruck to notice.

"Then where is . . . ?" she spurted, before the dryness in her throat stole her voice.

A deathly silence filled the crypt. How many heads did this beast have? She raised her lamp as high as she could.

CHAPTER FIFTEEN

GUARDIAN OF THE UNDERWORLD

The earth wasn't the only thing quaking – Ted Briggs was shaking from head to toe with excitement. This was the greatest moment of his looting career. The Itzamna Emerald had to be here somewhere. But Briggs was spellbound by another treasure, way beyond his wildest expectations. The trembling earth was causing the huge statue standing before him to shed its dusty coat and to reveal its golden fur. Briggs's jaw dropped, as he felt himself being drawn towards the three-headed beast. He was desperate to touch it. To rub his cheeks up and down its golden coat. To kiss its paws. To examine the exquisite shape of its curvaceous claws. So what if he couldn't put it in his pocket and take it home – as long as he could be near it. But Ted Briggs never got to touch the Golden Jaguar. The opportunity was stolen from him, right under his nose.

Back on the surface, the earthquake was causing absolute chaos in the rainforest. Howling monkeys, squawking birds; every form of animal life was flapping and scurrying in all directions. The ground was moving all around, causing the man operating Briggs's harness to fall from the hydraulic pulley.

Heaving himself up from the thick mud, he sloshed his way through the torrential rain, screaming like a madman. "The gods are against us!" he yelled. "Run for your lives."

It was the helicopter pilot who slid his way through the mud bath to pull himself up into the cabin and reel Briggs's harness in. "No!" screamed Briggs as he felt the almighty tug of his harness. Losing his balance, he stuck out his hands to break his fall. Bella turned but could see nothing through the dust, as Briggs was dragged back into the flooded tunnel like a hooked fish. He tried desperately to disengage himself from the harness, but he was being pulled too quickly. As his chin was bashed from rock to rock, his screams sounded more like a bleating lamb than an intrepid archaeologist on the brink of fame. But no one heard him. His pathetic cries were lost in the mayhem in the tomb.

"Earthquake!" the animals shouted, scampering and bounding in all directions, as huge torches of fire jetted across the tomb. Bella panicked. Her own father was supposed to have been killed in a Guatemalan earthquake. But looking up, she had no doubt where the fireballs were coming from.

"Evacuate!" ordered the tarantula, jumping onto Bella's shoulder.

All over the tomb, bats, rats, mice, spiders, ants, mosquitoes, centipedes and millipedes were all pushing and shoving their way towards any gap in the rocks big enough to slip through. By now Ted Briggs was set on a path that would take him to the higher chambers. His body was getting a real battering against the rocks. But that wasn't his only pain. He was being dragged against his will from the one place on earth he desperately wanted to be.

Back in the tomb, a calculated escape for Bella and the tarantula simply wasn't an option. Having clung onto the jaguar's paw to steady themselves, Bella and the tarantula now found themselves dangling several metres above the ground, as the beast raised it up.

"Aah!" Bella screamed as she watched her pendant swinging from her neck. With the sprain in her arm, it was all she could do to hold on. Her cries echoed around the tomb with a thousand shrieks of terror, as the three-headed beast released a fireball that lit every corner of the tomb. Her lamp was useless now, but still she hung onto it. The dust on the Jaguar's paws fell away to reveal his golden claws, each one longer than Bella herself. He started to shake himself violently, as if trying to wake himself up from centuries of inactivity. The effect on Bella was worse than any fair ride she'd ever experienced. "I think I'm going to be sick," she warned the tarantula.

Her head was spinning, and the temperature was rising fast. The tarantula dug her bristly feet into Bella's neck, as Bella's grip on the jaguar's paw began to slip. Sliding off the paw, Bella's dressing-gown belt somehow got caught on one of the jaguar's claws, leaving her dangling helplessly under his giant paw. Irritated by this movement, the jaguar peered down.

"He's going to stamp his foot," warned the terrified spider. "We're going to be crushed."

Just then, Bella's belt slipped from its precarious grip. "Aaaah!"

Crashing onto the filthy ground by the sarcophagus, Bella rolled away just in time, as the full weight of the beast thundered down beside her. Immediately a huge cloud of dust blew up.

"Bella, it's up to you!" choked the tarantula, her tiny voice almost lost in the drama. With a terrifying roar, the Golden Jaguar stretched himself up on his hind legs, filling the entire tomb.

"Help me!" cried Bella, closing her eyes. "Tell me what to do." She clung onto her pendant for dear life. She wanted so much to see her mum and to tell her just how much she loved her, but there was no time to think of such things now. Everywhere she turned, there was fire.

"Come on!" coughed the spider. "Only the human touched with the spirit of Itzamna can enter the temple and be led to its treasures. Now show him who you are, or we're done for!"

Bella racked her brain. She'd been reading about this in her book the other day.

"Use the scriptures!" shrieked the tarantula. "The ones you read to get you in."

A red-hot flame struck the ground only a few metres from where they were standing, setting fire to one of the wooden chests. Bella tried with all her might to recall the words she had read at the entrance to the temple. "Harak, karadak, lopatos, almanos," she chanted, although she could hardly speak, her throat was so parched.

"That's it!" yelled the tarantula, scampering up to her left ear. "Keep going. And show him your pendant!"

Bella thrust the glittering pendant up into the air. Immediately, the Jaguar's right head extinguished its flame and started to cower. Bella breathed a sigh of relief. But it was premature. The beast let out another colossal roar and sent his middle head straight for them. Bella stared into his eyes and let out an almighty scream – "Aaaaaah!" – as she dropped the lamp and dived.

Feeling the tarantula release her grip after they hit the dust, Bella looked up to see that the entire tomb was alight with flames. The heat was unbearable.

"Follow me," shouted the tarantula directly into Bella's ear. Bella watched the spider scuttle off through the dust. Jumping up, Bella grabbed the lamp and chased after the spider, squinting and rubbing her eyes as she followed the trail of dust left in her wake. But the Golden Jaguar had no intention of letting them escape. Even though one of his heads had seen the pendant the other two were still ignorant of Bella's true identity. He lunged after her.

"Harak, karadak, lopatos, almanos," she shouted up into the face of the flame-throwing beast. Then, without any warning, the spider darted through a small crack in the floor. The gap was hardly wide enough for her, let alone an eleven year-old girl. Bella was stranded. "I'm toast!" she thought.

She looked up into the towering inferno and thrust up her pendant one last time. "Harak, karadak, lopatos, almanos!" she screamed as the two remaining fire-breathing heads shot towards her.

It was a miracle. The heat, combined with the stresses and strains on the rock made by the jaguar, was causing the earth to fracture. Just as the flames were about to engulf her, the ground beneath her feet suddenly opened. Bella disappeared just as the jaguar's claws hit the ground where she'd been standing.

Down, down, down through the slippery rocks she slid, clinging onto the dimming lamp until the gradient at last began to flatten out. When Bella's roller-coaster ride finally came to an end, she found herself at the bottom of an enormous trench in the rocks, hundreds of metres below any temple corridor designed by the Maya. The glow-worms had kindly spread themselves around the walls to illuminate the scene, and to Bella's amazement, her arrival was greeted with a gentle round of applause. Perhaps half of the original party was still together.

It took a good few minutes for the applause to settle down.

"Don't worry about the others," wheezed the tarantula, breathless from her own hurried descent. "The gods must be on our side, or we'd have been fried alive for sure."

They were distracted by the scurrying sound of tiny paws behind them. "Well done, Bella," squealed the newly arriving rats, who had stayed behind to witness her miraculous escape. "The jaguar is cowering in shame," they told her. "It had no idea who you were until it was too late."

"Three cheers for the human," cried the tarantula. "Hip-hip . . . "

"Stop!" Bella shouted, raising her hands to her ears. "I haven't any time for this. Ted Briggs has got my friend, the Quetzal, and even now is escaping with artefacts from the higher chambers."

"And he'll be back," added the tarantula grimly. "With dynamite too. What are we going to do?" she pleaded to Bella.

"Gather round," said Bella, taking control of the situation. "With your knowledge of these tunnels and my understanding of Ted Briggs, we have to work together!" Bella was a member of the Hawksmore Children's Council so she knew all about heated discussions. At school, they thrashed out issues such as fizzy drinks and crisps, mixed football teams and the need for more Jacqueline Wilson books. The children often conducted these meetings as if they were wild animals, but Bella had never attended one in which real creatures were present.

The tarantula had scuttled up onto one of the higher rocks so that she could be on a level with Bella's head. Bella called the meeting to order and put the fading lamp into the middle of the gathering. Time was definitely running out because the lamp was beginning to make hiccupping noises and flicker with the wick down to its minimum.

"What's the latest news?" asked Bella, kicking off the meeting by addressing those rats and glow-worms arriving from reconnaissance missions to the surface.

"They're loading the treasures onto a helicopter," one of the rats told them. "The human who followed you into the tomb of King Kabah has escaped, and he's talking about taking the treasure to Quezaltenango before coming back to find the Itzamna Emerald."

Bella's heart sank. While she hadn't had time to look for the Emerald herself, she'd led Briggs right to it. If the Golden Jaguar really was as wiped-out as he sounded, Briggs might yet achieve his ambition.

"Right," said Bella, decisively. "Let's get down to business."

The commotion caused by the continually arriving bats, rats and mosquitoes made it difficult for Bella to get everyone's attention.

"For goodness' sake, settle down!" Bella yelled.

The humming of wings gradually faded.

"I'd like to continue by forwarding the motion that we have a no-fly zone around the meeting area," Bella suggested. "All creatures with wings are grounded until further notice."

This motion went down well with the rodents.

Her plan was simple – at least in theory. The rats, who

knew all the tunnels beneath the temple better than anyone, were to lead Bella back to the rainforest. Everyone else, except the tarantula, who was to keep Bella company, was to make their own way out and get on with the business of gathering up animal support.

"I suggest we send the bats out on a reconnaissance mission," suggested one of the senior rodents, "to keep an eye on this evil human and report back to the tarantula before sunrise."

"Hear, hear," the animals cheered.

"And I think we should call upon the armadillos and the lizards to act as Miss Bella's guides and messengers on the surface," whirred one of the flies. "She's going to need an escort up there, and I think the monkeys should be kept out of it."

This idea too went down well.

It was decided that once Bella was back on the surface, she would run to the local village and raise the alarm. As long as she could get the artefacts back to the main entrance, the animals would work together to return them to their rightful place and seal the tomb. From then on, the animals were sure that the mortal jaguars of the jungle would guard the entrance. But Bella knew that even this wasn't enough. She needed to expose Briggs and stop him from ever visiting Guatemala again.

The meeting was finally closed with a prayer in which all the animals, regardless of their personal differences and beliefs, bowed their heads in a rare moment of unity.

"We, the creatures of the dark," droned the tarantula in her gravest voice, "ask that you, Itzamna, the god of all living things, will lead Miss Bella not into danger but protect her from all evil. For thine is the kingdom, the supremacy and the splendour, for all eternity. Akra arakiti."

"Akra arakiti," echoed the congregation.

Bella felt her whole body go tingly with goosebumps. It was just like being in a church. All these animals were working together to help her. She felt that it was a tremendous honour that they had welcomed her into their world.

"I won't let you down," she told them solemnly.

Before they set off, Bella again rubbed the pendant along her injured arm. This time the warm tingly feeling was much stronger, and almost immediately her arm began to feel a little better. It was just as well. This next part of the journey was even more hazardous than the first. Bella was glad that the tarantula had decided to come along even though she was getting a free ride in Bella's hair.

"I used to be scared of spiders," she told her bluntly.

"I used to be scared of little girls," replied the tarantula. "Now look at me!"

Onwards they went, up steep inclines of slippery granite and along deep passages barely the width of Bella's shoulders. The steady trickle of water and the sound of thunder were alarming. In one of the narrow tunnels the water level was almost to the roof. After all her falls in the tomb, the wick in Bella's lamp was almost completely dry, but still she held it above her head as she made her way through the tunnels, catching her breath in a ten-centimetre air pocket between her mouth and the roof.

"You can do it, Bella," encouraged the tarantula resting on her nose.

Worst of all was the last bit. Deep within the temple, with barely a flicker of light, the rats led them down to an underground cavern. Here, cascading water thundered down from the ceiling and gushed through deeply-cut drainage channels into a large pool. No sooner had they arrived than the earth began to tremor.

"There's another earthquake brewing," squealed a rat scampering up Bella's dressing gown. "I can feel it." He sounded scared.

"Can you swim?" quivered the tarantula into her ear.

"*Now* you ask me," Bella shouted through the sound of falling rocks. "What if I was to say 'no'?"

"Then you'll drown," replied the spider grimly.

There was another earth tremor.

"Told you," said the rat, now hanging from Bella's belt.

Through the sound of crashing rocks, the tarantula told Bella what she had to do. "Hold your breath, dive to the bottom, and follow anything that looks or feels like a whirlpool," she yelled.

"There's a small hole at the bottom," interjected the rat. "Pull yourself through and then swim with all your might towards the light."

"And what about you?" Bella asked the spider, confident that the rats at least could swim. "Can you swim?"

But there was no time to answer. A huge downpour of water washed the spider and the rats away.

"Aah!" screamed Bella.

And with that, the lamp went out.

CHAPTER SIXTEEN

DARKNESS DESCENDS

Back at the surface, an angry and battered Ted Briggs was being hauled out of the temple by the loyal pilot. "Who gave the order to pull me out?" Briggs howled through the storm.

The pilot, tugging to release the safety hook from Briggs's harness, realized at once how angry his boss was. "We panicked," he stammered, the hook finally unclipped. "This earthquake has got everyone on edge."

Briggs looked around. The place was a mud bath. Apart from the helicopter, surrounded by a paltry amount of boxes, there was nothing and nobody to be seen. A sudden shot of fear flashed across his face.

"Where's the rest of the treasure?" he growled, grabbing the pilot by his shirt collar and raising a threatening fist right up to his face.

"Most of it's in the helicopter," replied the terrified pilot, praying Briggs wasn't going to fly off the handle just because he'd not managed to load the whole lot by himself.

"And where the hell *is* everyone?" Briggs roared.

"They think this earthquake is a sign from the gods that

you shouldn't have gone in," choked the pilot. "We're going to have to finish off the loading together."

Briggs was agitated to the point of madness. His eyes bulging with frustration, he released the pilot and grabbed hold of his own hair. "Superstitious mumbo jumbo!" he screamed. "I was in the tomb of King Kabah. The Itzamna Emerald was within my grasp."

Through the driving rain, Briggs and his loyal pilot dismantled the pulley system and finished loading up the helicopter. It was hard work for Briggs – especially with all the bruises his swift exit had caused. They were just putting the last box on board when a final tempestuous rumble of the earth caused the rock by the tomb entrance to collapse with an almighty bang. "Damn!" cried Briggs, squelching through the mud to assess the damage. But all was not lost. Quite by chance the rock had fallen at a slight angle, leaving a small gap into the tomb. If they covered the opening with smaller stones and camouflaged the rock with bushes and leaves, no one would ever know it was there.

The two men got to work right away.

"Right," Briggs ordered when this was done. "Let's get out of here. The rain should cover our tracks."

Briggs checked that the Quetzal was still firmly secured inside his box and ordered his pilot to leave. Having observed at close hand the way Bella and the Quetzal interacted with each other, Briggs was deeply suspicious of him. Some further investigation into this animal's skills might well prove rewarding.

Bella felt her spirits plummet the moment the lamp went out.

"I'll be buried alive," she thought to herself, as the earth shook yet again, sending a new flurry of boulders plunging into the cavern. She was petrified. Trembling down to the water's edge, she stuck her slippers into her dressing-gown pocket along with her camera and lowered herself into the freezing water. Armed with nothing but her senses and the vague mental picture of where this slowly draining plughole might be, she took a deep breath and plunged into the darkness.

The second her body hit the cold water she felt her lungs compress, forcing half her oxygen supply to shoot out of her mouth in a flurry of bubbles. While her muscles suddenly felt weak and limp, she focused all her energies on trying to swim, but the water felt thicker than glue. "I'm not going to make it," she panicked, overwhelmed by a sense of futility.

Again, she recalled how the Quetzal had helped her use her senses. Through the sound of falling rocks, Bella became aware of a strong pull and the sound of water coiling its way through an outlet. With her wet clothes dragging her down, she let herself sink to the bottom and began to feel her way around. Her heart was pounding; she'd never held her breath for so long her entire life. Just when she thought her head was going to explode from the thumping in her temples, a weird suction noise gave her hope. And then, there it was. She felt the gap with both hands. It was no bigger than the diameter of a bucket, but she could do it. Dizzy and desperate for air she pulled herself through and swam towards the light.

Gasping for breath, Bella must have swallowed a half a

pint of water before the oxygen hit her lungs. For a moment the relief was indescribable. She couldn't get enough of it. Panting like a dog, the cool delight of fresh air had never felt so good.

"Where am I?" she wheezed. Her heart sank, as her gasped words reverberated around the walls of yet another tunnel; this one was even narrower than the last. The rocky walls looked slippery and steep, impossible to climb without a rope. Her only consolation was the moonlight above.

Bella was about to give in to despair when she heard a boy's voice speaking a language she didn't recognize at first. She reached for her pendant.

"Hello down there," repeated the voice from above. "Did you fall in during the earthquake?"

Bella wasn't sure, but her instinct was that the boy was speaking K'iche'. Since reading the inscription on the temple entrance, Bella held the notion that the portrait in the attic spoke to her in this language. Certainly, she had seen many more K'iche' words painted onto the interior walls of the temple. She rubbed her pendant.

"Yes!" she bellowed – K'iche' words coming into her mind as if by magic. "Help!"

It suddenly dawned on Bella that she was in a well. The young boy called for assistance, and before Bella knew it, a bucket was being lowered to fish her out. It was a slow jerky ride, but eventually she managed to reach out, grab the lip of the well and haul herself up onto the cylindrical wall.

Standing in the moonlight, drenched to the bone, Bella's clothing was dripping so fast it reminded her of a drip-drying jumper hanging over the patio at home. Her clothes, her hair –

everything clung to her like cellophane. But despite being utterly bedraggled, she was in high spirits.

"Thank you, thank you," she cried, as she set eyes on the young boy and his helper for the first time. Even though she'd been through the whole night without any sleep, she greeted her rescuers with a beaming smile.

"She looks Mayan," said the boy timidly to his sister.

"I think she looks more like a quetzal wearing those colours," sniggered the girl.

Bella was sick of hearing it but continued to beam at her rescuers. She followed the boy's gaze, as it set on her pendant. His face literally lit up when he saw it. Bella quickly tucked it away and stepped out of her muddy puddle.

"My name's Bella," she told them, offering the boy her hand.

"And my name's Antonio," replied the boy, shaking her hand warily. "And this is my sister, Angelica." Angelica, too, shook Bella's hand.

Bella noticed at once that Angelica was also wearing a necklace. Hers was green and sparkled in the moonlight with a dazzling luminosity. Bella examined the two strangers closely. Both of them had dark rounded features a little like her own. Antonio was simply dressed in brown shorts and a grubby white shirt, but Angelica looked stunning in her colourful wrap and headdresses. It made Bella feel awkward about her drenched and shabby appearance.

"I must be in one of the local villages," she thought.

Out of the corner of her eye she could see a small group of armadillos and lizards desperately waving their feet to attract her attention. She wanted to ask them for news of the tarantula but was sidetracked by the children. And then she heard it – the ominous sound of a helicopter, fading away through the jungle.

CHAPTER SEVENTEEN

BELLA'S QUEST

While Antonio and Angelica chattered about what to do with their unexpected guest, Bella had a quiet moment to gather her thoughts. She was losing track of time. With the sun starting to rise in the east, she reckoned it must be Thursday.

"I bet mum's called the police," she thought. She felt the tears welling up again. "My picture is probably all across the TV news."

The Quetzal had told her that he could play some tricks with time, but he couldn't stop it indefinitely. The more Bella thought about the Quetzal, the more worried she became. Without him she'd never be able to get home to her mum. Reaching for her pendant, Bella knew that for now at least, her quest was simple: to rescue her friend and return the treasures. To do this, she had to track down Ted Briggs – and fast. Hopefully there was still time for her to get to Quezaltenango and inform the police.

Antonio and Angelica wanted to take Bella back to their village for some breakfast. They'd never met a fellow Guatemalan child dressed in green pyjamas and a bright red dressing gown before.

"I'd like to come," Bella told them. "But I can't. I'm in a rush."

"How did you get here?" Antonio asked. "And *why* can't you stay? Our community needs children." Bella was surprised to hear that so many children had gone to the city to try to make their fortune, there were hardly any left.

Bella told her story as briefly as she could, and to her absolute astonishment, they believed it.

"We've heard many such stories of humans talking to their nahual," Antonio told her. "And of the extraordinary things that can happen when we finally get to meet them."

"It's important that you do everything you can to help the Quetzal," agreed Angelica.

"What about the tarantula who helped you in the temple?" asked Antonio. "Do you think she made it?"

With tears in her eyes, Bella shook her head.

"We should run back to the village and raise the alarm," said Angelica.

"Yes," agreed Antonio. "We could all help."

Bella looked across to the armadillos and lizards who were nodding ferociously from the bushes. This was indeed the plan as decided by the animals, but something in Bella's head was telling her to go on alone.

"No," she said quietly, drying her eyes. "Thank you, but you need to keep an eye on the temple. Just look out for me. I intend to get back as soon as I can." Bella could have sworn she saw one of the armadillos slap his paw against his forehead in exasperation.

Bella couldn't explain why, but she knew that her future and that of the two children were connected. With Angelica for company, Bella rested on a log by a banana tree nearby, while Antonio drew them all some water.

"When you get back I'd like you to stay," said Angelica, as she reached out and plucked a banana from the tree. "My family could adopt you."

"But I have a mum," replied Bella, gratefully accepting the banana.

"So what's it like living in London?" Antonio asked, passing Bella half a coconut shell and a bucket of water from which to scoop herself a drink. "Do you see the queen?"

The children had lots of questions about England and what it felt like to be adopted.

"They tease you at school," Bella told them, water dripping from her mouth. "And no one believes in their animal twin."

"My mother and father won't tell me who my animal twin is," Antonio complained. "I know I'm a monkey, but they won't tell me in case I start acting like one."

"Same with me," said Angelica, taking her turn to scoop out a drink of water. "Our parents don't tell us who our animal twin is until we're eighteen, but we know how to find out."

"How?" asked Bella.

"The elders in the village have this magical stone that they call 'Luz Verde'," said Antonio, lowering his voice.

Angelica and Antonio looked at each other cautiously and then nodded. "You must promise to keep it a secret," Angelica whispered. "No one knows about it but for a few people."

Antonio and Angelica huddled closer in.

"I don't like secrets," Bella hushed, thinking of Charlie and how she wouldn't tell her mum about Eugene's bullying. "But I'm good at keeping them." Keeping the pendant's powers a secret from her friend was one of the hardest things Bella had ever had to do.

"If you hold the Luz Verde up to the light," Angelica whispered, "you can see the reflection of your animal twin."

"We sneaked in and had a look," Antonio interrupted in hushed tones.

Bella listened with interest but thought no more of it; she had other things on her mind. The Quetzal was in trouble, and she needed to rescue him *and* stop Briggs from escaping with the treasures. He might not have stolen the Itzamna Emerald this time – but he'd be back. That, she was sure of.

Her energy levels restored, Bella sat on the log and tried to come up with a new plan.

"Can you get me on a bus to Quezaltenango?" she asked the children.

"How many quetzals do you have?" Antonio asked.

Bella thought this was a strange question until she realized "quetzals" meant money. Unfortunately, Bella had nothing but her waterproof camera which she had no intention of selling.

"Then we are going to have to stow you away on board," said Angelica. "We'll put you in a sack and pretend you're one of my father's pigs. That way, you won't have to answer any awkward questions."

Bella squirmed. She'd had enough of sacks.

"Lovely," she said sarcastically, thinking of all the times that Eugene Briggs had called her "pig-face". He was someone else who was always trying to put a sack over her head. "His days as a bully are numbered," Bella thought to herself ruefully.

Bella's idea of a bus was either of a red double-decker, like the one she sometimes got on with her mum when they travelled into London, or the local green single-deckers with an electronic door. It hadn't actually occurred to her that the small wooden bus she'd bought from The Quetzal shop in Greenwich was actually a model of a typical Guatemalan bus. If she had, she might not have been so shocked.

The children led Bella around the outskirts of the village to a bush from where she could see the old dilapidated bus.

"I'm not travelling anywhere on that battered up thing," she complained as she crouched back down for cover. As soon as she said it, she felt bad. It was probably the only kind of bus Antonio and Angelica knew.

"Sorry," she said, quickly. "I'm sure it will be fine."

Bella wondered how the engine inside the faded orange bonnet was ever going to move it. Everything about the bus looked destined for the scrap heap. At least the wooden one she had at home had a shiny gloss painted over it and a happy driver waving to her at the wheel.

"These are old American school buses," Angelica told her proudly.

Even from a distance Bella could see that the tyres had no treads, and most of the glass had been punched out of the windows. 'Old' was an understatement. Apart from being jam-packed with passengers on the inside, the villagers were loading bananas, wood and livestock onto the roof and securing them with rope to a series of railings. It reminded Bella of the roof rack on top of her mum's Mini.

"That's where you're going," said Antonio, pointing to the roof. Bella felt sick at the thought of it. It shocked her that so many of the men were carrying knives or machetes, and the sound of squealing pigs and goats tied up in sacks was very upsetting.

"It leaves in half an hour," Antonio told her. "We must hurry."

Still damp and cold from all the swimming, Bella agreed to lie behind the bush, while Antonio and Angelica dashed back to the village for a sack. Tucking herself up to keep warm, she soon dozed off.

"Wake up," hushed Angelica, bending down to give Bella a gentle shake. "It's time to go."

Bleary-eyed, Bella stepped into the sack.

"Good luck, Bella," Antonio smiled. "Pull the top down and tie the knot from the inside. That way it will be easy to open it yourself."

Bella did as she was told, and then Antonio made a superficial knot with string to make the sack look like it had been tied from the outside. Tearing a small hole in the top so Bella could breathe, the two children carried Bella up to the bus and helped to haul her onto the roof.

"We'll say you're a pig," Antonio told Bella through the sacking.

Bella let out an impressive snort. "What is it with me and pigs?" she was thinking.

"That was good," Angelica laughed, almost dropping her end of the sack. "Can you do any other animal impressions?"

But there was no time to answer.

"Shhh!" hushed Antonio. "They'll hear us."

"Put the pig with the rest of my father's things," Bella heard Antonio order. "Muchas gracias."

She felt herself jerked up and thrown down onto the roof.

It didn't take long for the humidity inside the sack to rise.

"Why is it always so hot and itchy inside these things?" Bella wondered irritably, as she rubbed her back against the baggage railings.

She was starting to sweat. To make things worse, she felt utterly exhausted. In other circumstances sleep would have come easily, but as soon as the bus revved up its engine and started the long, bumpy haul from the village to the nearest road, she felt sick. Tossed from side to side as if in the midst of a violent storm, Bella had nothing to hang onto. Every now and then the bus would stop abruptly, and she would hear the sound of hacking machetes as some of the passengers got out to forge a pathway through the rainforest. But these moments of respite were rare. Following the rainstorm the ground was muddy, and the bus often careered into the trees. Bella would be flung across the roof along with the loose cargo, crashing against boxes and sacks filled with distressed livestock.

"Ow! Watch it, will you?" squealed a wild pig.

"I want my mum," bleated a kid.

"I'm over here," cried the goat from the far side of the bus.

"Why did they have to tie my feet together?" clucked a helpless chicken.

It was awful! Bella guessed the animals were going to market. She wanted to talk to comfort them but didn't dare. If she were discovered, the driver would probably throw her off for not buying a ticket.

Eventually, after many hours of turmoil, Bella became aware that the ride was getting smoother, and for a short time she fell into a deep sleep. Antonio had told her that the last hundred kilometres would be on tarmac. "That's the worst bit," he'd warned her. "The drivers race along like madmen."

In fact, it was the loud horn of an overtaking bus that woke Bella up. Peering through the slit in her sack to see if there were any other passengers on the roof, Bella caught her first glimpse of the Guatemalan highlands. With no one around, she undid the loose knot she had tied and wriggled out.

"Wow!" thought Bella, taking in the spectacular scenery.

The road ran through an enormous plain flanked by steep mountains topped by a string of forested peaks. Stretching across the flat valley was a huge expanse of maize fields amongst which Bella could see a scattering of villages and what she guessed to be the odd shop and school. Occasionally, they would pass Mayans in their colourful robes going about their business. Some were selling maize by the roadside, while others were ploughing the fields or herding cattle. Those that saw Bella would smile and wave, happy perhaps to see a young girl enjoying her freedom at a hundred kilometres an hour with the wind blowing through her long black hair.

A battered old, blue sign read "Quezaltenango 20 km". Bella felt emotional knowing that she was heading to the place where both she and her birth mother were born. Somewhere in this city there was an orphanage where someone, even now, might be able to tell her more about her family.

As they entered the suburbs, Bella kept her head down. The sound of motor horns and backfiring traffic reminded her of the vibrant streets of Central London, but here all the vehicles looked clapped-out and decrepit – held together by tape and string. It was obvious by the commotion they were making that the animals on the roof were becoming stressed.

"Don't worry," she called out. "This is your lucky day."

Bella had already decided what she was going to do.

"Did you hear that, Alicia?" she heard one of the pigs snort. "That's the first time I've heard a human talking Pig."

"You do speak a lot of animal hogwash, Sebastian," Bella heard Alicia grunt.

When the bus pulled up at a crossroad, Bella quickly scurried around the roof releasing the animals. She couldn't have known how much trouble this was going to cause. As soon as the pigs were free the bus started to move again. "Help!" they squealed. "We're scared."

The chickens were no better, flapping around in all directions. "What are we going to do now?" they clucked.

As the driver wrenched the clutch into first gear, and the bus jerked forward, Bella was beginning to regret helping any of them at all.

The commotion on top of the bus had also arrested the attention of passing pedestrians. "Thief!" croaked the feeble voice of an old man, pointing up at Bella from the street with his walking stick.

The chorus was soon taken up by a chasing crowd. "Thief!" they cried.

Bella panicked and hoped that they might have been referring to someone else, but looking around, she knew there was no chance of that. The driver slammed on the breaks as several men quickly clambered up onto the roof.

"There she is!" shouted the first man up, pointing angrily right at her. Bella was shocked and scared to see how cross the men looked.

What happened next was a surprise to everyone. In a show of spontaneous unity, the animals charged at the men. "Run

Bella, run!" they yelled.

Checking she was still wearing her pendant, she grabbed the outer railing of the roof rack, lowered herself down as far as she could and jumped into the road. Throwing herself against the bus to avoid being flattened by a passing petrol tanker, she saw a gap in the traffic and made a dash for the other side. Despite her awkward landing, Bella was quickly into her stride, sprinting through the streets away from the pursuing mob. All around her feet, piglets, goats and chickens were making a fleeting run for freedom. "Muchas gracias, Bella," they called.

Sprinting through a roadside market where stallholders were selling colourful fabrics and kitchen utensils, Bella passed a gang of children playing football in the road with a tin can. "After her!" shouted the tallest boy amongst them.

The children chased Bella through the streets.

"Stop, stop!" they called after a few minutes of flat-out running. "They've given up chasing you. We're your friends. Stop!" The children were speaking Latin American Spanish.

Feeling too tired to run another step, Bella staggered up to the nearest lamppost and slumped heavily against it. "OK, I hear you," she panted, holding onto her pendant so that she might understand them. When they had all caught up and gathered around her, Bella realized there were two girls and three boys, all of them in ragged old clothes with matted mops of jet-black hair. She was shocked that none of them were wearing shoes, but the skin on their filthy feet looked as tough as leather. They all appeared tired and drawn, as if they hadn't eaten for days.

"Did you steal food?" asked the tallest boy in the group.

"No!" replied Bella, upset to be accused of such a thing. "I just released all the animals from the top of a bus going to market."

The children all laughed.

"No wonder they were after you," giggled one of the girls. "They would have given you a right old beating if they'd caught you."

Bella wondered at the sight of their filthy dresses. It looked like they'd been playing out in the woods all night.

"Your clothes are funny," smiled a small boy in grubby white shorts and a red threadbare T-shirt. His cheeky grin was so endearing to Bella, she couldn't help but smile back.

Bella guessed they were all street-children. She'd heard about them from her mum and read about them on the internet. The Quetzal shop in London sold lots of brilliantly crafted toys made by street-children from Guatemala. She wondered if some of her favourite toys might have been made by any of these children.

"What's in your bag?" Bella asked the oldest looking boy.

The boy, who looked about twelve, opened his bag proudly. To Bella's surprise, she saw that it was full to the brim with small toy vehicles, carefully and quite skilfully carved out of wood. She knew that homeless children had to sleep on the streets and scratch out an existence by doing odd jobs and stealing when they had to, but despite this hard life, some of them had developed incredible skills. Bella thought back to last year when she and her mum had organized a sponsored swim to raise money for a project to train street-children in wood carving.

"They're amazing!" she exclaimed, rummaging through and finding a bright orange bus. Sure enough, the driver was smiling and waving in exactly the same way as the one she had at home. Bella tipped the bus and tried to shake the driver out.

"It won't come out," said the cute-looking boy who'd laughed at her dressing gown and pyjamas. "It's all one piece."

"No!" exclaimed Bella. "I thought it was glue."

"We don't know you," said the boy with the bag, eyeing her distrustfully. "Do you belong to a gang?"

"No," replied Bella, feeling dizzy from lack of sleep and the effects of her exertion. "I've only just arrived here."

"Did you come from Guatemala City?" asked another.

Bella thought about it for a moment. She wanted to tell the truth but just didn't have the energy for a long story.

"Yes," she said.

The street-children inspected Bella's ragged and filthy dressing gown suspiciously. In many ways, she did look like a street-child from the capital, but experience had taught them to be suspicious. The fact that Bella was wearing *anything* on her feet was unusual enough – but slippers? The street-children had never seen shoes quite like them.

Bella had been aware of her fatigue the moment she had slumped against the lamppost, but now she was feeling dizzy and faint. The world before her eyes was becoming misty and beginning to spin.

"Are you alright?" asked the tall boy, suddenly concerned.

Bella collapsed into his arms.

"Ricardo," he ordered, addressing a shy-looking boy wearing an old Brazilian football top. "Go and ask the man at the cantina if we can have a soda for our sick friend. The rest of you, help me drag her into that doorway across the street."

CHAPTER EIGHTEEN

SECRET GARDEN

The sweet taste of fizzy cola ran down Bella's throat like a magical elixir. "What happened?" she wheezed feebly as her senses slowly returned.

"You passed out," replied one of the girls. "Ricardo went to get you a soda."

"Thanks," said Bella weakly as Ricardo helped to prop her up outside the derelict shop. Ricardo looked a little younger than the boy holding the bag.

"I guess you should introduce me to the others," Bella suggested, looking up at the tall boy. "I don't like not knowing your names."

"My name is Carlo," he announced. "I'm twelve, so I'm the leader."

Bella nodded respectfully, while Carlo ushered forward the small boy in the red T-shirt.

"This is Lucas," he told her. "He's five." Lucas stepped forward.

"That looks like a Manchester United top," said Bella, admiring Lucas's scrappy red sport shirt. Lucas looked blank but grinned at her nonetheless.

Carlo introduced the girls as Irma and Sofia. "Sofia's seven years old and Irma's eight."

"Nice to meet you," said Bella, shaking each of them by the hand. "You do *look* like sisters."

"People think we're sisters because we're always falling out with each other," giggled Sofia.

"But we're not!" Irma chastized her. "Not *real sisters*." Irma was slightly taller and more serious.

"We stick together like a family," Carlo interrupted by way of explanation. "That way, we have more of a chance. We used to live in the orphanage until we had to leave."

Bella's head was still a bit fuzzy, but the mention of the orphanage really perked her up.

"Why couldn't you stay?" Bella exclaimed, pulling herself gingerly to her feet.

The children looked at her as if she were mad.

"We're too old," said Lucas as the children gathered around Bella.

"No one wants to adopt children older than four or five," Irma told her. "Didn't you know that?"

Bella felt her stomach turn. In all probability she would have ended up on the streets with these children if she hadn't been adopted.

Bella liked all the children, but Carlo was special. He was like a gentle giant, looking out and caring for everyone. Bella watched with admiration as he left the group to help an old Mayan woman up a steep hill with all her shopping. The woman gave him a banana for helping her. When he got back, he gave the banana straight to Lucas. Even he, after taking a bite, passed it on to Sofia. It made Bella feel bad about throwing most of her lunch away each day at school. There were so many things on this adventure that were changing the way she saw the world.

"How come we haven't met you before?" Irma asked Bella suspiciously.

Bella decided to tell the children that she'd travelled up from Guatemala City to try to get a job at one of the tourist campsites. She told them an edited version of her adventure at the Great Temple of Tikal with Ted Briggs and how she'd been parted from the Quetzal. Like Antonio and Angelica, the street-children were very open to the concept of understanding and communication between humans and animals – especially between animal twins.

"I don't know who my nahaul is yet," Ricardo told her, kicking a stone aimlessly across the street. "But I know all about quetzals. We used to keep one as a pet at the orphanage."

"Yeah, but he kept on escaping," Irma reminded him.

"You shouldn't keep birds in cages," exclaimed Bella crossly.

"I've never been to Tikal," said Carlo, "but I know it's important because so many tourists go there. I've heard people talking about a famous emerald that's supposed to be hidden there."

"The Itzamna Emerald," blurted Bella. "You know about it?"

Bella's outburst drew the attention of a male cyclist as he passed, almost causing him to lose his balance.

"I know that it's important to us," replied Carlo, following the man with his eyes before returning his attention to Bella. "If anyone were to take it from Guatemala then terrible things would happen to the earth."

"Like what?" asked Lucas, jumping up and down, enthralled by the story.

"The gods would be so angry with us they'd probably send earthquakes and floods for a thousand years," Carlo told him. Then, seeing that Lucas looked upset – "Or tickle five-year-old boys behind the ears," he winked at Lucas and reached out to do just that.

"Whatever they do, it's not right that someone should take it," said Bella. "Someone's got to stop Briggs before he gets his hands on it."

All the children were nodding in agreement.

"We're with you, Bella," said Carlo. "What do we need to do?"

"I'm reporting him to the police," Bella decided.

"That's the last thing you should do," gasped Carlo. "They'll think you're one of us and give you a beating."

Bella was shocked. "But that's awful!" she cried, feeling her anger rise.

It had never occurred to Bella that policemen could be anything other than helpful. All the policemen who visited Hawksmore Primary to tell them not to talk to strangers were always friendly. On holiday in Tenerife last year, Bella had got lost looking for the portaloos on the beach. A kind Spanish policeman had helped her find her mum again.

"Not all the policemen are bad," said Carlo. "But the bad ones stick together."

"Your best bet is to go to the airport and stop him yourself," Sofia told her. "You can hitch a ride on a petrol tanker from the other side of town. We can show you."

The first thing Bella noticed as she walked through town was the lack of Christmas decorations. London was full of them right now. By her calculations, if this was Thursday, there were only six school days left until the end of term. After that, there were only three days left until Christmas. Bella wondered if she would make it home in time.

"What are you thinking about?" Irma asked her. "You look sad."

Bella wanted to say she felt homesick but was distracted by an old, one-storey building across the street. The whitewashed walls were faded and grimy, while the rotten door looked like it might drop off its hinges at any moment. Looking out from one of the barred windows, Bella saw a woman in a white uniform holding a baby. She looked tired and withdrawn, but when she saw the children she seemed to come alive and waved enthusiastically. The children waved shyly back.

"She's a nice lady," Lucas told Bella. "She gave us biscuits."

Above the window there was a battered sign that ran the entire length of the building. The writing on it was faded and difficult to read.

"That's the orphanage of Santa Maria," replied Irma, seeing Bella squint at the sign. "The one we were all born in."

Bella stopped in her tracks. She'd been so preoccupied with finding Ted Briggs she hadn't even considered looking for the orphanage.

"What's the matter, Bella?" asked Carlo. "You're shaking."

Bella couldn't speak. She'd always promised herself that one day she would come and find the orphanage where she and her mother were born. The woman at the window had gone, but Bella ran up to the bars and stared through. Despite the blazing sunlight outside, the room looked dark and dingy. From one end to the other, it was crammed full of babies in cots. Bella was upset to see so many children cooped up with nothing and no one to play with.

"There are no toys and nothing nice to look at on the walls," she complained.

She looked to Carlo and the gang. All of them had blank expressions on their faces.

"That's what most of the orphanages here are like," replied Carlo. "You know that."

The tears in Bella's eyes made it clear to Carlo that she didn't. Carlo and the street-children watched Bella turn to peer back at the babies inside the orphanage.

"My mother and me were both born here," sobbed Bella, unable to control her emotions.

"So was I!" exclaimed Ricardo.

"And me!" shouted Sofia and Irma together.

"Was I?" blurted little Lucas, a little confused. Carlo put a reassuring hand on Lucas's shoulder.

"We all ended up here," said Carlo, "one way or another. But we're not going back."

His voice was determined and forthright.

"We're looking to the future," he announced with pride.

Bella looked into his eyes. There was an anger in them that she understood.

A voice inside her head said: "Never forget that there are children living like this. You can't do anything to help them now, but you will. It's time to get a move on. Briggs is getting away." Hearing the voice made her think of the portrait in the attic at home.

"Come on, Bella," said Carlo kindly, waking her up from her daydream. "We better go."

The children turned to walk away.

"Wait!" Bella blurted.

The children stopped. The look on their faces, as Bella took the camera from her dressing gown pocket and handed it to Carlo would have made a great photo.

"*Please* take a photograph of me standing by the door," she begged.

The children were amazed by the camera.

"You better show me how to work it," Carlo told Bella, giving her a quizzical look.

Bella showed him and then went to stand with her back against the orphanage. The friendly woman with the baby returned to the window just as Carlo took the photo. The instant he clicked the button, the film started to rewind.

"I wish I had a camera," said Sofia as the children continued their walk across town. "How did you get it?"

"It was a present from my mum," said Bella.

"Wow!" exclaimed Lucas. "I wish I had one."

"You can have it," said Bella, handing him the camera. "I just need the film."

Lucas looked bemused. "I meant . . . I wish I had a mum," he said, turning away.

Bella felt awful. She slipped the camera into her pocket and realized that she had never really appreciated her adoptive mum quite as much as she did now.

As they got closer to the centre of town, the hustle and bustle of the market district was replaced by crowds of mingling tourists. Many were taking photographs and admiring the impressive grey stone buildings. Almost everywhere Bella looked, there was a young foreigner with a backpack reading a travel guide or a young Guatemalan boy polishing someone's shoes.

"I used to do that," Carlo told her, pointing to a young boy unpacking his shoeshine box by the roadside. "But a few bad policemen would always get round to stealing our money eventually."

The town was crowded.

"All the cantinas are full," Carlo observed, gesturing with his head to one of the bars.

Bella was surprised to see that you could sit and drink beer *and* buy groceries in the cantinas. It wasn't like that in London. There the food shops and pubs were separate. She was also surprised to see how many portable stalls there were on the streets, selling ice cream and barbecued corn. Everywhere you looked there was someone eating.

Through the bustling streets, the beautiful sound of marimbas filled the air with their tranquil melodies, enticing people towards the main square. All around them, Mayan men and women wearing their traditional tribal robes were chatting away, enjoying the carnival atmosphere. There were children everywhere; some clinging onto their parent's hands, others helping their younger brothers and sisters along the way. Bella was fascinated by the way the Mayan mothers carried their babies in colourful slings draped over their shoulders. They were just approaching the main square when a commotion broke out in the crowd ahead of them.

"There they are!" shouted an angry-looking man, pointing directly at them. "The girl and the gang who stole all my pigs."

Bella recognized him at once from the incident on top of the bus. The man was surrounded by a pack of mean-looking policemen. Bella looked at the panic-stricken children.

"We better split up," said Carlo urgently. He turned to Bella: "Just hold onto my hand – and run!" They turned and dashed back up the street. Bella still felt weak. She reached under her pyjamas for her pendant and found renewed vigour spring into her legs.

Away from the main square, the streets were deserted, making it easy for the police to pick them out.

"Quick!" yelled Carlo. "They're catching up!" He dragged Bella down a narrow alley full of bins and Coca-Cola crates, which brought them out into a parallel street. From there they cut through another alley, then another and another. They ran for what seemed like an eternity until they reached a rubbish dump by the outskirts of town. To Bella's dismay, Carlo led her up onto the heap.

"Right," he said. "Bury yourself."

And she did.

The smell was unbearable. Bella found herself concealed amongst rotting chicken bones, mouldy vegetables, smashed cans, bent bicycle wheels and dead car batteries – almost anything you could imagine. To add to her discomfort, a family of scavenging rats were nibbling around her ears.

"Shhh," Bella whispered. "I'm trying to hide." Her body tensed as the shouts of angry policemen rummaging through rubbish got closer and closer. Suddenly, she heard a gunshot.

"Carlo!"

Luckily, Bella's muffled cry went unheard.

Silence followed. Nothing stirred. Not even the rats.

Just at the point she thought she would explode with grief, Bella heard a howl of uproarious laughter.

"Stop shooting rats and get on with it," came the order from the police captain. "They're not here."

She breathed a sigh of relief. Not so the rats, who were weeping uncontrollably at yet another pointless murder.

Even when they thought the coast was clear, Bella and Carlo stayed buried in the rubbish for a few minutes, just to be sure.

"That was close," said Carlo eventually, pulling himself up and wiping away the slime from his forehead.

"What about the others?" asked Bella, doing much the same.

"Don't worry about them," Carlo reassured her. "We're all used to running away from the police. And we've had enough beatings to know what to expect if we do get caught."

"Why do they hate you so much?" Bella asked, depressed that anyone could be so cruel to children.

"They think we're pests," Carlo replied in a matter-of-fact tone. "That we only beg and steal. But let me show you something."

Carlo spent five minutes searching through the rubbish for wood. When he'd gathered a few small pieces, he led Bella to a gap at the bottom of the barbed-wire fence at the back of the dump and carefully lifted it up.

"Roll yourself under," he told her.

Bella did as she was asked and, picking herself up on the other side, was surprised to see a small, cultivated area with maize, beans and bananas growing.

"It's our secret garden," Carlo announced proudly, following her through. "The ground belongs to the Kellogg's factory, but they don't mind us using this bit because it's by the dump. We can't grow enough food for all of us, but it helps."

"You planted all these?" Bella asked, impressed with the extent of the crops and just how much work had gone into making the place look so lush and inviting. The children had arranged crates and boxes to use as table and chairs as well as picking out some old utensils from the dump.

"This is our little farm and kitchen," said Carlo. "It's our home."

"It's lovely," sighed Bella. "Just imagine what you could do with a little more land."

The children sat down on the boxes. Carlo was anxious about time. "What about your mission, Bella?"

But a voice in Bella's head was telling her to be patient. "Rest," it told her. "You will need your strength."

"I think I need to sit down for a while," she told Carlo, smiling wearily.

Carlo nodded and went over to a nearby rock. With an almighty effort, he turned it over. Using his hands to burrow into the ground beneath it, he pulled out a battered old box, caked in mud. He opened it up and took out a hammer before tipping out his assortment of rusty chisels.

"This is my workbox," he told her proudly. Taking a single piece of wood, he gave Bella her first carving lesson.

"What do you want to make?" he asked her.

"A bus," said Bella. "With a smiley driver at the wheel."

Carlo laughed. "My speciality," he said.

The sound of police sirens driving towards them from the factory car park broke their hour-long concentration.

"Run!" shouted Carlo, dropping everything and grabbing Bella by the hand.

Bella glimpsed the terror in his face and was shocked. "But why?" she yelled. "We're not doing anything wrong."

"We're street-children!" cried Carlo. "That's enough."

Bella felt the injustice too much to bear. She tried to pull herself free from Carlo's grip, but he wasn't letting go. Rolling back under the barbed-wire fence, Carlo dragged her back onto the rubbish dump and pulled her to the ground.

"It's not a fight we can win, Bella. Please don't try!" he begged.

The children buried themselves as deeply as they could.

Through a rotting pile of fruit and vegetables, Bella wept, as she watched the policemen destroy the children's makeshift kitchen and rip up every living thing in the garden.

"Stop it, stop it!" she wanted to shout.

She felt so angry, she could have screamed. Distraught and completely powerless, she buried her head into the waste and screwed her eyes tightly shut.

When the police finally left, the two children pulled themselves out of the rubbish and slowly made their way down to examine the remains of the garden. Feeling soggy, smelly and utterly depressed, Bella put her arm around Carlo's shoulders.

"I'm sorry," she said. "If you hadn't been trying to help me, none of this would have happened."

"It happens every year," said Carlo dejectedly. "It just depends on our luck if they come before or after the harvest."

Bella helped him search through the devastation to find his tools and put them back into his box. "At least I still have these," he said sadly, sitting down on a broken crate to count his remaining chisels.

Bella sat down next to him. She felt miserable and was as close as she had ever been to giving up. Somehow, Carlo found the energy and will to continue showing Bella how to carve the bus. "I'm not going to let you leave Guatemala without it," he told her. "It will be something to remember us by forever. You can paint it when you get home."

Bella felt confused. It sounded like Carlo suspected her home was somewhere other than Guatemala.

"Thank you," she said. "But I'm Guatemalan. I am home."

Carlo looked directly into her eyes. "Are you?" he asked intuitively. "I don't think so, Bella."

Bella was stunned.

The sun was setting when Sofia, the youngest of the girls, arrived. She told them that she'd broken into a parked car and fallen asleep on the back seat. Then, one by one, the others started to appear, each of them with their own story to tell. Sadly, Irma had been picked out of the crowd by two policemen and taken to the station. There, she had been forced to sweep out the cells and do a pile of washing-up before she was allowed to leave. The two boys had managed to slip out of the crowd unseen and had made a few quetzals loading Coca-Cola crates into a hotel.

"I've got a present for Bella," declared a very happy Lucas. He skipped over and handed her some corn on the cob wrapped in fresh newspaper. Bella smiled. He was such a cute kid.

"It's not my birthday till October," she said, taking the food and giving Lucas's hair an affectionate ruffling.

"When's yours?" she asked him.

"I don't know," said Lucas. "I've never had one."

Bella took a bite out of the corn and passed it around. When the tasty snack was finally returned for her to finish off, a soggy photograph in the paper caught her eye. There, as large as life, beaming out at her from the page was none other than Ted Briggs himself.

"Lucas, Ricardo, this is the best present ever!" Bella cried.

All the children were happy with Bella's delight in the paper.

"This is him," she told them, pointing to Briggs's inanely grinning face. "The man I'm looking for."

Lucas had wrapped the food in a copy of the evening's newspaper, which he had found on a bench. The article Bella was now reading was full of adulation for Briggs's commitment to Guatemalan history and the recovery of treasure that he would hand over to the museum in Guatemala City.

"He's bribed someone at the museum with some minor artefacts," Bella conjectured. "He's going to get himself a licence to excavate properly and go back for the Itzamna Emerald."

Reading on, Bella learned that Briggs was flying to England tomorrow lunchtime with the promise that he would soon return to continue his quest "on behalf of the good people of Guatemala".

"What a liar!" cried Bella, throwing the paper down. "Unless he's stopped, the good people of Guatemala will have nothing left of their Mayan heritage. It will all be in Ted Briggs's private collection."

That night, as the children buried themselves into the rubbish to keep warm, Bella vowed that she would do everything she could to be a friend to these children. Tomorrow, they would help her get to the airport early to find Briggs – although what she was going to do then, she had no idea. Hungry and exhausted, the children soon fell asleep, too tired to notice the persistent drizzle that was, even now, causing the rubbish to slowly sink around them.

CHAPTER NINETEEN

KISS OF LIFE

Bella was woken by the ear-piercing screams.

"Lucas!" the children were shouting at the top of their lungs. "Bella!"

She tried to lift herself up, but the cardboard and waste beneath her kept giving way. "I'm sinking!" she shrieked in horror. More wet rubbish kept falling down around her head.

"Over here!" she cried but then realized that to call for help was a death warrant to anyone who responded. The rain was pounding down, turning the junk so soggy it was like quicksand. Even the rats were running scared.

"Evacuate!" they were yelling to each other. "Head for the sewers."

Bella fell on her face, as an old car battery slid down and landed on the back of her head. "Ow!" she cried, reaching up to push it away.

With all her might she tried to climb. "Come on, Bella," she growled through gritted teeth, trying her best to pull herself upwards. Her arm was feeling stronger, but she was still making no progress.

"Bella! Lucas!" came the anguished cries of her search party.

But Bella couldn't shout out now even if she wanted to. She was being buried alive.

It was like trying to clamber up a smelly slimy escalator going in the opposite direction. Through the sound of hammering rain, Bella took her pendant, put it between her clenched teeth and tried again to scramble her way up. "There's no air," she thought as she struggled. "I'm going to suffocate." Despite her fatigue, her muscles seemed to draw on a hidden reserve of energy she'd never known before. Onwards and upwards, slipping and sliding, she pushed her way through all the drenched and putrid rubbish, until somehow, she made it to the surface.

"There she is!" shouted Carlo through the torrential rain, pointing towards Bella's hands, as they emerged from the debris.

Carlo was lying as flat as he could on the surface of the heap so as not to sink. "Stay back all of you," he ordered Irma, Sofia and Ricardo, who had somehow managed to get out in time and were now anxiously scouring the whole area from the relative safety of the outer edges.

"Where's Lucas?" Bella bellowed, slowly getting up and steadying herself on the compacting waste.

"He's still in here," Carlo shouted back. "But I can't reach him."

Bella could see that one of Carlo's arms was buried deep into the rubbish. Rolling across the top of the heap to distribute her body weight as evenly as she could, she got herself over to where Carlo was lying.

"I'm going in," Bella yelled through the torrential rain.

"No, Bella!" Carlo cried, grabbing her arm. "You'll suffocate."

There was a crack of thunder. Bella took a deep breath, yanked her arm free and dived back into the soaking rubbish. Wriggling her way down like a worm, she used the power of the pendant and her newly-discovered listening powers to filter out all the noise of the rain and the shouting from the surface, to find Lucas's heartbeat. Sure enough, there it was. Beating even faster than hers. "He's out of oxygen," she panicked. Following the frantic pulse of Lucas's heart, Bella fought her way down towards it. She reached out into the unknown and fumbled around until she found him. Wrapping one arm around his waist, she tried to fight her way to the surface with all her might. But it was impossible. The slippery debris kept giving way beneath, while the many heavier items sinking above her were forcing her down.

"I'm drowning," she panicked, "this really is the end."

"Believe," whispered a voice inside her head. "The power of your will is a remarkable force."

With one final almighty effort she frantically started to climb.

From the edge of the heap the onlooking children were on the verge of giving up on Bella and Lucas when Irma noticed a fist, punching up through the rubbish.

"There she is!" shouted Irma, directing Carlo with an outstretched arm.

Bella, gasping for air, couldn't see a thing through the blur of the rain. With her last drop of energy, she dragged Lucas to the surface.

Carlo scrambled across. "He's not breathing," he spurted, as he took Lucas from Bella's arms. "We've got to be quick.

Follow me."

Clutching his little friend tightly to his chest, Carlo defied the squelchy terrain and led Bella to the edge of the dump, where he then laid Lucas down and started to give him the kiss of life. The other children stood helplessly to one side.

"Come on, Lucas," Irma shouted, "breathe!"

Irma and Sofia were clutching each other in a desperate embrace, while Ricardo and Bella looked on in panicked disbelief at the unfolding nightmare. Nothing Carlo was doing was having any effect. He stopped blowing into Lucas's mouth, put both hands over his heart and began to pump. Bella had never seen anyone work with such ferocity and determination, which made it all the more scary when he stopped and flopped over by Lucas's side, too exhausted to speak.

"He's dead," the other children cried.

Bella was having none of it. Feeling utterly shattered, she knelt beside Lucas's limp body, held his nose and started to blow into his mouth, while her pendant fell onto his chest. Immediately, Bella began to feel the surge of power flowing through the pendant into Lucas's body. With the rain pounding into her face, she pumped his chest and lungs, praying that she might yet breathe life into him. And then, just when she thought there was no hope left, Lucas gasped. For a moment it seemed as if it might have been a last breath, but then he gasped again and then again, before he started coughing and wheezing in a desperate attempt to fill his lungs with oxygen.

"He's alive!" shouted Irma.

"Bella, you did it!" cried Sofia.

Bella rolled over onto her back next to Carlo, who was crying into the rain-filled heavens. She *had* done it, but in doing so, she felt as if there was not a drop of life left in her body.

It was still the middle of the night. All seven of them sat in the rain, too exhausted to speak. After Bella's exhilaration at Lucas's miraculous return to life, she turned her attention to her pendant. Lifting it up to her face, she let the distant streetlights illuminate it, as she gazed in wonder at its dazzling beauty and mind-boggling powers. Feeling both her faith in herself and the pendant returning, a powerful injection of energy invigorated her body.

"Time is running out," whispered a voice inside her head.

"I've got to fly," said Bella in a sudden burst of energy.

"Wait, and we'll all come with you," sighed Irma, trying to raise the strength to get up.

"Yes," murmured Carlo, unable to stir.

Ricardo and Sofia looked sleepy but willing, while Lucas and Carlo were clearly too exhausted to do anything.

"You need to take care of Carlo and Lucas," Bella told the others. "Meet me at the airport as soon as you can get there. I'll find Briggs and do my best to distract him."

"No," croaked Carlo, finally dragging himself up.

But Bella was already running.

Leaving these children was the hardest decision Bella had ever made.

"Fly!" ordered the voice inside her head.

She ran from the dump and skidded into a nearby alley by a small cantina. Grabbing hold of her pendant, she closed her eyes and focused all her energies on trying to fly.

"The power of your will is a remarkable force," the voice reminded her.

Force was one thing, but every bone in her body ached with

tiredness. Since the attack on the Quetzal by the harpy eagle, Bella hadn't flown at all. Maybe she couldn't do it alone.

"Come on!" she cried, gritting her teeth. She put the pendant into her mouth, bent her knees and jumped.

The first jump sent her tumbling into a line of cardboard boxes and rubbish from the cantina, but she didn't give up. Ten minutes later, Bella was soaring over the city in the form of her nahaul.

"This is great!" she chirped loudly into the star-studded skies.

She truly felt as free as a bird.

Finding the airport was harder than Bella thought, and it took several hours of circling the city to locate it. Day was breaking when Bella finally spotted it and swooped down.

"It's so small," she mused as the first rays of sunlight illuminated her path. There was only one runway and one terminal building with three planes and one helicopter on the tarmac. She landed on the roof of a small, ten-seater aircraft, easily the largest plane on the ground. Looking down from the cockpit, she watched as the porters loaded aboard the last of the wooden crates marked "Delicate – Handle with Care".

"I wonder . . . ," she said to herself.

Bella surveyed the loading area for any sign of Ted Briggs and saw a short, dark-haired man in a pilot's uniform talking to a small group of men.

"And if there are any breakages, Professor Briggs will be speaking to your boss," the man concluded.

Bella recognized the pilot.

"So it *is* his plane," she mused. "But where is he?"

CHAPTER TWENTY

UP, UP AND AWAY

With the plane almost loaded but for the suitcase he kept firmly gripped in his right hand, Ted Briggs was prowling around the departure lounge, while the petrol tanker fuelled the plane. "I need a full tank," he'd growled at the airport staff. "This plane's got to get me to New York without any unscheduled stops."

Briggs had spent most of the night either hunched up over boxes with his clipboard itemizing his precious cargo or shouting at people on the phone. His anger at being deserted by his men and dragged from the tomb just as the full glory of its treasures were unfolding was more than he could bear. In short, he was slowly going mad with frustration. Since his arrival in Quezaltenango, he'd had nothing but hassle trying to charter a plane for London and ringing through his client list to find buyers for his artefacts. Any more setbacks would push him over the edge.

From New York, Briggs would be refuelling and flying to a private airfield in Surrey, England, from where he planned to put his precious cargo into storage and return directly to

Guatemala in pursuit of the Itzamna Emerald. Stretching out his long arms, Briggs flexed his jaw and turned to the window where he gasped at the sight of a quetzal sitting on the roof of his plane.

"Impossible," he muttered, pulling himself up stiffly.

For a moment he thought his own quetzal had escaped. But having tied the bird's beak and feet himself before wrapping him in a box and firmly wedging him under the pilot's seat, there was little chance that this could be the same bird. Still, thinking of the quetzal sent his mind back to Bella Balisitca. An irrational impulse led him to consider checking the cockpit of the plane in case she'd somehow survived the temple and tracked him down. "No," he muttered to himself. "There's no way she could still be alive. Not with that ferocious beast and then the earthquake."

He smiled to himself as he cracked his knuckles and then turned his attention to his mobile to send a text message to an old antique dealer he knew in New York. After that, he planned to text Margaret Sticklan about Bella Balistica.

While the tanker was filling up the plane, Bella hopped into the cockpit. She'd had to concentrate and hold tightly to her pendant with her beak to keep her animal form, but she'd done it. It was a new skill she was acquiring. She'd seen Ted Briggs glaring at her with his dark shady eyes through the window of the departure lounge. He looked menacing, like a caged wolf about to pounce. "He knows," she said to herself, her body shaking. "He can see it's me."

Bella's next challenge was her most dangerous yet. Never in her life had she flown anything but paper aeroplanes and the aircraft simulator by Southend pier, but these days anything and everything seemed possible to her. There were no two ways about it: she had to stop Briggs taking these historic treasures out of the country. If she could expose him in Guatemala, he would never be allowed to return for the Itzamna Emerald.

Once in the cockpit, Bella returned to her human form and gazed at the overwhelming display of lights and buttons that adorned the flight deck. "Remember," came the familiar refrain inside her head, "the power of your will is a remarkable force."

Bella's inner voice, that prior to this trip had only ever spoken to her while she gazed at the portrait in the attic, was turning into a right old chatterbox. But Bella found that even just thinking about the Guatemalan woman in the portrait gave her strength. "I am going to fly this plane," she said to herself. "I *know* I can."

It was then that Bella heard the tapping beneath her seat. She leant over and peered down between her legs to see a grey box with a tiny hole poked into the top. Pulling it out and ripping off the elastic bands, she found the Quetzal buried and bound beneath a blanket of damp grass. She quickly freed him.

"And where have you been?" snapped the flustered bird the second his beak was free. "I could have suffocated in there!"

"Nice to see you too," retorted Bella sarcastically.

It took the Quetzal a few moments to catch his breath.

"What's that awful smell?" he complained, wafting his wings around his face to drive away Bella's unpleasant aroma. "You need a shower."

It was true. Bella hadn't washed properly in days – a time during which she'd flown halfway around the world, spent several hours sweating inside musty sacks and a whole night buried in rubbish. Needless to say, she smelt rather fruity.

With his beak still buried beneath his plumage, the Quetzal squawked: "Tell me, you *do know* how to fly this preposterous contraption?"

"No," said Bella haughtily. "I'm hoping you do."

Bella pressed two large switches labelled 'engines', and immediately the propellers started to rotate.

"Tank full," called the man on the runway as he re-screwed the petrol cap.

At the sound of the engines turning, Ted Briggs and the pilot looked out from the waiting room towards the plane.

"What's going on?" Briggs asked the pilot. "I thought we were flying without a co-pilot."

"We are," replied the pilot, as stunned as his boss at what was going on.

"Then who's that in the cockpit?"

Ted Briggs felt the hairs on the back of his neck prick up. The last thing he wanted was a freak accident that would mean some interaction with the authorities – not with the illegal load he was carrying. A niggling thought at the back of his mind went directly to Bella Balistica. He should have followed his instincts and checked the plane the moment he'd seen the quetzal. As quickly as they could, Briggs and the pilot ran out of the waiting room towards the plane.

"Quick!" squawked the Quetzal to Bella, "They're coming."

The brakes on this aircraft worked using a similar lever to the one in her mum's old Mini. Before she knew it, Bella was steering the plane all over the runway like a Southend bumper car.

"Watch out for those children," ordered the Quetzal. "And put your seatbelt on."

Bella couldn't believe her eyes. There on the runway,

running right towards them, was Carlo with Lucas firmly gripped in his arms, followed by the rest of the gang. She slammed her foot down on the brakes and sent the Quetzal flying into the windshield.

"We're taking them with us," cried Bella.

"Are you mad?" screamed the bird, as he tried to disengage his foot from the air-conditioning grid. "This isn't a bus!"

Ignoring the Quetzal, Bella leant over and opened the passenger door. She reached out to take Lucas from Carlo's arm and helped pull the other children on board. Most of the seats on the plane were occupied by boxed-up artefacts, but there was just about enough room for everyone if they huddled up.

"Bella, I finished it," Carlo called to Bella as she retook her place at the controls. "I wasn't going to let you leave Guatemala without it." He took the hand-carved bus from his pocket and passed it up to her.

"Who are these people?" groaned the Quetzal.

But Bella was delighted with her gift. "It's brilliant," she called out through the engine noise, "Thank you. Now hold tight!"

While Bella tried to orient herself to the flight deck, the Quetzal was assessing the immediate danger. "You'd better hurry," he warned. "Briggs has got a Land Rover."

Sure enough, racing up the runway towards them, Briggs and his pilot were in hot pursuit.

"Turn around" ordered the bird.

"It's a quetzal," blurted Lucas gleefully, pointing to the chattering bird.

The children in the back were still trying to get themselves comfortable in what little space there was.

"I love quetzals," Lucas continued. "They bring good luck."

Bella looked across to the Quetzal, who was shaking his beak in disgust. "No respect," he muttered.

Ted Briggs was fuming. While his pilot drove the speeding Land Rover up the runway towards the plane, he got out his binoculars.

"Damn and blast if it isn't that pesky kid again," he snarled, throwing the binoculars down into his lap. "Step on it!"

"Look," yelped the pilot. "She's heading right for us."

Bella was clutching her pendant with her eyes firmly shut.

"Pull the throttle!" shouted the Quetzal.

Bella peered through squinted eyes at the levers before her. "Which one is it?" she yelled.

"How should I know?" squawked the bird.

Bella pulled back one of the levers, and immediately the plane started to speed ever faster towards a head-on collision with the Land Rover.

"We're going to crash!" she squealed. She shut her eyes and braced herself for the impact.

"She's going to mow us down!" cried Briggs. The pilot driving the Land Rover swerved away just in time. The plane was now bumping off the runway, heading straight for a row of electrical pylons.

"Excellent," exclaimed Briggs when the skidding Land Rover came to an abrupt stop, and he saw the fatal turn his prey had taken. "She's toast."

"The wing flaps!" gasped the Quetzal, looking out from the cockpit window to see that they were still horizontal.

"Come on, Bella!" shouted the children in the back.

Bella pulled on every remaining lever and stick that she could see. All around them windows were coming down, seats were going up, heaters were coming on. She closed her eyes, gripped the pendant and pulled back the steering control – "I love you Mum," she shrieked through gritted teeth, and . . . to the sound of everyone screaming, the plane took off. It veered and wobbled uneasily, ascending so slowly that the wheels only just missed crashing into nearby electricity cables.

"Wow!" yelled Lucas, opening his eyes as the plane began to straighten. "I knew you could do it, Bella."

Bella had no doubt that it was the power of the pendant that had saved them.

As the children's faith in Bella and her command over the plane grew more assured, they became transfixed by the unfolding view from the window. Never in their lives had any of them flown before. "Everything looks so tiny from up here," Irma observed.

But admiring the view was not a luxury Bella could afford to indulge in, as the plane was being pulled and pushed around by the wind in a way the simulator by Southend pier never was. Peering down through the clouds to take in the breathtaking sight of the Guatemalan highlands, Bella scoured the sun-drenched valleys to find the road connecting Quezaltenango with the north.

"Just hold on to the steering control as tightly as you can," the Quetzal advised, when Bella found the road and had set her course. "Our altitude is good, but watch out for the mountain peaks. We might need to fly higher."

Bella nodded, her arms rigidly clutching the steering control in absolute terror at what she was doing. With the pendant firmly gripped between her teeth, she tried to master her fears as she guided the plane north, over the highlands and onwards towards the tropical rainforest and the temples of Tikal.

"Are these the artefacts you were telling us about?" Carlo asked, breaking open one of the boxes and carefully lifting out a delicate ceramic bowl with an ornate hummingbird perched on the rim. "The ones you needed to return to the temple?"

Bella nodded, too preoccupied to talk.

"There's something following us," said Lucas, a half hour or so later. The Quetzal and the children turned around.

"It's a helicopter," confirmed Carlo. "It looks like your man is chasing us."

"He's racing us back," chirped the Quetzal. "He wants to return to the tomb of King Kabah to find the Itzamna Emerald. I overheard him talking to the pilot."

Ted Briggs was already flying alongside, to the east. Bella peered across and shivered when she saw his furrowed brow and livid expression. Then, for no apparent reason, an evil grin slowly formed on his face. It was as if he knew something that she didn't. And then it occurred to her. "I'm an idiot," she blurted, dropping her pendant from her mouth. "What was I thinking of?"

Then, remembering that there were other people on board, she chirped quietly to the Quetzal. "There isn't a runway at Tikal. Only helicopters can land there."

"You're talking like a bird," shouted Lucas with glee from the back. "I can do that." He whistled nonsensically in mock bird talk until Carlo told him to stop.

The Quetzal had been very quiet since the children had boarded. "Look to the west," he tweeted quietly to Bella, pointing his beak. "Aim for the cut-down area of the forest." Bella remembered seeing the felled area of rainforest the day she and the Quetzal had arrived.

"The government thinks that if it devastates the rainforest from the middle it'll avoid an international scandal," the Quetzal moaned. "Shameful, isn't it?"

"You're not landing there, are you?" asked Sofia, staring down in horror at the small clearing.

"We'll all be killed!" cried Irma.

All the children were on edge now. The clearing in the forest looked barely bigger than a football pitch.

"I don't think we have any choice," grimaced Bella. She looked to the Quetzal for moral support, but the bird remained silent.

It was Carlo, putting his hand on Bella's shoulder, who calmed everyone on board. "I trust you Bella," he said gently. "You can do it."

"Yes," agreed Lucas firmly. "And we've got the quetzal for luck."

The last time Bella had tried to land a plane was on an arcade game ride. On that occasion, she'd gone up in a huge, onscreen explosion. The stark reality of this actual experience was causing her hands to go clammy. As Ted Briggs swooped off to the east, Bella turned the steering control west and pushed it forward. Immediately the plane started to turn and descend towards the clearing much faster than she'd anticipated.

"The wheels!" squawked the Quetzal, pointing frantically with his beak to a red lever on the flight deck. Somehow she'd pulled them in during take-off while arbitrarily pulling and pushing every lever she could see. Bella pushed the lever. A clunk from under the cabin indicated that the wheels were responding. Three hundred metres, two hundred, closer and closer to the ground they sped – "I love you Mum!" cried Bella – and then, with everyone's eyes closed – BANG!

The plane ricocheted over the bumpy terrain like a skimming stone, while their shaky view of the trees that marked the end of the clearing grew ever larger in their sights. Bella flinched as the left then the right wing was ripped right off, leaving the main cockpit to skid through the trees like a torpedo. She closed her eyes to wait for the explosion and the end of everything.

The final impact was brutal. Bella, held firm by her seatbelt, watched in distress as the Quetzal was jettisoned with great force into the ceiling. Irma and Sofia, huddled together in a final gesture of sisterhood, crashed into the back of Bella's seat, while the three boys felt the full impact of the boxes smacking against their backs, as they too were thrust forward.

Surely, no one could survive such a crash.

Bella had no idea how long she had lain unconscious in her seat. She had the vague memory of her face being licked clean of blood by a baby howler monkey and a hundred brightly coloured birds flocking around the cockpit window. When she finally woke up, she couldn't quite make out the face looking directly at her. "Mum?" she croaked.

"It's me, Bella," wheezed the out-of-breath voice behind the blurry image. "Antonio. The boy who pulled you out of the well with his sister, Angelica – remember? Are you alright?"

Bella heard these words like a distant voice in a dream.

"We saw the plane coming down while we were picking fruit," the voice went on. "It's a miracle you're alive."

Outside the plane, Angelica heard her brother's voice as she finally made it to the cockpit window. "Thank God!" she cried, peering through the shattered glass and steaming it up with her panting breath.

Again, Bella squinted. "I recognize that voice," she thought dreamily.

"There are another five children in the back," Antonio told his sister, gesturing over Bella's shoulder.

Bella was still in shock but was starting to remember the boy's voice.

"We'd better get her out quickly before there's an explosion," he concluded.

The two children dragged Bella from the cockpit and carried her some distance from the smouldering wreckage. She was so bruised even their careful grip caused her pain.

"Where are the others?" Bella mumbled, her senses slowly returning, as they laid her down in the tall grass.

"We're going back in for them now," said Antonio urgently. "They look a little stunned, but I think they're alright."

Bella wanted to help, but she was too dizzy to stand.

It took Antonio and Angelica about ten minutes to drag the injured children from the wreckage and carry them to safety. Some of them had cuts, and they all looked bruised and badly shaken, but they were all alive. While Angelica started to clean their wounds with moist leaves, Antonio went for help. But he needn't have worried. The sound of the crash had attracted the attention of everyone in the village, and they were soon besieged with helpers.

Lying out in the clearing by the wreckage, Bella watched as Carlo and the gang were cared for by the Mayan women from the village, while the men used their machetes to hack down branches to make stretchers. The Quetzal was nowhere to be seen.

"Is this yours?" Angelica asked Bella, holding up the miniature bus that Carlo had given her.

Bella nodded.

"And what about this?" Angelica had seen Bella's camera lens sparkling in the sunlight and had found the two things together amongst the wreckage. "It looks broken," she conjectured, passing the camera over.

There was a split right across its face, and the lens was completely shattered. Bella opened up the back, took out the film and put it into her dressing-gown pocket with the miniature bus.

"What about the boxes?" asked Bella, looking around for the artefacts.

"Boxes?" replied Antonio. "We didn't see any boxes."

Bella was stunned.

CHAPTER TWENTY-ONE

A NEW HOME

Antonio and Angelica's parents wanted all the children to be brought back to the village to recuperate. Carlo and the rest of the street-children spoke a little K'iche', but for the most part, the villagers kindly used a mixture of Spanish and K'iche' to be understood.

"It's quite a way," Antonio warned them. "I'm afraid my father's going to insist that you're all carried on stretchers."

In addition to being bruised and badly shaken, Irma and Sofia were both in shock.

"How did you do that?" gasped Irma, as Bella laid her pendant against her wounds and they began to heal.

"I don't know for sure," murmured Bella. "This pendant has some strange powers."

But when Sofia took the pendant and rubbed it against the cuts on her leg, it did nothing.

"No, Bella," said Sofia rather decisively. "It's not the pendant. It's you."

Ricardo and Lucas were in good spirits and had far fewer cuts. This didn't mean, however, that they were keen to walk when a free ride was on offer.

"Which one's your dad?" asked Bella, studying the men making the stretchers.

"He's called Stephano," replied Antonio proudly. "He's the best hunter in the village. He's gone to find the men in the helicopter we saw flying over the wreckage and ask them to fly you all to the American doctor in Flores."

"That's Ted Briggs!" cried Bella, "The man who stole the treasures from the temple. If he comes back at all, it won't be to help us."

With four stretchers ready, Bella and Carlo argued that they were well enough to walk and that it would be better to get going. Throughout the journey back to the village Bella kept staring into the skies in search of the Quetzal. "Where is he?" she wondered quietly.

The jungle was eerily quiet, until suddenly, in the distance, an almighty howl broke the tranquillity and set off a cascading rumpus.

"It sounds like a wolf," said Bella, thinking immediately of Ted Briggs.

"Jaguars," replied Antonio warily.

Antonio dropped back to join his sister and to introduce himself to the other children in Bella's party. Bella and Carlo walked on ahead with the leading group of women, who were widening their path through the undergrowth with machetes.

"What do you think happened to the boxes?" she asked him.

"I think it was the animals," Carlo conjectured. "I was unconscious for a while, but I could swear my face was licked clean by a jaguar. The whole area was covered in their tracks."

Bella hadn't noticed the tracks, but something deep inside

made her believe that Carlo's idea was true.

Even though she had a lot on her mind, Bella was struck with the simple charm of the village. As they entered, she counted twenty wooden houses with roofs made from thatched leaves. There was one big fire in the central area where villagers were gathering to cook, while outside each house there were smaller fires, some of which were being used to dry clothes.

"Antonio, it's lovely here," she called to her friend. "And this is twice now that I am indebted to you."

"You're welcome," Antonio smiled. "It would make us very happy if you would all stay here forever."

Bella was too full of conflicting emotions to answer.

The children were all introduced to an old man sitting in a wooden chair outside a hut. Dressed in a colourfully-patterned shirt with an equally impressive wrap around his waist, he welcomed the visitors with warm words and a courteous bow of the head. The children in turn paid their respects by returning his bow and shaking his hand. Bella wondered at his age. His face was as craggy and weathered-looking as a dried prune. Looking into his dark wondering eyes, she guessed he was blind.

The children were all offered local clothes while their own were washed and their wounds attended to with hot soapy water. When the village chief was happy that none of the children needed urgent medical attention, he ordered the women to prepare steam baths – which they called *temascals* – for them to bathe in. Bella made sure she put Carlo's little bus and her film somewhere safe before she got in. Alone in her hot bath, which was hidden behind a bush at the back of one of the houses, Bella couldn't relax. It wasn't that she missed the privacy and comfort of her own bathroom at home, it was more the worries at hand that lay heavily on her mind. What had happened to the Quetzal? And where was Briggs? It was then that she heard the gentle flapping of familiar wings as the Quetzal flew down from a nearby tree and landed by the tub. Bella felt her spirits rise instantly.

"I'm so happy to see you!" she cried, clapping and splashing her hands in the warm water. "I thought you were dead."

The Quetzal kept his eyes to the ground, partly to evade the water but also so as not to embarrass her.

"What's been happening?" Bella pleaded, desperate for news. "Has everything been put back where it should be? And where's Briggs?"

The Quetzal looked serious. "The first part of the mission has been accomplished," he revealed smugly. "We made sure you were all alright after the crash and then we went to work. I don't often have a good word to say for the jaguars, but this *was* one occasion in our turbulent history when the arrogant beast was helpful. All the artefacts are back in the temple. As for Briggs, he's on his own. There's no one to help him where he's going."

"What do you mean?" gasped Bella, as she contemplated the unthinkable.

The Quetzal lowered his head. "He's gone back into the temple," he said grimly.

"Alone?" Bella shuddered.

The Quetzal slowly nodded his head.

The horror was unimaginable.

Just then, they heard a loud commotion in the compound.

"Pass me my towel!" cried Bella urgently.

The Quetzal flew up to the bush where Bella had draped her towel, gripped it in his beak and passed it directly to her.

"I must go," he told her. "I'll meet you out front when you're ready."

Bella quickly dried herself and put on one of Angelica's beautiful Guatemalan dresses before running out to see what all the fuss was about. A crowd of dumbfounded villagers were surrounding the scene, but that didn't deter Bella. She pushed her way through to the centre, where to her horror she saw Antonio's father, Stephano, holding Ted Briggs's limp body over his shoulder. By his side, he'd dropped his spear and Ted Briggs's suitcase.

"He's killed him," she gasped.

Briggs's suit was torn to shreds, and the left sleeve was covered in blood.

"Is he dead?" she spurted.

Stephano shook his head. There was a frenzied dash to find hot water to wash Briggs's wound, and the crowd pulled back to allow the exhausted hunter to lay his patient down by the fire.

"His hand!" screamed one of the woman. "Where is his hand?"

Bella thought she was going to vomit. There was nothing at the end of Ted Briggs's left arm apart from a blood-soaked cuff. Stephano's wife pulled back Briggs's sleeve. The wound was so ugly, Bella had to turn away. When she finally gathered herself to return her gaze, she stared with dread at his face. It was completely whitewashed, and his grey hair was standing on end, as if he'd been scared out of his wits.

As the village chief was carried on his chair to join them, Bella sensed the sombre mood of the villagers as they gathered around the fire.

"What happened?" Antonio asked his beleaguered father.

Stephano looked shaken, as if he too had witnessed something too awful to speak of. He sat down on the ground next to Briggs and shook his head. The children brought him a coconut and some cold tortillas for refreshment, but he had little stomach for either. The villagers watched him slowly chew what few morsels he could eat before he put everything to one side and let out a long sigh.

"I'm ready to tell you," he told them. "But be warned. My story may have the trappings of the fantastical – but I can assure you, every word of it is true."

He looked deeply into the flames of the fire to help him collect his thoughts and began: "I left the crash-site as soon as I knew Bella and all her friends were safe. I have twice now, in recent times, seen this mechanical bird with the spinning top . . . "

"He means the helicopter," Bella whispered to Lucas, who had made his way through the crowd to clutch her leg.

"It was my hope that these men might help take these poor children to the American doctor in Flores, but as soon as I revealed myself, they drew guns."

This news aroused angry mutters among the villagers.

Stephano continued: "We in the village have long feared the motives of these strangers from foreign lands. They enter our world in the name of science and take from us much more than knowledge."

The story was interrupted by a long delirious groan from Ted Briggs.

"He has a fever," announced Stephano's wife, putting a

damp cloth to Briggs's forehead. "Carry on with your story, husband."

"I retreated into the forest and watched them set up camp in a small clearing," the hunter went on. "From there, I followed them to the Great Temple where they foraged around in the undergrowth until they found a small gap by a fallen rock."

"The entrance to the lower chambers," interjected the village chief, furrowing his brow. "They must have discovered it."

"They set up some kind of lowering device and tied this man to it," Stephano went on, tilting his head towards Briggs. "Then he lit a powerful torch and lowered himself in."

There was a communal gasp of horror from the villagers gathered around the fire. Bella too felt a cold shiver run down her spine.

"Couldn't you stop him?" came a lone voice in the crowd.

"He was like a man possessed," Stephano persisted. "*And* he had a gun."

Again, the crowd were calmed by the hunter's reasoning.

"What he could have hoped to achieve in there alone – I've no idea," he paused. "But then, in the grip of madness, it's impossible to predict what an enraged and obsessed man might believe he can accomplish."

There was another moan from the injured Briggs. Bella thought she saw his eye twitch, but apart from that, he looked close to death.

Despite being overwhelmed with revulsion at the sight of Briggs's injuries, Bella was struggling to find forgiveness in her heart. "It serves him right," she was thinking, while at the same time trying to convince herself that she should love, learn, forgive and move on. Bending down to give Lucas a reassuring hug, Bella decided that whatever Briggs might have done to her in the past, she would try to forgive him. This punishment, if that's what it was, was too much.

"As soon as he'd gone into the temple," the hunter went on, "a pack of jaguars arrived, and the other man ran away."

"Did he escape?" asked Angelica. "The other man, I mean."

Her father nodded. "He flew away in the mechanical bird."

"And you followed this man into the tomb?" asked Bella, frustrated by the deviation from the main plot.

The hunter paused for some time before he nodded. The reason for his hesitation soon became clear because of the condemnation this confirmation provoked in the crowd.

"You know it is forbidden to enter the temple," interjected one of the elders sternly.

Again the hunter nodded, this time with shame.

"I was worried for the man's safety," he replied sullenly. "And I had every need to be."

The tempo of his story was increasing: "I waited for nearly a half hour until I heard his cries, and then I went in, using his cables to steady me. The man was howling like a deranged wolf. 'Help!' he cried. 'Have mercy!'"

Then, abruptly, the hunter stopped talking, took the coconut the children had brought him earlier and cracked it open on a rock. He needed to drink before he could say anymore.

"I think you were very brave," Bella declared. "Please go on."

"The second I slipped through the gap, the heat hit me," gulped the trembling hunter, coconut milk dripping from his chin. "I almost fainted, it was so hot. It was like lowering myself into hell itself."

"How deep did you go?" Angelica asked.

"For sure, I don't know," her father replied, wiping his brow with a shaking hand. "But it took me quite a while to get down to him. And then I saw it."

"Saw what?" gasped Lucas, hugging Bella's leg so tightly she was starting to get pins and needles.

All the adults were nodding knowingly to each other. The hunter could hardly bring himself to speak.

"The Golden Jaguar," he hushed.

A deathly silence filled the clearing. Nothing but the crackling embers of the fire and the incoherent murmurs of Ted Briggs could be heard. Even the mosquitoes seemed to have stopped to listen. It was one of the village elders who spoke next.

"And is it true?" he asked wide-eyed. "What they say about its heads?"

Again the hunter needed a moment to collect himself. "It had three heads," he answered, almost under his breath.

Many villagers in the crowd exuded a wail of revulsion.

"Each as big as a house," he went on with a little more vigour, "shooting out great torrents of fire. One of the heads had the man's jacket gripped firmly between its teeth, until I poked it in the eye with my spear."

The spontaneous burst of criticism from the crowd surprised Bella. "You attacked the guardian of Itzamna's treasures?" they queried in disbelief.

But the hunter had no intention of defending his spontaneous actions. Instead he spoke more quickly, as his tale progressed towards its hideous climax.

"I grabbed his right hand and tried to pull him out as

quickly as I could, but the beast was on fire with rage. I wasn't strong enough. The Jaguar grabbed him by the left arm and before I knew it . . . "

Bella had her hand over her mouth, as the hunter slammed his fist into his hand to mark the dramatic climax. It seemed as if the whole crowd had taken a sharp intake of breath.

" . . . it was gone."

The silence that followed seemed to last an eternity. Bella was aware that her heart was pounding so fast, it hurt. Poor Lucas was in tears, as were many others. She bent down and wiped Lucas's eyes, but the story wasn't quite over.

"That seemed to be enough for the beast," said the hunter. "My guess is that it was already weakened, perhaps by some recent defence of the temple."

Bella lowered her head to avert her eyes from enquiring looks.

"The creature simply whimpered back into the darkness from whence it came. I pray to the gods that I never see the repugnant monster ever again," said the hunter finally.

It was a while before anyone spoke.

"May this be a warning to all of us," announced the village chief, breaking the silence. "To keep to our promise to guard but never set foot inside the Great Temple. We must return to the entrance immediately and close it forever."

All the young men from the village left to do as the chief had advised, while the rest of the community sat in quiet vigil over Ted Briggs, mulling over the immensity of events in the hunter's story.

After half an hour or so, the crowd gathered around Ted Briggs began to dwindle, as villagers returned to domestic chores. When she was sure no one was looking, Bella got out her pendant and laid it against Briggs's arm. The second it touched his skin the pendant frosted over. "Ow!" exclaimed Bella, releasing the pendant and shaking her hand.

The spine-chilling intensity of the ice numbed her to the bone. The pendant clearly wanted nothing to do with him. Briggs gave out a painful moan. Bella tucked the pendant safely away and went to sit on a small log away from the main fire. She needed some time by herself.

Despite returning the treasure to the Great Temple, there was no pleasure for Bella in seeing her enemy at death's door. She was missing her mum.

"I want to go home," she was thinking.

The Quetzal, sensing the moment, flew down and sat beside her.

"Will he be alright?" she asked him sadly. "I wanted to help."

"He'll survive," replied the Quetzal gravely.

Bella felt relieved.

"And what happens now?" she asked him. "I want to go home."

"And so you shall," replied the Quetzal. "But first, let's eat."

At the thought of going home, Bella felt a warm glow inside – but she was worried. By her reckoning, if she'd spent Wednesday night in the Great Temple and Thursday night with the street-children in Quezaltenango, then this must be Friday night. She had no idea how she was going to explain to her mum what she'd been up to. For now though, there were other, more pressing concerns. She was getting close to having to say goodbye to her friends. With a weary heart,

A NEW HOME

Bella dragged herself up and returned to the group, unaware of the incredible secret the night was yet to reveal.

CHAPTER TWENTY-TWO

THE LUZ VERDE

Refreshed by their baths and clean clothes, the children watched as the Mayan women laid earthenware discs over the small fires around the village. "They're making fresh tortillas," Angelica announced, as the village children began to join their guests.

Conversation was slow to begin with, but as soon as Antonio produced his football made out of rubber bands and blue plastic bags, everyone seemed to forget their shyness and injuries. It was a strange experience for Bella trying to kick a wonky ball on uneven ground in her slippers. She seemed to spend a great deal of time either on her backside or searching for her loose-fitting footwear in the bushes. All the other children played barefoot but Bella found the soles of her feet weren't tough enough. Straight after the game it was time for supper. Everyone in Carlo's gang was ravenous and gobbled their tortillas and beans with relish. Antonio and his mum made a sumptuous local drink called *atoll*, made from maize dough cooked with water, salt, sugar and milk. It tasted like a hot milkshake and made them all feel warm and energized inside. "Gracias," they all said.

"But why are there so few children in the village?" asked Irma.

It was Antonio's mum who told them how so many of the young people left the village in search of the wealth and excitement of city life.

"But it's lovely here," Lucas beamed, with *atoll* dripping all down his face. "Can we stay?"

And then it was decided. Tomorrow, the villagers would take Ted Briggs and the injured children to the American doctor in Flores. Once they'd made arrangements for the Englishman to be flown to an American hospital, they would return. For tonight, all the children were offered dried banana leaves to sleep on by the fires.

"If it rains, we'll find you all some floor space in houses around the village," Antonio reassured them. But the street children didn't mind. They were accustomed to sleeping under the stars. It would be a tight squeeze for some of them if it did rain, but by the end of the week, a new house would be built for them to share.

"This is brilliant, Bella," Carlo told his friend, as they all sat around on their banana tree leaves and gazed into the starry skies. "I told Stephano about our secret garden in Quezaltenango, and he says we can clear an area in the forest nearby and start our own little farm. Bumping into you was the best thing ever!"

"It was, it was," cheered the other children.

"But what about you, Bella?" asked Carlo. "Will you stay?"

Carlo seemed to have some sixth sense that somehow Bella wasn't quite at home here. Bella felt torn. She thought the world of her new friends and the lovely people of Guatemala:

in so many ways it felt like home.

"I'm missing my mum," said Bella finally, with tears in her eyes. "And my friend, Charlie. My home is in London."

Everyone looked sad and confused to hear this.

"But you're Guatemalan," insisted Irma and Sofia together.

"I know," said Bella proudly. "And I'll never forget it."

After dinner, the village children and their guests played another moonlit game of football.

"I wish my friends from school could be here," Bella thought. She was having so much fun, she was reluctant to go with Antonio, as he ushered her away from the game and into his house.

"We've got to be quick." he told her. "I want to show you the Luz Verde."

"The what?" asked Bella, for a moment confused by the unfamiliar word. Then she remembered. The Luz Verde was the stone that Antonio and Angelica had told her about the day she'd met them. The elders used it to show the children their animal twins.

"The one on display in the house of the village chief is a replica," Antonio whispered to her, as he closed the door, "just in case any tourists or thieving monkeys stray into the village. The real one is always buried somewhere closeby – but I always seem to be able to track it down. I borrow it sometimes when the elders are sleeping," he told her. Then, with a very serious expression on his face, he added: "They would give me a beating if they knew."

He went to his sleeping mat and lifted it up. Despite being caked in sludge, the sparkling green light forced Bella to squint and turn away. Then came her revelation. "Luz verde" meant "green light". The elders must have used the Spanish phrase to avoid any unwanted interest. "But that's the Itzamna Emerald!" Bella blurted a little too loudly, her eyes wide.

There, in the mud, Antonio had buried the most priceless emerald on the planet. He dug it out and rubbed it clean with an old rag. Holding it in both hands, he carried it over to the window and lifted it up to the moon. "Yes," he said. "The Itzamna Emerald."

Bella couldn't believe it. The villagers had been looking after the Itzamna Emerald all along. She examined it closely. It really was as big as Antonio's head. Despite the dirt, its resplendent beauty was stunning, quite unlike any precious stone Bella had ever seen in a jewellery shop window.

"How did you get this?" she gasped in disbelief.

The irony was almost too much to bear: Ted Briggs had nearly died looking for the gem in the temple when it had been here all along!

"They say that many years ago, a golden jaguar crept out of the shadows to deliver it into our care," Antonio told her.

Bella was flabbergasted. But then, it made complete sense. With so many archaeologists and scientists excavating the site at Tikal, it was better to hide the emerald where no one would ever imagine looking.

"And do you know how important it is?" she asked, moving closer to study the emerald in more detail.

"I know that if this emerald ever fell into the wrong hands it would be a disaster for everyone, animals and humans alike," Antonio told her gravely.

"I can't wait to tell that know-it-all Quetzal," exclaimed Bella. "He still thinks it's in the temple."

As Antonio held the Itzamna Emerald up in the moonlight, she could see that his reflection was indeed that of a monkey.

"I told you," he said, grinning. "I've always known really deep inside that this was my nahual. No wonder I'm always getting into trouble."

Bella smiled at her friend. Monkeys were fine animals. In fact, they'd saved her from trouble at least once on this trip alone.

"Here," said Antonio, "take a look yourself."

A few days ago, all Bella would have expected to see was a fiery girl with scruffy hair. But Bella had come a long way since her mysterious visitor dropped in from the skylight. She took the Itzamna Emerald and lifted up to her face.

"Look at you!" cried Antonio with amazement. "You're a quetzal!" He gazed at Bella's reflection in complete awe. "The village elders say that humans born with a quetzal twin are one in a hundred million."

That didn't surprise Bella. She'd always felt quite unlike any other child at Hawksmore Primary. The difference between this reflection and the one the Quetzal had shown her in the attic was that the image seemed to fit much better. It was no longer a comical embarrassment but a comfort.

Bella knew that the Quetzal would not have approved of what she and Antonio now had in mind, but she couldn't resist it. With the Itzamna Emerald tucked safely away beneath Bella's borrowed dress, they crept over to the fire where Ted Briggs lay, apparently sleeping beneath several layers of blankets. Looking around, Bella could see that most of the children were already asleep, while the few villagers that were still outside were making their final preparations for bed. The men who had gone to seal the entrance to the temple had not yet returned. "The coast is clear," Antonio whispered.

Bella pulled out the Itzamna Emerald and lifted it up to Briggs's face. The two children stared, their bodies trembling with anticipation. At first, all they could see was the reflection of the flames, raging like some hellish inferno in the eye of the jewel. Then, to their horror, Briggs suddenly roared out in pain, and from nowhere sprang the heinous and petrifying reflection of a ferocious wolf, its eyes flaring up like fireballs.

Before Bella knew it, the stone was so blisteringly hot she had to throw it to the ground. From all corners of the village people were running to the fire. Antonio looked up to see his own father returning from his mission to close the temple entrance and quickly tried to cover the jewel with earth. But it was too late. The little monkey had been caught. Ted Briggs's blood-stained arm was in spasm, and his eyes were wide open. He jerked up, raised his head to let out another almighty roar then collapsed and fell back into a deep sleep.

"You better put that back where you found it," Antonio's father said quietly, gesturing to the half-covered emerald. "We'll talk about this later."

"It was my fault," Bella pleaded. "I begged him to let me borrow it. Please don't punish him."

Antonio's father looked into Bella's eyes and nodded. "I won't," he promised. Then, moving his attention to Briggs, he said: "There are forces and terrors moving within this poor pitiful creature, the power of which we can scarcely imagine."

They all stared at Briggs. During his violent outburst, all the blankets had been dispersed, leaving his limp body lying on a bed of dried leaves by the crackling fire. His threatening snores reverberated round the village, adding chill to the already nippy night air.

As the evening grew late, the gentle rumble of the rainforest brought tranquillity back to the village and the children snuggled up around the fires. Bella was just dropping off to sleep, when she felt something bristly scuttling across her face. "A spider," she thought.

A few days ago, Bella would have probably screamed and knocked the creature away. Instead, she opened her eyes and peered down her nose. What she saw filled her heart with joy.

"You made it!" she cried, as her eyes settled onto the furry features of her eight-legged friend. "I thought I'd never see you again."

"Saved by a rat," announced the tarantula who had been her guide through the Great Temple. "Just shows you what can happen when everyone pulls together."

Bella listened to the spider's story for as long as she could keep her eyes open. She was sound asleep when the Quetzal returned to poke her in the ribs with his beak.

"You idiot," he scolded. "As if you didn't know what Briggs's nahual might be."

"I'm sorry," replied Bella meekly, rubbing her eyes. "I couldn't resist it. The Itzamna Emerald is just so amazing." She looked around for the tarantula.

"Don't worry about her," snapped the Quetzal. "She's got a mountain of work to do back in the temple. All this commotion over the last few days has destroyed a hundred year's worth of cobwebs. She told me to pass on her best wishes."

"And what about the Itzamna Emerald?" asked Bella. "Do you think it will be safe here?"

"Well, considering it's been hidden here for all this time without being discovered by a single quetzal, I think we should have every confidence in these humans," said the bird, "especially the children. And it's just one of those occasions when I'm going to have to bow my head to the jaguars."

"And what will happen to Mr. Briggs?" asked Bella.

"Stephano the Hunter has gone to Flores to ring the American doctor," the Quetzal informed her. "They'll have him out of here in no time. The state he's in, I don't think he's going to be much of a problem to them. And when they find what he's got in that suitcase of his, he's going to be in a great deal of trouble. I'd be surprised if he'll be allowed back into the country ever again. Now come on. Your clothes are dry. As I said, I can play some tricks with time, but there's a limit to just how far I can stretch it."

Bella picked out her dressing gown and pyjamas from the array of clothes drying around the fire and quickly got changed. She then tiptoed around the village saying her goodbyes to the sleeping children.

"I'm going to miss you," she whispered. "But I'm never going to forget you."

Witnessing at firsthand the conditions for babies at the orphanage and meeting the street-children who had once lived there had affected her deeply. She'd decided that from now on, she wasn't going to get mad or get into fights over things that didn't matter. Like being called "pig-face" by sad and pathetic bullies. She'd fight for things that *did* matter. Like getting toys to children who didn't have any, and raising money for projects to help children without families and homes.

Gripping the pendant firmly between her teeth, Bella opened

her arms, bent her knees and jumped. It was her best take-off yet. Her confidence in herself and the pendant was literally flying away with her. Bella and the Quetzal circled the little clearing in the rainforest to get their bearings before setting course for England. Over the rainforest and onwards across the Caribbean Sea they flew, waving to the manatee, as she relaxed in one of the island bays, and later swooping low over the North Atlantic to see if they could find the blue whale. By late afternoon, with the sun already set, Bella found herself flying over England towards London.

"Was this a dream?" Bella asked the Quetzal suspiciously. "Is that how you've been able to play around with our time away on this adventure?"

"No," said the Quetzal bluntly. "It's all to do with the interchange of time and perception. It's a conceptual thing. I'll explain it to you one day."

"Well, if it *wasn't* a dream, I've had it," blurted Bella, her teeth already chattering with the return of the December chill. "When my mum finds out Mrs. Stevens rushed back from her shopping trip and I wasn't in, she's going to be cross."

"Well, come on then!" ordered the Quetzal "Stop dawdling. She's just on her way back from the hospital right now. She doesn't even know you've been away."

CHAPTER TWENTY-THREE

HOME TRUTHS

Bella scrambled in through the skylight just in time to hear her mum coming in through the front door.

"Bella," she shouted up the stairs. "Why don't you answer the phone? I've been ringing all afternoon."

Bella couldn't believe it. Surely it couldn't be Wednesday evening. Maybe the Quetzal really could play tricks with time.

It was good to be home. The familiar smell of the attic timbers made her feel warm and safe.

"Sorry, mum," she bellowed down through the hatch. "I've been in the attic."

But Bella's mum was already at the foot of the ladder. She'd been worried because Mrs. Stevens had left several frantic messages for her at the hospital to say that she was still at the shopping centre speaking to the police about her stolen handbag.

"Bella Balistica!" she exclaimed the moment her eyes fell on her daughter. "Haven't you even showered and got dressed yet? And look at the state of your dressing gown and pyjamas!"

Bella couldn't think what to say. She was just so happy to see her mum. Luckily for Bella, words were pouring out of her mum's mouth, twenty to the dozen. "Did you feed the cat?"

"Sorry," said Bella. "I forgot."

"Bella, I'm so sorry about today. Did you go back to bed again? Poor Mrs. Stevens has been beside herself with worry. Apparently, she thought her handbag had been stolen, but all the time it was sitting under a table in Orinoco's coffeehouse."

She paused to take in the sight of her daughter, who looked so tired and yet so obviously happy to see her. "Hurry up," she said gently. "Charlie's round for tea. I thought I might order a Chinese takeaway." And then, as she turned to go down, she added: "Bella, I've been thinking. I've not been very good at sticking up for you recently. The things that have been going on with those bullies is beyond the pale. Do you know, Eugene was caught by the police last night at three o'clock in the morning trapping badgers in Oxleas Wood?"

Bella felt bad. Eugene would not yet know about his father's accident.

"I think it's disgraceful!" her mum concluded.

"Oh, and one more thing," said her mum. "I've got the rest of the week off. We can do whatever you like."

As quickly as she could, Bella put her pendant back in the secret compartment of her little box and popped the camera film into the top drawer. Looking up to her favourite place in the room, she stared straight into the eyes of the woman in the portrait. "It was your face that I saw on the temple wall," she told her. "You must be Itzamna. But you look so like me."

"Itzamna can appear in many forms," said a voice inside her head. "Harak, karadak, lopatos, almanos."

"Love, learn, forgive and move on," Bella translated. "*I know*!"

"You remembered that the power of your will is a remarkable force, and you used it well," said the voice. "Now hurry up and have a shower – you smell!"

The Quetzal was nowhere to be seen, so Bella went down to her bedroom. On her bedside table the small orange bus caught her eye. She picked it up and examined it closely. Peering into the driver's cabin, she could see the incredible skill of the carver who had chiselled the figure out of one piece of wood. She smiled with new appreciation and reached into her dressing gown pocket to get out the little hand-carved bus that Carlo had given her. "It's almost identical," Bella exclaimed as she put it down alongside the orange bus. Bella wondered whether Carlo had made them both. But one thing she was sure of: she would never forget the amazing street-children of Guatemala.

"We're like family," she sighed with pride.

As quick as she could, Bella got undressed, grabbed a towel from the airing cupboard and stepped into the shower. Before she'd even turned the tap, she noticed a spider crawling up through the plughole. Rather than scream the house down, she simply bent down and picked it up in the palm of her hand. "One of my best friends is a spider," she told the dumbstruck creature, laying him down gently onto one of the bathroom plants.

After her shower, she put on her favourite Charlton Athletic T-shirt and jeans and then ran downstairs just as Charlie and her parents were arriving.

"Charlie!" Bella cried, giving her friend the biggest hug. "Are you feeling any better? I've really missed you."

"I've missed you, too," said Charlie, a little bewildered. "Although I have seen you every day this week."

Charlie's mum had sorted out Eugene's spiteful attack on her daughter's hair by cutting it into a stylish bob. There were still bruises on her face and arms from her fall, but she was looking much happier. Bella was surprised to see that Mr. and Mrs. Stevens were also staying for tea.

"We've got some things we want to talk about," Bella's mum explained.

After their Chinese supper, the two children went up to the attic, while their parents continued to discuss school issues in the living room.

"I decided to take your advice and tell mum and dad everything about Eugene and his bullying," Charlie told her friend. Bella was delighted. Secrets about bullying were dangerous.

"Did you hear the news about Mr. Briggs's aviary?" Charlie asked.

"No," said Bella keenly.

"Apparently, he was keeping lots of illegally imported birds. The police found out about it after lots of them escaped. They say he'll never be allowed to have an aviary ever again."

"That's good," said Bella, but she was distracted. She was still thinking about Briggs's terrible injuries.

"You don't sound *that* happy about it," exclaimed Charlie. "I thought you'd be jumping for joy."

"I'm happy for the birds," Bella explained. "I just wonder what Mr. Briggs is going to do now."

"My mum and dad think that this bullying problem at school is all Mr. Briggs's fault," Charlie continued. "It was his decision to appoint Mrs. Sticklan as an acting head without any interviews. They say Hawksmore Primary has been going downhill ever since." Charlie's mum and dad ran the parents and teachers association and had their finger on the pulse of parental gossip. "They don't think Mr. Briggs should be a governor," Charlie went on. "They say he should resign."

Bella was surprised to hear this but was bursting with so much news, she didn't know what to talk about first.

"Charlie," said Bella. "I've been thinking about our project . . . "

Bella had a thousand and one things she wanted to tell her friend.

Needless to say, Charlie didn't get the whole story.

Bella had been excluded until the Monday of the last week of term, so Mr. and Mrs. Stevens decided to let Charlie stay at home for the rest of the week, so that she could recover from the bullying and keep Bella company. While all this was going on, Bella's mum made another official complaint to the Local Education Authority and the school governors.

On Thursday, to pass the time, she took the children to Southend for the day. Charlie and Bella spent nearly the entire afternoon flying planes in the arcade simulators. It was later that evening when news of Ted Briggs's arrest and deportation from Guatemala was reported. Bella had been helping her mum fix the Christmas tree lights the cat had smashed, when Mrs. Stevens called on the phone.

"Quick," ordered Bella's mum, hanging up, "switch on the TV. Ted Briggs has been arrested at Heathrow and taken to Greenwich."

According to the report, Ted Briggs been taken to hospital in Houston, Texas, by a helicopter to have an artificial hand attached to the end of his left arm. He had then returned to Guatemala to steal from a tribe of Mayan Indians who had saved him from certain death at the jaws of a "ferocious jaguar". It seemed that the jewel he had tried to take was not valuable but held great significance for the village. Sadly for the villagers, only hours after Briggs was caught red-handed trying to steal it, a mysterious jaguar crept into the village and whisked the jewel away into the rainforest.

"I've never liked that man," said Bella's mum, reaching for the remote to turn down the volume after the report. "But I feel really sorry for Eugene and his mum. I think Mr. Briggs will go to prison."

The article in the national newspaper the following day featured a picture of Antonio and Angelica along with Carlo and his gang smiling and waving to the American photographer who had come to cover the story. Bella cut out the article and stuck it on the wall in the attic. The police had also discovered some ancient Mayan jewellery in Briggs's suitcase. To add to this, the article reminded everyone of Briggs's previous archaeological wrongdoings *and* picked up on the local story regarding his "aviary shame". It concluded by saying that the UK authorities were looking into allegations that Briggs had amassed a huge private collection of illegally acquired artefacts.

On Friday, Bella and Charlie stayed in and helped Bella's mum with her Christmas cooking. They crushed cinnamon sticks and cardamom pods and ate so many mince pies they thought they were going to explode.

"I love the smell of Christmas," Bella told Charlie and her

mum. "It smells of foreign lands and faraway places."

They sat drinking hot chocolate with the kitchen door open, enjoying the blending aroma of pine needles and spices, before crashing out in front of the TV to watch Disney videos.

Although Bella really enjoyed getting into the Christmas spirit, her favourite times were when she and Charlie just hung around in the attic and worked on their endangered species project. Talking about the manatee and the blue whale made Bella remember her amazing adventure. It was incredibly frustrating not being able to tell her friend anything about it.

"Charlie," said Bella nervously. "I have a secret that I want to share with you – but I can't. At least, not everything"

Charlie turned to her friend with a deadly serious expression on her face. "A secret is a secret," she replied. "As long as whatever it is isn't making you unhappy, then I don't want you to tell me."

Bella smiled.

"It makes me happy," she told her friend. "And one day I'm going to tell you everything."

There was no sign of the Quetzal for the rest of the week. To Bella's surprise, she actually missed his bossy presence. By Saturday, Bella had all but given up on him. "Fair-weather friends," she complained to the portrait in the attic. But she didn't get an answer. "So you're giving up on me as well, are you?" she protested.

"Are you alright, dear?" called her mum from the landing. "Have you remembered we're going to the match this afternoon?" Her mum had got tickets for a home game at Charlton Athletic. Bella was thrilled.

"Mum," Bella shouted down the stairs. "You're the best."

On Sunday, Bella had a brainwave about her camera film and was actually thankful that it wasn't a digital camera.

"Mum," she said over breakfast. "I've found a roll of film at the bottom of your old chest in the attic. Maybe it's from your travels through Central America?"

"I don't know, darling," her mum replied, curious. "Let's have a look."

The two of them went upstairs to the darkroom. Bella wasn't allowed to touch any of the chemicals, but she could use the special handling device to move the photographs around in the solutions. She loved how the images would slowly emerge like faded memories into fully developed pictures.

Bella was confident that she wouldn't be given away by any shots of herself or the house, because she hadn't used the camera before her trip with the Quetzal.

"Whatever we find in these photos, it's going to be a surprise," said Bella's mum as she rolled out the film. "I'll try not to peek at the negatives."

This was much more exciting. One by one, the pictures would unfold before their eyes as if by magic.

The first picture to come out took their breath away. "It's a blue whale!" Bella's mum cried, lifting the photograph up to the dim light to examine it more closely. "I don't believe it! I remember going on a boat trip to see them, but I don't recall getting *this* close. I must have had a better zoom lens than I thought."

The whole whale appeared in the photo, with a spectacular fountain of water jetting out of its blowhole.

"Bella, isn't it an amazing photograph? We'll have to get it enlarged," her mum concluded, as she hung it on the line to dry.

The manatee was next, although Bella's mum wasn't even sure what it was. "It's an aquatic herbivore," said Bella, remembering the article she'd read on the internet. "They can be found all around the Caribbean and the Central American coastline."

"You sound like a talking encyclopaedia, Bella," teased her mum. "I don't remember taking any of these. I must have lent my camera to one of the girls I was travelling with."

Bella was elated. These pictures would be fantastic for her project, and there were so many more to come. Bella's mum was overwhelmed by the pictures, as they were developed, one after another. Parakeets, parrots, monkeys, beautiful shots of beaches and tropical rainforest – the range of photographs was vast and wonderful.

"This is definitely Guatemala," said Bella's mum, as she stared into the unfolding image Bella had just put into the developing chemicals. "I recognize the Temple of Tikal."

Everything was going well. Bella and her mum had all the pictures hanging up to dry.

"How many more?" Bella asked.

"I think this is the last one," her mum replied.

Bella put it into the solution. "I wonder what this one can be?" she thought to herself.

At first it looked like there was no image at all.

"It looks like I got the light wrong on this one," sighed her mum. "It's overexposed."

Then, slowly, through the ripples in the chemical tray, the

shape of a building began to appear. Bella started to get flustered. She recognized the battered old sign above the door. It was the Santa Maria orphanage in Quezaltenango. Carlo had taken the picture, and she was in it!

"I'll finish this one," blurted Bella, trying to bustle her mum out of the room. "Why don't you go and put the kettle on?"

But Bella's mum was going nowhere.

"Oh Bella!" she cried, tears running down her face. "I know this building. Bella, my love, this is the orphanage you were born in."

She had her arm around Bella's shoulder and was clutching her tightly. From under her mum's embrace, Bella stared at the picture, waiting for her own image to appear. If her mum saw it her secret would be out. First came the grubby whitewashed walls, then the image of the kind-looking woman with the baby standing at the window – nothing could stop the inevitable now. She closed her eyes and prayed that somehow the picture was so overexposed she would not be seen.

As the picture grew more defined, it became clear to Bella that Carlo had never taken a picture before in his life. All she could see of herself were her eyes and the top of her head. He'd shot too high, and there was too much light in the picture.

"I recognize the woman with the baby," Bella's mum quavered, tears already forming in her eyes. "That's the nurse who took care of you before I adopted you. Doesn't she look lovely? And that little girl, she's almost as beautiful as you."

Bella thought her mum was looking at the baby in the arms of the nurse, but she wasn't. She was pointing directly at the top half of Bella's head.

They were both crying now.

Bella's mum was so affected by the photographs, she wanted to spend the rest of the morning rummaging through her old chest and talking to Bella about all the knickknacks and photos. Bella had heard her mum's stories a hundred times before, but this time they seemed much more vivid.

"I'm sorry I didn't know your real mother for long, Bella. But I do know that she was an exceptional woman. She was learning Spanish and studying to be a lawyer when she met your father. I saw how gentle and kind she was. I'm just sorry I never met your dad."

Bella was shocked. Her mum had never admitted to knowing her birth mother before. She had only ever said that she'd heard about Bella's mother from other people. Bella was speechless. But there was more to come. Her adoptive mum took a deep breath.

"Bella," she said, her voice trembling. "The story about finding you in the orphanage . . . well, there's something else."

Bella felt scared because her mum looked so nervous and upset.

"The midwife who took care of you and your mother in the orphanage – the one I've told you about a million times. Bella – it was me."

Bella was sobbing uncontrollably. Somehow, deep inside, she'd had a feeling that this was so. "Your mother was so happy to be having you," her mum went on. "There was a quetzal who used to come and perch on her bedroom window every day. I would sit and listen to your mother sing to him, as if she were a bird herself."

Bella's jaw visibly dropped.

"Bella, your mother was like you in so many ways," Annie

continued. "I'm just so sorry for you *and* her that she isn't here to take care of you. But Bella, I'm really happy for me, because I love you, and wherever the spirit of your real mother is now, I know that she loves you too."

It was funny, but Bella was sad and happy all in the same moment. With all the things that had happened to her over the last few days, she felt, for the first time in her life, that she knew who she was and where she had come from. As for the future, one thing was for sure, it wasn't going to be boring! "Remember," said a voice inside her head, "the power of your will is a remarkable force. Learn to control it and use it to do good."

While Bella hardly even acknowledged it, there was another voice inside her head. Its tone was very different from the maternal one she associated with the portrait. "He's alive," it growled.

The dream that her father was, even now, fighting his way back against powerful forces to find her was starting to rise up in her consciousness. Bella squeezed her eyes shut and shook her head to make this eerie and vaguely threatening voice go away – for now.

As Annie dried her eyes, Bella picked up the jewellery box and showed her how she'd found the pendant.

"I'm sorry I didn't show you before," Bella told her mum, as she handed her the glistening pendant. "I was being horrid."

"You were angry with me, Bella," replied her mum with a smile. "And you were right to be. I should have told you about these things a long time ago. We could have looked for the pendant together."

Bella's mum had seen Bella wearing the pendant the day of

the bullying incident over at Charlie's house. She had wondered when Bella was going to show it to her. The moment had turned out to be perfect.

Bella asked her mum a hundred questions about her birth mother and what life was like at the Santa Maria Orphanage.

"We need to send those babies some toys to play with," Bella announced. "We should do a fundraiser for money and unwanted toys straight after Christmas."

"We should," agreed her mum. "Did you know that there is a project to help street-children learn to be photographers?" she added. "They take pictures of their lives and put them in an exhibition that goes all over the world. That way more and more people are becoming aware of their problems."

"What a great idea!" Bella exclaimed. "I'll speak to Mr. Alder. Maybe we can make supporting that project the focus of next year's school appeal."

Everything was falling into place for Bella. But down the road, life in the Briggs household was anything but festive. Ted Briggs had been released on bail but was still under investigation following a raid on his house in which a large number of artefacts had been confiscated. Charity was probably the last thing on Ted Briggs's mind when he told his son what he could do to get even with Bella Balistica.

CHAPTER TWENTY-FOUR

FREE AS A BIRD

By the time Monday morning of the last week of term arrived, Bella and Charlie had finished their projects and were ready to hand them in. At registration, they were told that Mrs. Sticklan was not at the school anymore and that Mr. Alder would be taking charge until they appointed a new headteacher.

"Where did you get those amazing pictures?" everyone asked Bella and Charlie.

"I'm not telling you," said Bella, enjoying the positive attention and a chance to weave some intrigue. Not even Charlie knew the whole truth.

Despite missing the final rehearsals, Bella got an honorary walk-on part in the Christmas concert. This basically meant that she gave out make-believe Christmas cards with mythical characters from countries as far away as India and China. It made Bella happy that Mr. Alder had given the part of the narrator to Rahina Iqbal.

"You look lovely in your costume," Bella told Rahina, as they stood in the corridor, waiting to enter the packed school hall for the opening night.

"Thanks," replied Rahina, shaking with nerves.

Bella put a hand on Rahina's shoulder to comfort her, but she needn't have worried. The second she stepped into the spotlight, Rahina was in her element.

Bella and Charlie got top marks for their endangered species project and had to stand up in front of the whole school at Friday's assembly to talk about their work. Mr. Alder, who'd heard about the terms of the girls' football match against the boys, insisted that the original result was reinstated and that the boys should relinquish the main area of the playground to girls-only football.

"But we want mixed teams," Bella told him, knowing that the way forward was to share. "And anyone who wants to play, can," she concluded adamantly.

Bella noticed that neither Eugene Briggs nor Connor Mitchell were at the assembly. "Maybe they've bunked off early," she thought to herself. Bella had thought it strange at lunchtime that the two of them had moped around behind the bicycle sheds rather than playing football.

Friday was the last school day before the Christmas holidays and Mr. Alder had sent a letter home earlier in the week, informing parents that classes would finish at 2.00 p.m, after the assembly. Bella had arranged for a mixed-teams football match on Oxleas meadows after school and told Melanie Roberts and Imogen Meeks that she wanted to invite Eugene and his gang to join in.

"Why?" asked Imogen.

"Because it's Christmas," Bella answered with a smile.

This wasn't entirely the truth.

"Love, learn, forgive and move on," she told Charlie, privately. "That's what I think."

She'd heard these words a hundred times before while swinging in the hammock in the attic. This time, though, they were her own.

"Sounds like good advice to me," Charlie mused, "but I don't think that's Eugene's style – do you?"

"Still, I want to try," said Bella. It must have been difficult for Eugene to find out his father was such a scumbag, she thought.

Just before the school bell rang, Prakash Malik strode up to Bella's table and slid her a note. "It's from Eugene," he told her.

"Are you coming to play football?" asked Bella enthusiastically. "You can play in goal if you want."

Prakash looked uneasy. "Can I?" he asked.

By the look on his face, it seemed to Bella as if Prakash had just opened the best present he'd ever had. But Prakash couldn't sustain his fleeting joy.

"I'd like to play," he grumbled, as the corners of his mouth turned down. "But I can't."

"You see what you're up against," said Charlie, as Prakash scurried off. "Eugene would kill him."

Bella opened the note. What she read made her stomach churn.

> We've got all the evidence on videotape.
> We know everything.
> Come to the old watchtower or we're going to the police.

Bella cast her mind back to the night she and the Quetzal broke into the Briggs's house. Those little red laser lights weren't the alarm system – they must have been small security cameras. She was done for. The school bell rang.

"I've got to go," Bella told Charlie grimly, as she swung her chair onto the table. "I'll get to the meadows as soon as I can."

Bella ran until she was clear of any other children. She need not have worried – hardly anyone took her cross-country route to the meadows in winter. "I'm going to have to apologize about the pet shop and the aviary," she thought to herself. "If they report me to the police, I'm in big trouble."

And then she stopped dead in her tracks. What if the video had shown her turning into a quetzal? Everyone would think she was a freak!

With her head bowed to hide her tears, Bella trudged on towards the old watchtower until a loud catcall from the trees caused her to stop and look up. It was Connor Mitchell. He was sitting in the branches, chewing gum, and had just sent out a clear message to Eugene that she was approaching. Eugene had everything covered.

"I'm trapped," she thought. She was going to get a real beating, and there was nothing she could do about it.

"Cheer up, pig-face," Connor snarled, running his fingers through his short spiky hair.

"We're playing football in half an hour," Bella told him feebly. "You can play too, if you want."

The unexpected invitation put Connor off. He quite fancied a game of football. "Where are you playing?" he asked in as neutral a tone as he could muster.

"Down on the meadows," replied Bella hopefully.

Connor fell silent for a moment, while he weighed things up. Eugene was going to give Bella Balisitca such a beating it was doubtful whether she'd be playing football this side of New Year. He finally replied by spitting his gum at Bella's feet. Normally, he'd have gone for her face.

"No," he said.

Eugene Briggs was sitting on the stone ledge that ran the circumference of the old watchtower when Bella arrived. He too was chewing gum. Strangely for Eugene, he was alone.

"Alright, pig-face," Eugene hissed, standing up.

Instead of letting herself get riled by the insult, Bella tried to focus her energies on defusing the situation. "Love, learn, forgive and move on," she reminded herself.

"I'm sorry about your father's accident and the incident at the pet shop," she told him. "I'm sure your mum and dad will open a new shop that will be just as busy."

Bella looked directly into Eugene's snake-like eyes and shivered despite herself. He really did look like a viper.

"We know it was you!" Eugene yelled with venom. "We've got all the evidence we need on this."

He pulled back his bomber jacket to reveal the video-cassette, half tucked into his trousers.

"But you were caging birds," Bella pleaded with a little less gusto than usual.

"Oh dear!" scorned Eugene, opening his mouth and raising his hands in mock horror.

Bella took a step back, as Eugene's arm shot out towards her neck.

"We know your secret, Bella Balistica," he shouted, as he pulled down the collar of her blouse and grabbed the chain around her neck. "You're a freak and soon everyone will know it."

Bella panicked. Eugene was after the pendant. She tried to pull away, but his grip was too tight. Surely the chain would break. Eugene dragged her to the ground and pinned her down. She tried to kick, but he was sitting too high up her body.

"How would you like me to cut off that silly little nose of yours?" he snarled meanly, taking a pair of scissors from his inside pocket. "Or perhaps a bit of a haircut is in order?"

There was nothing Bella could do. She was completely at the mercy of Eugene's fury. The anger that she so often called upon to fight back when the chips were down was suddenly not there anymore, not for this fight. She felt sad for Eugene. He was always so cruel and self-centred. A bully who no one would ever give two hoots about should anything horrid happen to him. And she felt sorry for herself. Soon everyone would know what she had done and that she was the weirdest girl in the history of Hawksmore Primary. Eugene took a bunch of her hair and opened up the scissors.

A terrific screeching noise from above took them both by surprise. Bella looked past Eugene's head to see a white mass of seagulls swooping down towards them from the top of the tower. Eugene had to bury his head under one of his arms, as they pecked at his head and squawked into his ears. Then came the sparrows and the starlings, the blackbirds and robins, even the crows – the whole place was full of bird life. Bella was stunned.

"Get off!" Eugene was shouting, waving his hands around his head.

It was then that the red and green plumage of the Quetzal

appeared, taking aim and flying straight at Eugene's face. Eugene put his hands up to protect himself, and that was all the opportunity Bella needed. She pushed him away and scrambled to her feet. Somehow, Eugene too managed to stagger to his feet, only to find himself staring helplessly at Bella through the melee. "Pig-face," he called pathetically. It was all the counter-attack he could muster.

Bella smiled at the sight of Eugene Briggs blindly staggering his way down Oxleas Mount, as he tried to escape from his attackers. She brushed herself down and breathed out in relief.

"About time you decided to show up," she chastised the Quetzal, who was hovering above her. The Quetzal had a beakful of videotape, which he spat out over the dismembered cassette on the ground.

"I leave you alone for five minutes, and look what happens," came his familiar retort.

Secretly, they were both happy to see each other.

"I thought you were going to leave without wishing me a Happy Christmas," Bella grumbled, trying to sound cross. "Some friend you are."

Bella soon forgot about her aches and pains and raced the Quetzal down the hill to Oxleas meadows where she was meeting Charlie and anyone else who wanted to play football. She saw Winston Geoffrey and Prakash Malik chasing rabbits around the small area of grass outside the deserted café.

"Come on," she shouted. "Kick-off in two minutes!"

"We're coming," they called.

"Can I play?" came the distant cry of Connor Mitchell, as he waved to her from the top of Oxleas Mount.

Bella bit her tongue. Her instinct was to tell Connor Mitchell to get lost. He'd been Eugene's right-hand man for as long as she could remember. There was an awkward silence before Bella finally shouted up the hill: "Only if you play on my team."

That was all the encouragement Connor Mitchell needed.

The Quetzal came to land on Bella's shoulder. She had a suspicion he had another adventure in mind.

"I've got this friend," the Quetzal mentioned, trying to sound casual. "He works in an Indian circus."

Bella threw up her hands.

"I don't want to know," she exclaimed. "There are three days to Christmas. I'm playing football with my friends, and then I'm going home to wrap up presents with my mum."

And with that, she pulled off her school jumper to reveal her Charlton Athletic football top.

"I'll watch for any off-sides," sulked the bird, as he flew up into a nearby tree. "And no cheating!"

"What do you mean?" shrieked Bella in all innocence before remembering the power of the pendant.

"Oh," she acknowledged sheepishly, nodding her head. "OK. But I'm not promising anything."

Bella ran down the hill so fast, she almost took off, even without her powers.

"Hey!" she shouted down to Rahina and Imogen, who were busy practicing long-ball passes on the meadow. "Pass to me."

With the cold December chill fresh against her cheeks and her black unkempt hair flying wildly in the wind, Bella Balistica looked up into the clear blue skies and screamed with pleasure: "Yeeehah!"

She felt as free as a bird.

BELLA BALISTICA AND THE INDIAN SUMMER

When her mum gets a new boyfriend, Bella's world is turned upside down.

"I don't need a father figure," Bella complains. "I have a real father!"

While on holiday in India, Bella discovers sinister forces are conspiring to steal her precious pendant and mystical powers. Lurking behind the scenes of the touring Mumbai Circus, the Quetzal reveals a formidable enemy – Diva Devaki, the acclaimed impresario, acrobat and illusionist. But all is not what it seems. Can Bella outwit the spellbinding Diva, heal the rift with her adoptive mum, and finally meet her elusive birth father face to face?

Out soon: *Bella Balistica and the Indian Summer*, the next book in the Bella Balistica series.

ACKNOWLEDGEMENTS

My first thanks are to my inspirational friend Catriona and her three beautiful and spirited adopted children, Irma, Bella and Sofia, for opening my eyes to the wonder of Guatemala and the Maya. To my friends Mary Colson and Rebecca Evans, whose comments shaped the novel's course – I am truly indebted. Thanks to my agent, Robin Wade, Sedat Turhan, Laura Hambleton and the whole Milet team – especially Patricia Billings for her meticulous editing – who all injected energy, enthusiasm and fresh ideas into the book. Thanks to Rachel Goslin for creating all the vibrant and engaging artwork. Finally, and above all, thanks to my beautiful and supportive wife, Charlotte, who must have read the book twenty times over, distilling my eccentric ideas, nurturing my narrative and correcting my dyslexic spellings and grammar.   A.G.